TO THE STARS

To The Stars

by

Patricia Robins

Dales Large Print Books
Long Preston, North Yorkshire,
BD23 4ND, England.

British Library Cataloguing in Publication Data.

Robins, Patricia
    To the stars.

A catalogue record of this book is
available from the British Library

ISBN 978-1-84262-812-6 pbk

First published in Great Britain
by Hutchinson & Co. (Publishers) Ltd.

Cover illustration by arrangement with Arcangel Images

The moral right of the author has been asserted

Published in Large Print 2011 by arrangement with
Claire Lorrimer

Dales Large Print is an imprint of Library Magna Books Ltd.

Printed and bound in Great Britain by
T.J. (International) Ltd., Cornwall, PL28 8RW

FOR DAVID R. EVERETT.

As the stars that shall be bright when we
  are dust
Moving in marches upon the heavenly
  plain,
As the stars that are starry in the time our
  of darkness,
To the end, to the end, they remain.

'For the Fallen'
(Laurence Binyon.)

PART I

THE BEGINNING

Chapter 1

Jonquil Mathews opened her white leather handbag and searched among the assorted jumble of vanity oddments for a cigarette. Presently she found one, and having lit it, lay back on the garden mattress and stared up at the clear blue sky, inhaling deeply.

Far away in the distance could be heard the dull rumble of guns or bombs – or both – over Dunkirk. It was hard to believe, lying here in the warm sunshine among the lilac bushes, that only a few miles away Englishmen were hiding in the sand dunes on the beaches being bombed incessantly, too weary, for the most part, even to care. The rumbling noise, thought Jonquil, was far more akin to the sound of an avalanche in Switzerland when the snow melts in summer time and slides down the mountainside into the valleys below.

For a few minutes, the girl allowed her thoughts to wander back into those lovely carefree days she had spent at the Swiss

Pension near Lausanne, overlooking the Lake of Geneva. The only daughter of rich parents, no expense had been spared on anything connected with Jonquil, and her expensive English education had been 'finished off' with an even more costly school in Montreaux.

'I'm lucky!' she thought suddenly. 'I just managed to see the Continent before it was too late.'

She smiled a little, mentally thanking the poor maligned Mr Chamberlain for holding the war up long enough to enable her to travel as she had done, for Switzerland had been followed up by Paris and the Riviera in the company of her mother who exercised no control over the daughter she had always pampered and spoiled. Eager for her company, Mrs Mathews had encouraged her to 'grow up' and had showered smart Paris gowns upon her seventeen-year-old child, and managed to smuggle her into the casinos.

For all this, however, Jonquil remained young for her years, and while looking twenty-five at least, at heart she was still 'sweet seventeen', and up until the time of her return to England and her meeting with Simon O'Dair, she had literally 'never been kissed'!

Simon O'Dair was, therefore, the first man in her life, and right from the beginning of their affair Jonquil had decided he would be the only one. She met him at one of the dances given by the officers of the neighbouring Royal Air Force Station, and Simon had singled her out, falling at first for her chic appearance, and then, when he knew her better, loving her for herself, the unaffected, charming child that she was beneath her sophisticated exterior.

Within three months they were engaged to be married. Their love was gay and irresponsible, Simon being only twenty-two to her eighteen, but to each of them the other meant all that was happiest and most exciting in life, and when war broke out, like so many other young people, they decided to be married.

'I'll get fourteen days' leave,' Simon had promised. But somehow there had been training to be done first, and then when everything started to go so badly in France, leave was pushed aside for far more important things. The Royal Air Force was expanding rapidly and men with even as little flying experience as Simon, became invaluable. England was training her sons as fast as she could, but good pilots are not made overnight. The few Squadrons who were available to go to the help of the B.E.F. at Dunkirk fought tirelessly and heroically, and Simon was among them.

It was two days now since Jonquil had

even so much as heard his voice on the telephone. Lying in the garden unable to settle to anything, she tried not to be afraid. She pushed aside the agonising, morbid ideas that kept worrying their way to the front of her mind, and thought instead of the fun Simon would be having. Because flying was fun to him – even in war time. It meant a great deal to him and she knew it, and jokingly spoke of it as 'my biggest rival'. But even as she said it she knew it was not so much of a joke.

'Darling,' he had once told her, 'up there is another world you know nothing about – two other worlds. One minute, billowy clouds and red sunsets, a haven of peace and beauty; the next minute an exciting inferno of death. When I'm up there I really come alive.'

'Don't you feel alive when you're with me?' Jonquil had asked a little jealously.

Simon had put his arms around her and given her a large bear hug.

'Of course, darling,' he said, laughing. 'But that's a different part of me. I can't explain...'

But Jonquil had understood. Had she not been ski-ing? Felt the wind and snow sting her cheeks as she flew down the mountain-side, her body twisting and bending lithely to the graceful rhythm of Christiania turns? Felt the exhilaration of speed, of sunlight, of new tracks in virgin snow? Was there not in her love for ski-ing some similarity to the emotion Simon had when flying?

Her mother's voice broke into her thoughts.

'Jonquil, telephone call for you!'

'Simon!' Jonquil thought, and like a streak of lightning she ran up the flagged garden path into the cool hallway where the telephone stood.

'Hullo! Hullo! Jonquil here!' she said breathlessly.

'Darling, it's me, Simon! Can I put the deep breathing down to excitement, or have you been hurrying?'

'Stupid! I've been hurrying,' Jonquil said with a laugh. 'Darling, how are you?'

'I've got half an hour's breather while the old 'bus is being patched up'

'Patched up?' echoed Jonquil. 'You weren't hit, Simon? You aren't hurt?'

He laughed reassuringly.

'No, I'm not hurt, but a bloody Jerry knocked one of my wings into pieces.'

'Simon!'

'All right, my sweet. Confounded Jerry! But I got him, and five others, too.'

'Darling, that's wonderful,' Jonquil said admiringly. 'I always knew you were going to be England's big air ace.'

He laughed happily. Then his voice quietened and became serious.

13

'Jonquil, if anything should happen to me...' he began, but she interrupted him.

'Nothing is going to happen,' she said firmly.

'No, but if it should,' Simon persisted, remembering the six of his squadron who had not returned that afternoon, 'I've asked Adrian Hepworth to let you know. He's a grand chap and one of my greatest friends...'

'Simon, I won't listen to any more,' Jonquil cried out. 'It's detrimental to my morale!'

To her relief he was laughing again.

'O.K., sweetheart. You win!' he said. 'I've got to go now. I'm on my toes to get back. Jonquil, if you could see those chaps ... I can't tell you. They're so confoundedly brave; so pathetically pleased to see us. Everytime we get anywhere near them, they raise a cheer. And it's we who should be cheering them. They make me proud to be English.'

'So do you me!' Jonquil said softly.

'Rose-coloured spectacles to you,' came Simon's voice, a little embarrassed as always by praise of himself.

'I love you,' Jonquil said irrelevantly.

'I love you,' Simon answered. 'Now I'll have to trot, darling. Keep your chin up! I'll ring you later to-night.'

'Happy landings!'

Jonquil replaced the receiver and walked back into the garden. She felt immeasurably happier now, and quite at peace with the world.

'I'm going to weed the herbaceous border,' she called to her mother who was sitting in the swing sofa under the large monkey-puzzle tree. She wanted to be active now.

'Was it Simon, darling?' her mother asked.

'Yes! He's all right!' Jonquil called back happily. Oh, life was lovely, quite, quite lovely! she thought as she bent down and started to pull up the weeds. The B.E.F. was being successfully evacuated and Simon was winning great honours for himself.

With the thoughtlessness of the young, and in particular the young of the idle rich, she did not think of the great casualties emanating from an evacuation such as that from Dunkirk. She could not visualise the beach; the calm sea swarming with exhausted, starving, war-weary men; the bombs falling, falling, throwing up clouds of sand and water and human fragments. Not until many months later when the news films were released, did the tragedy of those days she spent so happily, really make an impression on her; and then, seeing the train loads of men, more than half asleep, more than half naked, tumble out on to the platforms and march bravely away to receiving depots, she knew she would never forget them, not as long as she lived.

Tea had been cleared away by a trim-looking parlour-maid and Mr Mathews was already back from work when the 'phone bell rang again.

'I'll answer it!' Jonquil said swiftly. 'I'm expecting a call from Simon.'

She left the drawing-room quickly, and her mother and father smiled at each other.

'Simon's a nice boy,' Robert Mathews said.

His wife nodded. They both agreed that the children were still a bit young for marriage, but under the circumstances they were willing to waive their objections. They themselves had been married during the Great War.

Outside in the hallway, their only daughter was answering the telephone. She was so sure it was Simon that she didn't bother to ask first.

'Darling,' she said. 'How are you?'

'Is that Miss Mathews?'

Jonquil held the receiver tightly to her ear.

'Yes! Who is speaking, please?'

'It's Adrian Hepworth here,' came the man's voice. 'I'm afraid I've got some bad news for you... Are you there, Miss Mathews?'

'Yes, I'm listening!'

Jonquil forced the words from between her lips.

'Simon – he – I promised him I'd tell you

right away if anything happened. I wish I could see you, Miss Mathews. The telephone is so...'

His voice trailed away.

'Is there *any* hope?' Jonquil asked desperately. 'Please tell me quickly.'

'No, I'm afraid there isn't,' Adrian Hepworth said, his voice utterly wretched. 'He was shot down over France... Is there anything I could do?'

'No, nothing, thank you. Nothing!' Jonquil told him, and she put the receiver back in its place.

Her hands were trembling and she curled her fingertips so that the nails dug into her palms. Then her whole body started to tremble and her legs felt so weak that she had to sit down on the oak chest. She didn't know how long she was there before the shaking stopped, and she could think again. She found then, to her surprise, that she felt nothing, nothing at all. She walked into the drawing-room and faced her parents.

'Simon's dead!' she said, and watched with detachment the look of surprise and horror that came into their faces.

'That's funny,' she thought. 'They feel something and I, who love him, feel nothing at all.'

They seemed to be speechless, able only to stare at her from large eyes in white, stricken faces. The silence became intolerable, so did their anxious, pitying gazes.

'Well, what are you staring at?' she shouted, hearing as if from a distance the hard, cracked voice, and recognising it with surprise as her own.

There seemed now to be two Jonquils, and the real her was watching her other self as it stood facing her parents. She felt sorry for this other person, but could do nothing to help.

'Jonquil, it can't be true!' her mother was saying. 'You're joking dear, aren't you?'

'Jonquil, are you sure?' her father said.

'Yes, it's quite true. It's not a joke, and I am sure,' she said. 'Adrian Hepworth, Simon's friend, just told me over the 'phone.'

And she turned and walked out of the room, her head held high, her large blue eyes vacant and tearless.

'It's so strange,' she said to herself as she sat down on the bed, facing the large framed photograph of Simon that stood on the little table by the lamp. 'I know he's dead, and yet I don't feel sorry. I don't feel anything at all.'

Downstairs the front-door bell was ringing insistently. Mrs Mathews drew her hand away from her husband's and stood up.

'I wonder why Helen doesn't answer the door,' she said absently. The ringing continued and she added with an effort, 'I suppose I had better answer it myself.'

She drew herself up straight as she went

out to the hall and opened the heavy oak door.

'I'm Adrian Hepworth,' said the tall young man who was standing on the door-step. 'I'm afraid you'll think this awfully presumptuous, coming round without an invitation, but Simon – I promised him I'd look after your daughter, and on the 'phone...'

Mrs Mathews shut the door behind him, drawing him into the hall and helping him off with his respirator and greatcoat.

'I'm so glad you've come,' she said. 'Jonquil was most peculiar – most. I really don't understand the attitude she's taking. She didn't cry or anything. I'm very worried. Do you think I should go up and see her?'

It didn't occur to her that she was asking the advice of a complete stranger. He was just one of those people everyone wanted to confide in – not handsome as Simon had been – but good-looking and strong-looking – a comfortable, sympathetic person. Such was her first impression of Adrian Hepworth.

'I don't think I would just yet,' he said. 'I imagine from what you tell me, that she is numbed by the shock. Perhaps, if you wouldn't mind, I could go and speak to her first?'

'Yes, yes, please do! It's the first unpleasant thing that has ever happened to her and I'm so afraid she'll take it badly. Her room is upstairs on the right. I'm sure conventions can't matter in an occasion like this. Can you find the way, or shall I show you?'

Adrian smiled in spite of himself.

'I think I can manage to find it,' he said gently.

Of course he will, thought Mrs Mathews, as she went back to her husband. He's the sort of person who would always do anything – find anything he wanted. A nice, reliable, dependable person. Relief brought the ready tears to her eyes and she relaxed against her husband's strong shoulder to enjoy a really good cry!

Upstairs, Adrian Hepworth found Jonquil's room and opened the door.

'May I come in?' he asked gently.

The girl nodded her head. Adrian sat down on the edge of the bed and took the photograph of Simon from her.

'It's good, isn't it,' he said. 'Does justice to his good looks. He *is* good-looking, isn't he?'

'Is?' Jonquil spoke for the first time.

'We never speak of anyone in the past in the Air Force,' Adrian explained. 'Because nobody does die. They are always alive in our thoughts.'

'It's not enough,' Jonquil cried suddenly. 'I want *him*. He's the man I was going to marry. I can't marry a memory. Oh, it isn't fair! It isn't fair! I wish he'd never joined the

Air Force. They've taken him away from me.'

'No, the Air Force didn't take him away,' Adrian corrected her quietly. 'Simon went of his own free will, and he went proudly. Flying meant everything to him, and to him, the Royal Air Force and flying were the same thing.'

'He loved me,' Jonquil cried wildly.

'Yes, he loved you,' Adrian agreed. 'But you weren't his only love. Oh, I'm not trying to take away from your memories. I want only to point out that he died happily, fulfilling himself in his other love, his duty.'

'If I'd asked him to, he'd have left the Air Force,' the girl said defiantly.

'Yes, he'd have left,' the man answered. 'But in the first place, you wouldn't have asked him, knowing how much it meant to him. It was part of him – part of his very being. Jonquil, suppose you could have these last weeks over again. Suppose you could ask Simon to leave the Air Force and thereby save his life, would you? Would you?'

He watched the struggle pictured in the haggard young face – the trembling lips, the large expressive eyes, and his whole being melted towards her. She was so young – so tragically unarmed against unhappiness.

He waited, not touching her, until at last as he had known she would, she turned towards him, her eyes now full of tears.

'No, I wouldn't. Of course I wouldn't!' she said, and buried her face in his shoulder, sobbing out the grief and pain that had swept away the first kind numbness of shock.

He let her cry, his fingers stroking her fair curly hair with clumsy tenderness, his voice saying comforting, unimportant things. His very sympathy only increased her tears, which was exactly what he had hoped. It would be so much easier for her if she could 'cry it out'.

When at last she raised a tear-wet, swollen face and blew noisily into the large white handkerchief he had lent her, he once again took charge of the situation.

'Sponge your face in cold water and powder your nose,' he said. 'You've no idea how much better you'll feel afterwards. I'll go down and tell your mother you're all right. She was worried about you.'

Jonquil attempted a smile.

'I suppose she thinks she ought to come and "mother" me,' she said.

Adrian laughed.

'That's just about it,' he said. 'But I'll tell her you're resting and that'll let you both out.'

She looked at him gratefully, realising for the first time, how good, how understanding this friend of Simon's had been. She was suddenly aware, too, that he was a complete stranger to her and that she must be presenting a thoroughly unattractive picture, with her red, swollen eyes and shining nose.

As if realising her sudden embarrassment, Adrian turned to go.

'If I may, I'd like to see you again,' he said. 'Can I give you a ring sometime?'

'Yes, please do,' Jonquil answered. 'I – later, I would like to know more about – how it all happened.'

'I'll ring you up,' Adrian said again, and with his quick smile he closed the door quietly behind him.

Jonquil went over to the wash-basin and bathed her face. She felt a little better afterwards, but her head ached and her eyes were still hot and inflamed. She took a couple of aspirins and lay down on the bed.

When Mrs Mathews came up with a dinner tray some little time later, she found her daughter fast asleep. She undressed her, pulled the bedclothes over the slight, still childish figure, and tiptoed quietly out of the room.

Jonquil slept exhausted until lunch time the following day.

Chapter 2

'That nice man, Adrian Hepworth, tele-phoned this morning, darling!' Mrs Mathews said, looking anxiously at Jonquil's white face and large, dark eyes.

'Oh! What did he want?'

'He wanted to talk to you, dear!' her mother said. 'I told him you were still asleep, so he promised to ring again this afternoon. He wants to see you.'

'Well, I don't want to see him,' Jonquil retorted in a hard voice that made her mother throw another anxious look at her daughter.

'Of course, darling, if you don't *want* to... But you can hardly tell him that on the 'phone, can you?'

'Why not?' Jonquil asked, again in that new voice. 'He was outspoken enough to me yesterday about – about Simon...'

She broke off as the tears rushed to her eyes.

'I won't cry. I *won't*,' she told herself fiercely, biting her lower lip hard as she fought for self-control. This morning, when she awoke, the thought of breaking down as she had done, in front of a complete stranger made her bitterly ashamed. She did not question the fact that her grief was justified, knowing only that she *had* lost control and cried like a child against Adrian Hepworth's shoulder. She was afraid he would think her 'terribly young' which, incidentally he did, but without knowing she considered such an opinion to be detrimental. She hadn't learned yet, that only the very young can afford wishing to be – and to be thought – older than they are.

'I'll harden myself,' she had determined as she came down to lunch. 'Then I shan't make a fool of myself again.'

'I was thinking, Jonquil dear, that I had better cancel the dance we'd arranged for your birthday next week,' her mother was saying as she toyed with her fish.

'But why?' asked Jonquil.

Mrs Mathews stared at her in surprise.

'Well, for one thing, the political situation hardly calls for celebrations,' she blustered. She was trying to be tactful and kind to Jonquil, but somehow everything she was saying seemed to be wrong.

'She has changed,' she thought. 'I don't understand her at all.'

'I don't see that that matters,' Jonquil was saying. 'After all, the papers are treating Dunkirk as a major victory. We can celebrate the "return of the heroes".'

'Of course, if you wish, dear,' Mrs Mathews

25

assented weakly. 'Somehow I thought under the circumstances you … we … well, I thought…' she broke off, floundering out of her depth in a situation she didn't know how to manage.

'If you mean Simon's death, why don't you say so, Mummy?' said Jonquil, gripping her hands together under the table.

'But what will people think?' protested the older woman, feeling thoroughly unhappy and shaken by now.

'What does it matter what they think!' Jonquil burst out angrily. 'I don't care, so why should you? After all, it's my fiancé who has been killed, isn't it? Not yours; not theirs, but mine, *mine*…' Her voice rose to a shout. 'And nothing you nor Daddy nor a hundred Adrian Hepworths can say will make any difference, *nothing*…'

Her voice trembled and afraid to go on she jumped up and ran out of the room and down to the lily pond where she knew she would be alone.

Mrs Mathews stared after her, her face aghast.

'Poor Jonquil!' she said aloud. 'I do hope this tragedy isn't going to make her "queer".'

The 'phone bell rang and glad of something mundane to do, she hurried into the hall to answer it.

'This is Adrian Hepworth speaking. Is Miss Mathews in?'

'Oh, Mr Hepworth...'

'Flight Lieutenant!' he corrected her gently.

'I'm so sorry – Flight Lieutenant Hepworth. I told Jonquil you were 'phoning – this is Mrs Mathews speaking – but she refused to speak to you. She has been most odd – *most*. I don't understand her at all. I've tried to be sympathetic and kind, but she seems to have hardened herself – even against me. It's not normal. It isn't, really!'

And she recounted their conversation at lunch time.

'Where is she now?' Adrian asked, when Mrs Mathews stopped talking.

'She ran out into the garden somewhere. Ought I to go down and stay with her, do you think? She might throw herself in, or something dreadful.'

Adrian smiled in spite of himself.

'I don't think Jonquil would do anything like that,' he reassured her. 'If I were you, I'd just leave her alone. I shall be free about tea time and I'll nip over and have a word with her. How would that be?'

'I *should* be grateful,' Mrs Mathews said with relief. 'Not that she'll see you, I'm afraid.'

'She will!' Adrian said calmly, and with an attempt at humour. 'After all, six foot two is quite a big thing to ignore, you know!'

When Mrs Mathews finally replaced the

27

receiver, she felt a lot better. Such a nice reliable young man! she thought, and went back to finish her lunch.

Jonquil, sitting by the lily pond hugging her hunched knees, noticed with detachment that the rumbling noise of the guns and bombs had ceased. So Dunkirk was all over! The evacuation of the B.E.F. had ceased – a day too late as far as Simon was concerned.

'I won't cry, I won't,' she told herself. 'Oh, I wish I had something to do to keep my mind off him.'

For the first time in her life, she felt really restless and discontented in this wonderful country home with its swimming pool, its tennis courts, and squash court; its rose gardens which were her father's delight, its long, close-cut lawns of which old Longhurst, the head gardener, was so proud. She felt hemmed in by the luxury of it all; by the day's activities that had become routine; by the endless parties and entertainments which were held so often that they had ceased to be exciting – except, of course, when Simon had been there...

'I'd like to get away,' she thought, 'to get a job in town and meet new people; to become independent.'

But she knew that it wasn't really a job she wanted so much as something – anything to take her mind off Simon; as to get away from this house and garden so full of memories of him and their love; away from her mother's anxious, sympathetic voice; her father's pitying affectionate eyes. Above all, she wanted to escape from this dreadful desire to hurt someone because she, herself, had been hurt. She was ashamed of the relief it had given her to be thoroughly rude at lunch time and shock her mother as she had done.

As yet in her life, however, she had had each of those twenty years carefully arranged for her. She had never had to think or plan for herself, and the thought of leaving home and the armour of protection provided by her parents' devotion, both frightened and dismayed her. After all, what did she know of the world? She was intelligent enough to realise that the little she had seen had been of only one part of humanity – the rich, society crowd who thronged to the Riviera and the casinos and the expensive places on the Continent. She had read books, books like Cronin's *Hatters Castle,* and realised that there was another side to like – a grim squalid side, and she was both interested and afraid of it.

No, Jonquil did not think she had the courage to leave home. Here in the country, the war had not really touched her, and she had no wish to experience air raids and bombing as must surely come inevitably to the big towns and cities. They had not been much disturbed here, for black-out curtains had been fitted by an expensive London shop, and caused no trouble at all. True, one or two of the younger gardeners had been called up, and Mrs Mathews' chauffeur. But the old butler was still with them, and at least three gardeners, and the female staff were still intact, from Mrs Mathews' personal maid down to the scullery maid. Petrol rationing had, of course, affected them a little, but not unduly. It was still possible to get an occasional extra gallon here and there, and anyway, with Simon within walking distance, Jonquil didn't need a car. So her own M.G. two-seater had lain idle for the most part, while her mother used Mr Mathews' large Alvis for her shopping. He received an extra allowance to take him to the station some six miles or so away each morning, and if his wife wished to use the car, she drove him in herself, and sent Jonquil to fetch him in the evening.

No, the war hadn't really touched Jonquil and her home materially at all – even after nine months of fighting. Not that it hadn't laid its finger-tips on her father. His business had been badly hit, since most of it was in occupied countries in Europe, but hard hit though he had been, he was a very rich man, and he saw no necessity as yet to start economising. Time enough for that later, he thought, and thrust his financial worries from him. The loss of three gardeners and his chauffeur had been a slight economy – a small one, but nevertheless a start, and no doubt there would soon be others going. He would not replace them. No, there was no need yet to start stinting his wife and daughter.

So Jonquil continued to have a large dress allowance and Mrs Mathews a still larger one. Her household accounts she handed over to her competent and capable housekeeper, who dealt with them directly with her husband. She, herself, had plenty to do ordering meals, managing the large staff, arranging the flowers and entertaining her own and her husband's friends. She had, since the war broke out, become chairman of some of the women's committees – the Womens' Institute and the Evacuees' Committee – and although she was mainly a figure-head, she was sometimes asked to give prizes and make speeches. There was one occasion when she had addressed a meeting which she thought she would never forget. It had not been a success. Firstly, the vicar, who was to introduce her to the audience, being slightly absent-minded, had presented her as 'Lady Montague', confusing Mrs Mathews with the next week's lecturer. And with this to upset her, she had herself given the wrong talk, momentarily mistaking this audience to be the Evacuees' Mothers instead of the Women's Institute, consequently welcoming to the village some of its oldest inhabitants.

As it happened, however, the microphone provided for the occasion had broken down after her first few words, and only the front row of the audience had heard a word she said. But she had been very upset by the affair and had since relegated her duties to sending along blankets and clothes and occasional donations.

In spite of these committees which had sprung up since the war, it was still a very peaceful country village and even the influx of airmen from the neighbouring Royal Air Force Station, had failed to shake them out of their complacency. Many of the officers were billeted out in the village, but Adrian Hepworth, being one of the original squadron members, like Simon, had quarters on the camp. He had just left them now in his old broken-down Morris, and was driving towards the Mathews' large house.

Twenty-five years old, Adrian seemed a lot older. He had been left an orphan in his infancy and had been brought up by an aged uncle who had once been a professor of science at one of the colleges in Cambridge. Since his earliest years, therefore, Adrian had possessed a fund of knowledge which sat quaintly on the shoulders of one so young. He had soon acquired a particular liking for all mechanical sciences and he passed out of Cambridge at twenty-two with firsts in both science and engineering, and a desire above all others to design aeroplanes.

'Can't design something you know nothing about,' his old uncle had said. 'Better get some experience first. When you know how to fly, you can think again about designing aeroplanes.'

So Adrian had entered the Royal Air Force for five years and when war broke out, was sent down with the squadron to one of the forward 'dromes on the South coast. It was here he had first become friendly with Simon O'Dair. Their friendship was based on their mutual love of flying and whenever they were together, they reverted to this topic. Adrian knew, of course, that Simon was engaged to the Mathews' girl, but not until Dunkirk – until Simon had that odd premonition of his death and asked him to look after Jonquil should anything happen to him, had he, Adrian, even so much as known her Christian name.

Girls had never meant much in his life. There had been one or two casual attachments at Cambridge, but no girl had come anywhere near touching his heart – until he had met Jonquil. Seeing her for the first time, sitting on her bed staring at Simon's photograph with large unseeing eyes, her face framed in a mass of fair wavy hair, he had known beyond all doubt that this was the girl he was destined to love, for better or for worse – and for all his life.

He didn't argue with this feeling, but accepted it as naturally as he would have accepted a sixth sense. Whether or not she would ever grow to love him, he had not even contemplated. Enough that he loved her and she needed his help.

Mrs Mathews greeted him affectionately. Already she liked and trusted him and was only too willing that he should have a talk with Jonquil.

He found her still sitting – like Narcissus, he thought – staring at her reflection in the lily pond. She looked up startled, as she heard his footsteps, and a blush crept into her face when she recognised him.

'She's remembering yesterday,' he thought instinctively, and wondered what he should say to make her feel at ease with him again.

'Did Mummy ask you to come?' she asked suddenly.

'No, I came of my own free will,' Adrian said with a grin. 'I thought you might like company.'

'Not yours, anyway!' Jonquil heard herself say rudely.

For a minute or two Adrian didn't speak. Then again instinctively, he divined the

34

cause of her rudeness.

'Suppose you work off your ill feeling against someone who deserves it,' he said quietly.

Jonquil looked up.

'What do you mean?'

'The Jerries, of course. They killed your Simon, not I. Why don't you fight *them?* They're your enemies. I want to be your friend.'

'How can I?' Jonquil asked scornfully. 'What do you expect *me* to do?'

'Well, you could join up,' Adrian suggested. 'I hear the W.A.A.F. are in need of recruits.'

'Join up as what? A cook, I suppose.'

'Are you a snob?' he asked quietly.

Jonquil felt suddenly ashamed, and was annoyed with him for having the power to make her so.

'No, I'm not!' she countered swiftly.

'Afraid to leave home then?'

She stood up, her eyes blazing with anger, and before he had realised her intention, she slapped him hard across the face.

'No, I'm not afraid to leave home,' she shouted at him. 'It'll be a pleasure since you're living so near.'

And she turned and ran up the path towards the house.

Adrian sat a moment longer by the lily pond, his hand nursing his cheek. His eyes were smiling a little, and he looked exceedingly pleased with himself.

'It's the best possible thing for her,' he told himself, and added with another grin, 'she'll look absolutely sweet in Air Force blue!'

He lit a cigarette and walked back slowly towards the house.

Chapter 3

Jonquil took a 'bus to Aldgate and walked the rest of the way to Victory House. Even although it was twenty-four hours since she had slapped Adrian Hepworth's face for insulting her, she still felt buoyed up with resentment against him. But the angry bubble inside her was slowly subsiding, leaving a sinking feeling in the pit of her stomach.

'Just the same sensation as I used to get going back to school!' she thought. 'Well, I don't have to join up. I can say I've just come to learn more about it. I don't have to make any decision.'

But even as she thought it, she knew her decision was already made. She could not, not under any circumstances, go back and face Adrian's taunts and jeers.

'Afraid to leave home!' he had said. And he had hit the nail on the head. She *was* scared – frightened to death of the unknown horrors awaiting her in service life. She had conjured up all kinds of dreadful ideas about the Recruiting Office on her way up in the train, and her nerves were now rapidly getting the better of her. She wished very much that she had brought her mother with her, but that would have meant telling her of her intention of joining the Women's Auxiliary Air Force, and Jonquil knew the commotion that would have caused.

She still had the parents' disapproval to face, of course, but it would be far easier to walk into the drawing-room and announce: 'I'm a Waaf!' – than to try to persuade them to let her join up. Once she had given in her name, she didn't suppose they would try to stop her.

Jonquil drew a deep breath and went in through the swing doors of the Recruiting Office at Victory House. Inside a large room were two or three desks at each of which was seated a Waaf officer. Opposite each of them was seated a girl in civilian clothes, and all around the walls of the room were more girls sitting on chairs and benches provided for those awaiting their interviews.

She went to the end of the line and sat down beside a pretty-looking girl in a smart blue coat and skirt and a neat, perky little hat. The girl studied Jonquil for a moment, then dived into her handbag and brought out a tortoiseshell case.

'Cigarette?' she asked.

Jonquil took one gratefully. The girl struck a match and lit both their cigarettes, and for a minute or two, they sat in silence, inhaling deeply. Presently the girl spoke.

'My name is Muriel Charlestone,' she

said, introducing herself. 'Who are you?'

Jonquil, usually a little shy with strangers, found she felt no embarrassment with this frank charming girl at her side.

'Jonquil Mathews,' she told her simply.

'Jonquil! What an unusual name,' the girl Muriel said with a smile. 'But I think Jonnie suits you better. There's something boyish about your close-cropped hair and – well, it just seems to suit you. Muriel, now, is a dreadful name. I'm better known as Em. I'm so glad you came and sat down here. When you first came into the room, I hoped you would. I've been waiting here for half an hour you know, and I'm fed up with my own company.'

'Half an hour!' Jonquil exclaimed aghast.

The other girl laughed.

'Oh, the queue's comparatively small now,' she said cheerfully. 'I don't suppose we'll be here more than another twenty minutes or so. Tell me what are you going to join as?'

'I don't know exactly,' Jonquil said slowly. 'I hadn't really thought about it. What *could* I do?'

'Well, there are all sorts of things,' Em said thoughtfully. 'Teleprinters and cooks and general duties, whatever they are! And – oh, heaps of others. But I'm going to do Special Duties.'

'What are they?'

'I'm not awfully sure,' Em said truthfully.

'But it's some kind of secret plotting work, I believe. I've got a girl friend who joined, but she's not allowed to say what she does. She thoroughly recommended it, though, and I think it sounds rather exciting. Why don't you go in for it, too? We might be together then.'

'Oh, do you think we might?' Jonquil asked eagerly. Everything would be so much more bearable if shared with someone, and this girl was so cheerful and friendly and self-assured.

'If you'd really like the idea, we could go for our interview together – say we are old friends and want to stay with each other if possible,' Em was saying.

'I *should* like it!' Jonquil said, her eyes shining. 'It's terribly good of you to suggest it.'

'Rubbish!' Em said with a laugh. 'We'd better start talking quickly, though, if we're supposed to be old friends. Tell me something about yourself.'

So Jonquil told Em about the twenty years of her life, shyly at first, but gradually with more frankness. She skipped over her childhood days, but went more deeply into the these last few months. When it came to telling Em about Simon her voice broke a little and the other girl laid a sympathetic hand on her shoulder.

'You don't have to tell me if you'd rather not!' she said kindly.

40

But Jonquil struggled on, conquering her tears, and told Em everything without reserve.

'That Adrian Hepworth sounds a nice person,' Em remarked when Jonquil had finished her story.

The younger girl looked up indignantly.

'Nice?' she echoed. 'Why, he's been perfectly horrible!'

'Not really, Jonnie,' Em said quietly. 'He was only hard for your sake. I'm sure of it. He knew how bad it would be for you to mope about by yourself, and I suppose he guessed making you angry would be the quickest way of making you join.'

Jonquil looked subdued.

'I never thought of that!' she said, and she turned impulsively to her new friend. 'I'm so glad I've met you, Em,' she said. 'I've never really had a particular girl friend since I left school. I was Mummy's constant companion abroad, and then, of course, there was Simon... Do tell me more about yourself.'

'O.K.!' said Em, with her cheerful smile. 'Here goes. I'm twenty-four; the oldest girl in a large family of four sons and three daughters. All my brothers are in the services, the three eldest in the R.A.F. and the youngest in the A.T.C. As a family we've never had enough money, but we've struggled along somehow – on family affection, I guess. The

41

other two girls are only babies still. Jill's fourteen and Barbara twelve. So being my brother's contemporary, I was always with them and they treated me like one of themselves. When Jim – he's the youngest – joined the A.T.C. I thought it was about time I got into blue, too. I'm still working at a secretarial job in the city, but I've given notice in lieu of my calling up. This boring you, Jonnie?'

'Not in the least,' Jonquil said. 'I'm enthralled!'

'I'm afraid the W.A.A.F. pay isn't much,' Em went on. 'And I shan't be able to help out with my salary as I have been doing. But Mother says I'll be one less to house and feed, and insisted I should go if I wanted to. Bless her! I know it'll mean more economising for her. But I'll get a commission or something, and work my way up until the pay is worth having! Pete – he's thirty – and Mark, who's twenty-eight – have already got their commissions. Joe's twenty-two, and only joined last year, so he's still a Sergeant Pilot. Shortly, I hope, yours truly will be a private (whatever they call that!) in the Women's Auxiliary Air Force.'

She stubbed out her cigarette and felt for the tortoiseshell case again. Then she changed her mind, and put it back in her handbag.

'Might as well start economising now,' she

said cheerfully.

Jonquil reached for her own silver case, but Em shook her head.

'That doesn't mean I'm making it up on you,' she said. 'If we're going to be friends, Jonnie, we're going Dutch – always. See?'

Jonquil smiled and nodded her head. But privately she determined to do all she could to help this girl and her family. She, who had everything, and as much of it as she wanted, realised for the first time how poorer people lived. She thought of her two large wardrobes, the shoe cupboard with the fifty odd pairs of shoes kept neatly in their racks by her maid; the row of evening dresses which hadn't been worn more than twice at the most; the costly fur coats, and Lillywhite's sports models. She longed suddenly, to ring up home and ask her maid to pack everything up and send it to Em's house. But she had enough sense to appreciate Em's pride. She would have to help this girl unobtrusively – in lots of little ways.

'Next, please!'

Em grabbed her hand and they went up to the desk together.

'Miss Mathews and I are friends and would like our interview together, if it's possible,' she said politely.

'Of course,' the Waaf officer said with a friendly smile. 'Draw up another chair and sit down. There! Now tell me all about your-selves. What branch do you want to join, or haven't you made up your minds yet?'

'We thought we'd like to go in for Special Duties,' Em said. 'I – we've a friend doing that and though she couldn't say much about it, she thought we'd like it.'

'It sounds a very good suggestion,' the Waaf agreed. 'We are badly in need of girls like you at the moment – girls with good educations and quick brains and plenty of intelligence.'

Already she had made them feel indis-pensable – welcomed into the Waaf. They both felt more confident and Jonquil felt heartily ashamed of her former fears.

'Would you like to think it over?' the officer was asking them. 'You needn't rush into anything, you know. Unfortunately, I can't give you much of an insight into Special Duties as it's on the Secret List. If you do join that branch you'll just have to risk it!'

Em looked at Jonquil, then turned back to their interviewer.

'I guess we'll take the risk,' she said.

'I'll take your names, then,' the Waaf told them with a smile. 'How soon could you come?'

Again Jonquil felt a little thrill of pleasure. *'How soon could you come?'* It was nice to know you were needed so urgently.

'I shall have to complete the month where I'm working,' Em said. 'Say in three weeks' time. How about you, Jonnie?'

'That suits me,' Jonquil said. It would just give her parents time to settle down to the idea of her going!

'Of course, you'll have to have medical examinations first,' the Waaf said. 'Could you do that right away?'

The two girls looked at each other and nodded.

'Well, take the first door on the right,' the girl said. 'And join the queue. There will be rather a lot of waiting about, I'm afraid. We're short of staff and everyone seems to want to join at once! Come back and see me when it's all over. Good luck to you!'

The interview was over.

Em and Jonquil found the door marked 'Medical Examinations' and walked in rather tentatively.

Once again there were chairs all round the room. One or two near the door were vacant and the girls sat down. At the opposite side of the room was another door beside which stood a Waaf. Presently a head popped out of the room and called:

'Next ten, please!' and the first ten girls were shepherded in through the door by the Waaf. Everyone else moved round ten places, and the subdued whispering started again.

More girls filled the chairs beside them and slowly they moved round the room. Jonquil tried to visualise her neighbours in uniform, but failed to do so. There was every kind of girl there – blondes, redheads, tall, thin, fat, round, cheerful, miserable, talkative, nervy, excited, apprehensive. Their emotions were pictured on their faces. Jonquil looked at Em's face, found that it was the only one with a calm assured expression.

'I was thinking,' Em said, 'what a marvellous picture this would make. My father is an artist, you know. (That's why there's never any money!) I'd like him to see all these girls here. What a picture! Women with a capital W, and each one with a different expression, a different character, a different reason, probably, for joining up.' Jonquil nodded her head. The scene was already alive in her own receptive memory. It was one of the impressions she never forgot.

The two girls were both a little weary by the time they reached the first ten, and they rose quickly when the Waaf called to them to move forward. The room they entered was scantily furnished – having nothing in it but a big table with ten chairs and a long bench by one wall. A Waaf officer stood by the table with a sheath of papers in her hand.

'Everyone is to fill in one of these forms,' she said as she distributed them. 'Do not leave a blank against any of the questions, but answer "Yes" or "No". If you don't understand the question, ask me. As soon as you have completed the form go and sit on the bench until you are called into the Examining Room.'

'Good heavens!' Em whispered. 'Fancy having to say all that three or four hundred times a day!'

'No talking, please,' said the Waaf, and silence fell in the little room, broken only by the scratching of pens. Jonquil wrote her name, her age, her address, and answered the questions as best she could. Place of birth, nationality, parents' names. Had she had any operation? No. Had she had any accidents? No. Did she suffer from fainting fits? No. Did she suffer from epilepsy? No.

She smiled as she read some of the questions, and met Em's glance with a friendly wink. Presently one of the girls started asking questions.

'Please, Miss, what's "epilepsy"?'

The Waaf officer explained patiently, and silence fell again, but only for a moment. The girl started again.

'Please, Miss, is falling off a bicycle when I was five an accident?'

'Not unless you were badly hurt.'

'Please, Miss...' until Jonquil felt like screaming. She wondered how on earth the Waaf kept so even tempered.

47

At last she and Em finished their forms, and sat down to wait on the bench. This time, however, they did not have to wait long. Another door opened and an R.A.F. orderly beckoned them to go in.

They were weighed; they had eyes, ears, nose, throat and feet examined. Then they went behind a screen and undressed, and were thoroughly examined by a Waaf doctor. When at last they were dressed again, they were asked by the Waaf doctor to provide specimens, and were shown into another room.

Nature, however, had a will of its own, and after a short while Jonquil emerged feeling extremely self-conscious to find Em in fits of laughter.

'Darned if I can do it to order!' she said, and burst out laughing to find Jonquil in the same predicament.

The Waaf doctor was very amused when they went back and explained the situation, and suggested they should go and have some tea and come back later. So Jonquil and Em walked down Fleet Street and spent an hour in a milk bar drinking glasses of Malted Milk and eating ice cream until they felt quite sick.

When they went back to Victory House, they were greeted with more laughs from the entire medical staff who had all been told the joke. Nature was overwhelmed by force of circumstances this time, however, and to the girls' relief, their papers were signed at last, signifying they were absolutely fit.

They stopped to tell the Waaf officer who had interviewed them, and left Victory House behind them.

'I've got to catch Daddy's train back to the country,' Jonquil said, looking at her watch. 'So I'll have to be going now, Em. Do you have every week-end off?'

'Saturday afternoons and Sundays,' Em told her. 'Why?'

'Would you care to come down and spend next week-end with me?' Jonquil asked shyly. 'It would be nice if we could get to know each other better. Besides, I need some help tackling my parents. They don't know I'm joining up and when they do, they're sure to imagine all sorts of ogres I might meet. Seeing you will make them realise the W.A.A.F. can't all be bad. Do come, Em!'

Em hesitated a moment, then, realising that Jonquil really did want her – that it wasn't just kindness – she readily agreed.

'I'd love it,' she admitted.

'Mummy has arranged a big party for my birthday which is on Sunday,' Jonquil told her. 'But I'll ask her to cancel it. Perhaps Adrian would come over and bring some-one along to make up numbers and we can have a quiet evening at home.'

'That sounds lovely,' Em said. 'See you

49

next week, then, Jonnie.'

'I'll ring up Adrian when I get home,' Jonquil thought, as she jumped into a taxi and was driven towards Victoria Station. 'I'll tell him I've met Em and – well, I think perhaps I owe him an apology. Besides, since he knows so well how to manage people, perhaps he'll tell me how to break the news to Daddy and Mummy.'

It wasn't until she reached the familiar landscape of home that she really thought about Simon. Then desolation swept away the excitement and with a great longing for reassurance and comfort, Jonquil drove her father quickly through the lanes towards the house.

'Immediately I get in,' she thought, 'I'll telephone Adrian.'

With this feeling of urgency increasing every minute she turned the car through the big iron gates into the drive.

Chapter 4

'Hullo! Flight-Lieutenant Hepworth? Oh, it's Jonquil Mathews here.'

'This is an unexpected pleasure,' Adrian said, wondering why she had 'phoned. 'Nothing wrong, I hope?'

'No! I just – wanted to say how sorry I am for behaving so badly the other day.'

'Nonsense!' came Adrian's reassuring tones. 'I was equally to blame, egging you on as I did.'

'Then Em was right!' Jonquil said, more to herself than to Adrian.

'Who is Em?' he asked. 'And why was she right?'

'I'd better start at the beginning and tell you all,' Jonquil laughed. 'I joined up today, and Em is one of the girls I met at the recruiting depot. We're hoping to stick together through our W.A.A.F. careers.'

'Well, this *is* news,' Adrian said. 'May I offer you my congratulations, Jonquil?'

'Don't tease,' she said.

'I'm not. I mean it,' Adrian replied seriously. 'I think it's wonderful, Jonquil. What is Em like?'

'She's coming down next week-end to stay

with me,' Jonquil told him. 'So you'll meet her then, I hope. I thought perhaps you would come over on the Saturday evening and bring someone along with you.'

'What kind of person do you think Em would like?' Adrian asked.

Jonquil gave a detailed description of Em, and Adrian decided to bring his navigator.

'They seem to have had much the same sort of lives,' he said. 'So they should get along very well together. What do the family say to all this, Jonquil?'

'That's just it!' Jonquil said. 'They don't know yet. I thought you might be able to help me – to tell me the most tactful way of breaking the news.'

Adrian felt a little thrill of pleasure. She needed him, was asking for his help. At last she must be looking on him as a friend. This love he had for her was so new and surprising to him, that Adrian needed no reciprocation as yet to keep him happy. He was still discovering in himself new, deeper emotions than he had hitherto experienced, had not realised he possessed. This great, melting tenderness, for instance, that had somehow transformed him, making him stronger, more capable of tackling any adversity for her sake. This instinctive understanding of her – her mind, her thoughts, her reactions, was born, he was sure, of his love. One day, perhaps, she too would feel that way about him. The more he saw of her, the more certain he was that she had never really been in love with Simon. In a boy and girl affair only – a sort of calf love. But he knew the gay, irresponsible Simon for one was not capable of reaching, probing into the very heart of this girl. And she, with so little experience of loving, could not have missed in him the mental understanding and compatibility of temperament that together with intense desire and passion make love and marriage the perfect thing.

Adrian had no feeling of disloyalty to Simon for these thoughts. He knew and felt that Simon, wherever he was, must know that while he had been alive Adrian would never have allowed such thoughts to pass through his mind, far less take possession of his heart. Anything he had felt for Jonquil he would ruthlessly have thrust into the background. But now no amount of wishing could bring Simon back, and Adrian knew his friend well enough to realise that he, least of all, would not wish Jonquil to remain unmarried all her life.

'Go ahead, old man!' he could almost hear Simon saying. 'Since I can't have her, let the next best man win!'

No, he did not feel disloyal to his friend for setting out to win Jonquil's love.

'You're taking a long time about it,' Jonquil said, breaking in on his thoughts. 'Is

53

it going to be as difficult as all that?'

Adrian dragged his thoughts back to the present.

'I should just announce quite firmly that you've joined the W.A.A.F. and, when the storm blows over a bit, tell them you've asked Em down. That'll give them something else to think about – to take their minds off you. I'll be holding thumbs for you, Jonquil.'

'Thanks, Adrian. And – am I forgiven for the other day?'

'There's nothing to forgive,' came Adrian's quiet voice.

'You're awfully nice!' Jonquil said suddenly and naïvely. 'Simon said you were, of course, but I hadn't really realised it until now...'

'I'll be getting swollen-headed soon,' Adrian interrupted. The pleasure of hearing her say such things was very bitter-sweet. They made him want to say all sorts of ridiculous things to her – that he couldn't but help being nice to her since he loved her, but he knew he must keep his emotions under control for a long time to come if he wanted to win her love.

'I'll have to be going now,' he said. 'What time on Saturday, Jonquil?'

'About six-thirty, if you can manage it,' she told him.

'We'll be there,' Adrian said. 'So long, Jonquil.'

'Goodbye-ee!'

'Hey, come back here. You shouldn't ever say "goodbye"!' Adrian told her, laughing. 'I'm superstitious. Say *"Au Revoir!"*'

She laughed with him.

'*Au Revoir,* Adrian!'

He waited until she had replaced the receiver before he replaced his own. Then he went into the mess anteroom and ordered a large stiff drink at the bar.

Jonquil went upstairs to her room and changed into one of her short silk frocks. They still changed in the evenings, even when they were alone, and into the more formal long dinner dress when they had visitors. To-night, they were *en famille,* and as Jonquil went down the wide staircase, crossed the hall with its big oak chest on which stood the telephone and the silver tray for visiting cards, she knew that this must be the moment to tell her parents she had joined up.

'Hullo, Jonquil dear!' her mother said as she sat down on her favourite seat – a little humpty in front of the fireplace. 'Did you have a good day in town?'

Jonquil took a deep breath.

'Yes I did, thank you,' she said quietly. And then: 'Mummy, this may come as a bit of a shock to you and Daddy, but you've got to know sooner or later. I'm – I've joined the

W.A.A.F. I shall be called up in about three weeks' time'

Her voice trailed away as she met her mother's horrified stare.

'Jonquil! You're joking,' Mrs Mathews said, and, appealing to her husband, 'Robert, tell Jonquil not to play such horrid jokes on me.'

'She's like a child!' Jonquil thought, with sudden pity. 'Whenever anything goes wrong, she pretends at first that it's a joke. Then she appeals to Daddy to make it right.'

She went over to her mother and put her arms round her protectively.

'Mumsie, I had to!' she said gently, using the old childish name. 'It isn't that I want to leave you and Daddy. It's just that I must do something – anything to keep my mind off Simon. Here in the garden where we spent so much time together... Well, I just can't stand it. And another thing, I've got to do something to repay the debt left owing by his death. They killed him and I'm going to do what I can...'

She broke off, realising that her mother wasn't even listening. Her face had creased into tiny lines and the tears were trickling slowly down her cheeks.

'I shall be losing my only child – my baby,' she cried emotionally.

Jonquil looked at her helplessly, and her pity gave way to contempt. Why couldn't she

56

be like Em's mother – brave and courageous. Did money weaken one to this extent?

'If this is the result of being rich, I'd rather be poor,' she thought. 'I'd rather be like Em.'

She turned to her father.

'Daddy, you haven't said anything,' she cried. 'You're not angry, too, are you?'

Robert Mathews laid a hand on his daughter's shoulder.

'No, I'm not angry,' he said softly. 'I'm proud, very proud of you. I shall hate your going, of course, but I like to think there's still some of the old blood fighting for England. The last war – well, it wasn't fun, Jonquil, but I met some of the grandest people, and the spirit and comradeship among the men was something I shall never forget – that, and all of us marching to "It's a Long Way to Tipperary." Oh, the war was sordid all right, but it made men of us. I like to remember I fought for England, and since I'm too old to fight again, I am happy that you...'

'Robert!' cried his wife, aghast. 'How can you be so – so cruel! Actually encouraging the girl! Think of the dangers, the discomforts she'll have to endure; the dreadful people she'll mix with; the illnesses she might get, and me not there to look after her...'

'Of course there'll be discomforts,' Mr

Mathews broke in. 'And illnesses, but she'll get plenty of medical attention. Our M.O. in the last war was a Harley Street specialist. It'll do Jonquil an enormous amount of good – broaden her outlook which I have often thought was too narrow. I've got faith in our daughter, Joan. She's had a good basic training and education and she won't forget it. Whatever happens, she'll come out on top.'

It was the longest speech Jonquil had ever heard him make.

'Daddy!' she cried, flinging herself into his arms. 'You're marvellous, you are really. If you knew how much your trust in me encourages me. Why, I feel ready to fight a hundred Germans single-handed and beat them all!'

She turned to her mother impulsively.

'Please, Mummy,' she pleaded. 'Try and understand. Say you won't stop me – because you can, you know, if you really wanted to. I'm not of age yet. And if anything awful *should* happen to me, I could always get out.'

'Come, Joan,' said Robert Mathews firmly. 'The child will have enough to worry her without the thought of you crying your eyes out at home. You know she'll go, whatever we say, so you might as well make the best of it!'

'Well, there's no need to be rude, Robert!'

said his wife indignantly, and he and his daughter knew she had accepted the inevitable.

The gong sounded for dinner and Jonquil drew her mother on ahead.

'It was all Adrian's idea, you know, Mummy,' she said with a smile.

'Well!' said Mrs Mathews. 'Let's hope you get sent to the R.A.F. station here. Then you'll be near home, and Adrian can look after you.'

'You'll be able to ask him all about the W.A.A.F. on Saturday,' Jonquil said. 'I've asked him to dinner and as I've also asked a future Waaf friend of mine for the week-end, I told him to bring a fourth...'

'Now that will be nice,' her mother said, cheering up enormously at the thought of entertaining. 'Let's see, Jonquil, we could have oysters – they're in season now, and then a roast chicken...'

She relapsed into silence, mentally planning the menu.

Robert Mathews caught his daughter's eye across the table and winked affectionately. Outside, in the servants' hall, the parlour-maid told the cook about that wink.

'The Master and Miss Jonquil's got something up their sleeves,' she said. 'Wonder what it is!'

Before the end of the week, they knew. Mrs Mathews announced that the guest room was to be made up for one of Miss Jonquil's Waaf friends who was coming for the week-end.

'In case you don't know, Helen,' she told the maid, not without pride. 'Miss Jonquil's volunteered for the W.A.A.F.!'

'Well,' gasped Helen, suitably surprised. 'Did you ever now, "Mum".'

'No!' said Mrs Mathews, taking her literally. 'In my day there wasn't any W.A.A.F.'

Helen giggled and rushed off to tell the rest of the staff the startling news.

Jonquil herself cut the flowers and decorated Em's room. Nothing elaborate, she told herself. Just a large bowl of garden marigolds and violas, and a vase of deep red roses. Em must not be allowed to feel at a disadvantage.

'I wonder if she'll remember to bring a dinner dress,' she thought, at the same time doubting it. Em's family would eat round the large kitchen table in a homely fashion, and they certainly wouldn't wear dinner dress.

She went upstairs to her wardrobe and studied the row of dresses carefully. There was one, a pale-blue frock with a cowl neck and long, tight sleeves, which she knew would suit Em beautifully.

'I'll give it to her,' she thought, but immediately a frown creased her forehead. Em wouldn't like that. She'd think it was charity.

'I know,' Jonquil thought on a sudden inspiration. 'I'll offer to sell it to her for five guineas. She'll never know it was a twenty-five guinea model...'

So Em, unsuspecting, bought the model, and the two girls, one dark, one fair, and both looking extremely glamorous, descended the large staircase together to greet their guests.

'Hullo! Many Happy Returns of tomorrow, Jonquil,' Adrian said. 'This is Flying Officer Charles Lewis – Miss Jonquil Mathews and...'

'Muriel Charlestone,' Jonquil supplemented for him.

'Muriel, this is Adrian Hepworth.'

The introductions over, the four of them joined Mr and Mrs Mathews in the drawing-room. Conversation before and during dinner reverted to the W.A.A.F., and Charles Lewis backed Adrian's theory that the two girls would enjoy Service life enormously. He and Em seemed to hit it off very well, and Jonquil, seated beside Adrian, found time to compliment him on his character perception.

'Em likes him!' she said. 'And I do, too.'

'*I* think *you're* nice!'

Adrian allowed the words to leave his lips, unable to resist the temptation of testing her reactions to such a remark. But she did not take him seriously.

'Flatterer!' she said, and changed the conversation.

'Just as well!' thought Adrian, but in spite of himself he was a little disappointed. He had hoped – well, what had he hoped? He shrugged his shoulders and turned to Mrs Mathews.

'I expect you'll miss Jonquil, won't you?' he said politely. The sumptuous dinner progressed slowly into its third course.

Mr and Mrs Mathews retired soon after the news, leaving the young people to themselves. Charles Lewis had had his eye on the baby grand that Jonquil sometimes played, and seeing this, she suggested he should play to them. He went over to the piano immediately, Em at his side.

'What would you like, Em?' he asked her as he ran his hands lightly over the keys?'

'Classical or jazz?' Em asked.

'Well, I can do either,' Charles said without boastfulness. 'Lady, name your piece!'

'Could it be *Swan Lake?*' Em asked eagerly.

For answer, he struck an opening chord and played the ballet music without hesitation or fault. Em sat by his side, her face mobile with expression, her gaze far away, and enrapt. Every now and again, Charles looked down at her, but it was not until he had finished the piece that she met his gaze. Then they smiled at one another with perfect understanding, and Em gave a little sigh of content.

'Please,' she said. 'Please go on!'

Adrian and Jonquil sat by the large log fire, smoking in companionable silence. Both were lovers of good music, but neither were really concentrating on Charles's playing at that moment. Each was lost deep in their own thoughts.

'She looks older, more beautiful in black,' Adrian was thinking. 'But it's too sombre for her really. I'd like to dress her always in blues and bright vivid colours – and white. White, he thought, would be most becoming of all. He remembered, suddenly Yvonne Printemps singing, 'I'll Follow my Secret Heart', and those words, spoken in her delightful broken English: 'White, white for a bride!' – and his heart contracted painfully. Jonquil as a bride – his bride.

A wave of desire swept through him with such intensity that he wanted to cry out. Oh, the pain, the ecstasy of loving as he loved! Would she ever belong to him – love him – long for him this way?

'I'll never fall in love again,' Jonquil was thinking. 'Oh, Simon, Simon. How terribly I miss you. How wonderful this evening would have been if you'd been here. How – how shall I go on living alone – without you? And what would you say if you knew I was going to be a W.A.A.F.?'

A sudden excitement for the future replaced the loneliness and unhappiness in her heart. It was so comforting to have something to look forward to. She had Adrian to thank for that.

She looked up at him, and her eyes were shining with gratitude as she met his gaze. They smiled at one another, and Adrian, seeing her changed expression, felt his hands trembling.

'Perhaps,' he thought. 'Perhaps one day...'

Chapter 5

Jonquil and Em were shown into the waiting-room at Victory House. They both wore light summer suits and each had with her a small suitcase containing serviceable pyjamas, wash things, make-up and a few photographs. Jonquil had left the large, framed picture of Simon at home, having with her only a few snapshots she had taken in the Spring, but which were particularly good of him.

The two girls put their suitcases on the floor and sat down on the green plush chairs, conscious of the curious stares of the five other girls in the room.

'It's like a dentist's waiting-room,' Em whispered to Jonquil with a shudder. Then she giggled suddenly. 'Let's outstare them,' she said. 'It'll be like school-days over again.'

The five girls opposite them also had suit-cases and it occurred to Em as she noticed them, that they, too, must have been called up today.

'I wonder if we are all going to the same place,' she said, breaking the silence.

Everyone started to speak at once,

nervously and excitedly.

They all appealed to Em, instinctively aware that she was to be the leader among them.

'Do you know where we are going?' one girl asked timidly. She had a heavy dark veil over her face and seemed more shy and nervous than the other four.

'I wonder if we will travel by ourselves or if a Waaf will come with us,' another remarked.

They were, however, to go alone. A Waaf officer came into the room and, taking stock of the girls, addressed Em without hesitation.

'What is your name?' she asked.

'Muriel Charlestone,' Em answered in her quiet calm voice.

'You will take charge of the others. Here is a joint railway warrant for you. You will proceed to the Waaf depot, where you will be met at the guard room by a Waaf. Give this envelope to her. Is that quite clear?'

'Yes, thank you!' Em nodded her head.

'Officers are always addressed as "M'am",' the Waaf told her kindly. 'You might just as well get accustomed to it right away, Charlestone. You, of course, will be called by your surnames. Now I'll just make sure you are all here...'

She took a list from her pocket and ran through the names quickly. They were all present.

'Well, good luck to you all,' she said, and handed the envelope and railway warrant to Em.

'Thank you, M'am,' they said together, feeling rather like a herd of sheep. But they were to get used to it, and in time this mode of address became so automatic that they no longer noticed it.

Em escorted her small party to the Underground, and shepherded them into the train. As it drew near their destination, the carriage emptied slowly of all save themselves, and counting them for the fourth time, she found to her relief that they were all there.

Jonquil was studying her companions. They had paired off already, and the girl with the heavy veil had been left odd.

'Aren't you awfully hot in that?' she asked, unable to think of any other subject on which to open a conversation.

'Yes, a little!' The girl's voice was quiet and highly strung. Jonquil felt sorry for her.

'Why don't you take your hat off, then?' she said simply. 'Em and I have taken ours off.'

'Because my face is scarred,' the girl said roughly.

For a moment Jonquil could think of nothing to say. What a dreadful blunder to make! Then her common sense came to the fore.

'Nonsense,' she said. 'It can't be as bad as all that! Besides, you won't be able to wear a veil with a Waaf cap, you know.'

The girl was silent for a few minutes, until with a little gesture of defiance, she pulled the veil away and turned her face to them.

'Why, it's hardly noticeable!' Em said firmly. 'If I hadn't heard you talking about it to Jonnie, I should never have noticed it.'

'You're just being kind,' the girl said. 'All my life – ever since I was twelve, when this happened...' she pointed to her pock-marked face – 'people have stared at me and made remarks. You'd think I might get used to it after all this time – and I suppose I am in a way. But it doesn't make their remarks any nicer ... hearing children in 'buses saying to their mothers, "What's the matter with that lady's face, Mummy?" And seeing hotel managers eyeing me with suspicion whenever we went away to the seaside for holidays because they thought I might have something catching. Once we were turned out because the other guests complained... Mother tried to pretend there was nothing wrong, and made me go to children's parties and when I was older, to dances. But it was always the same – people were either curious or repulsed by me. Now, I think, mother is scared to take me anywhere because we are both dreading the inevitable and trying not to let the other know...' Her voice trailed away miserably.

'Why did you join up?' Em asked abruptly. 'I mean, won't you be rather putting your head in the lion's den, so to speak.'

'Because I want to stop other people feeling like I do,' the girl cried swiftly. 'Think of the disfigurements that came from the last war. Men with no arms, no legs, crippled; men with burnt faces and ugly scars and twisted, distorted mouths and no noses. And it'll be worse in this war with the modern aeroplanes. It is already. The sooner the war stops the better, and if my joining up will help towards ending it, then my whole life won't be wasted. I'll have achieved something.'

'I think you are wonderful!' Jonquil said. 'Do tell me what your name is. I'd like to know you better.'

'Marion Phillips,' the girl said speaking again in her quiet, nervous voice, the excitement and animation dying as suddenly from her eyes as it had flashed into them.

'Em and I are quite old friends,' Jonquil said. 'But we'd love to have you join up with us, wouldn't we, Em?'

'We certainly would,' Em agreed.

Marion looked at them both gratefully.

'Are you quite sure you don't mind?' she asked gently. 'I mean I shall quite understand if you'd rather not be seen about in public with me. It – other people would always be avoiding us – me, and we'd be stared at and...'

'Just let them try,' Em said. 'As to being seen with you in public, Marion, well, the subject doesn't bear discussion. We're friends now, see?'

Marion nodded her head, unable to speak for the sudden lump that had come into her throat.

For the rest of the journey, the three of them sat together, discussing the possibilities of their remaining together in the future. Marion, too, was in for Special Duties, and they determined to do all they could to prevent their new friendship being split up.

The train drew into the station and with hasty collecting of suitcases, the seven future Waafs descended from the carriage and caught the connection to their destination. On arrival they were told the depôt was about a mile from the station. There were no taxis in the yard, so, with plenty of grumbling and grimaces, they shouldered their luggage and started to walk up the hill.

They were hot and tired when finally they reached the gates of the depôt. They were told by an R.A.F. corporal to wait outside the guard room while a Waaf was called down to sign them in.

'Down, where from?' Em asked, with an eye on her suitcase which had become heavier, so it seemed, with every yard she walked. The sun was burning down on her and she thought longingly of her own home where the family would no doubt be sitting down to afternoon tea.

The corporal smiled sympathetically.

''Tisn't far round the corner,' he said, with a friendly grin.

'We haven't exactly chosen the coolest weather!' Jonquil gasped. Her arm ached and she felt very dispirited.

'You wouldn't grumble at this if you could 'ave seen the weather the lot what came last winter 'ad,' the corporal told them. 'Pourin' with rain, it was, and snowing, and them without greatcoats or uniform shoes, marchin' up an' down, up an' down, mauve in the face, they was, with the cold, and their 'ands and feet frozen stiff. Now they did 'ave somethin' to grumble at. It's all bin nicely organised since then. You'll be lookin' smart as paint in your new uniforms tomorrow, mark my words. And 'ere's your runner.'

A young Waaf in a navy overall with a red band round her arm, came walking smartly toward them.

'Who is in charge here?' she asked the little group of girls.

'I am!' Em answered. 'I have an envelope for you, I believe.'

The Waaf opened it, read their names and had them signed in at the guard room.

'You needn't march, but you must line up

71

in threes,' she informed them. 'The odd one must go in the middle by herself.'

The girls shuffled into some kind of order and the Waaf called out:

'Squad, by the right, quick march!'

The group started to move to the right, but the Waaf headed them off quickly.

'By the right, means straight forward,' she explained, and following these incomprehensible directions, the new recruits moved forward once more.

They were halted outside a large stone hut marked 'Decontamination Centre', and told to sit down and wait on the bench outside the hut.

Em found her cigarette case and offered it to Jonquil and Marion. They smoked in silence for a minute or two. Then Jonquil pointed to a column of girls, most of whom were dressed in navy overalls, though some of them still wore civilian clothes, marching down the asphalt road towards them, each holding a knife, spoon and fork. They became accustomed in the following days to seeing girls half in, half out of uniforms. Recruits were fitted up at equipment stores the day after they arrived, but as often as not, the stores were temporarily out of the required size of shoes, collars, or overalls, and then the girls would have to continue wearing what they had arrived in until the necessary article could be provided.

They became accustomed, too, to seeing groups of airwomen marching to and fro. It was one of the rules of the depôt that no girl walked about on her own. She was escorted always by an N.C.O. or a runner if she was by herself, and a number would always march in threes. They marched everywhere – to meals, to lectures, to the drill hangar, to the games fields, the idea being to accustom them to being disciplined before they actually went to an R.A.F. station.

After what seemed to the girls to be hours, the airwoman reappeared, and beckoned to them to go inside in single file. Jonquil, third in the row, watched the first two being grabbed by Waaf medical orderlies who parted their hair with combs and looked carefully at their scalps.

'Whatever is that for?' she whispered to Em.

'De-lousing!' Em said, with a laugh.

'But surely that isn't necessary,' Jonquil protested, feeling faintly revolted.

'It certainly is!' Em whispered. 'Look!'

As they watched, one of the girls was taken aside. While Em was having her head examined, she questioned the orderly as to the fate of the other girl.

'Oh, she'll go to the isolation ward and have her hair thoroughly cleansed and disinfected and remain there a few days until it is clear again.'

Em and Jonquil were thankful that this was not to be their fate. When they were joined by the rest of the party outside, the Waaf runner suggested tea, and marched them off towards the dining room.

As far as Jonquil had been able to observe, the camp appeared to consist mainly of a street of council houses with numbers of wood huts and large hangars built round it, and the whole wired off like a prisoner-of-war camp. The dining-room was in one of the huts, holding about five or six hundred people, fifty or more to each long table. Outside the hut was a long wooden bench on which were ten large tin bowls for washing up. The runner explained to them as she handed them each a knife, spoon and fork, that they washed these up themselves and stacked their plates by the bowls. These and the mugs or glasses were washed by air-women on fatigues for the day. This was a voluntary fatigue, but every girl was more or less expected to volunteer to wash up at least once during her stay at the depot.

'Meals,' she told them, 'are served in three parts because the dining-room isn't large enough to hold everyone at once. Breakfast is at seven, seven-twenty and seven-forty. If you have early breakfast, you have early lunch too, and so on. Lunch is at twelve-thirty, one and one-thirty; high tea at four, four-thirty and five, and supper at six-thirty, seven and seven-thirty. The last tea will be over now, I'm afraid, but I dare say I'll be able to get hold of something.'

She told them to sit down at the end of one of the tables, and disappeared through a door marked 'Kitchen'. Presently she returned and told the waiting girls to collect their tea from the hatch. They had some cheese on toast, and bread and butter and jam, and a large tin jug of hot, very sweet, tea.

'I don't know whether I feel better or worse after that!' Em remarked with a smile. 'Let's have a cigarette.'

But before they had time to find one, the Waaf runner was lining them up again and marching them off to find their sleeping quarters.

'You're all in Hut Thirty,' she told them. 'You can leave your suitcases there now, but you are not officially allowed in your huts until six o'clock in the evening. If you want to go back for any reason before that time, you must go with an N.C.O. or a runner. There will just be time after we go to the hut to visit the air raid shelter. Then you will be free for the rest of the evening.'

The hut to which the girls were taken had twenty-five beds in it. Eight of them were unoccupied, and Em, Jonquil and Marion quickly chose beds near to each other. They noticed that the mattresses were divided into three parts (which later they learnt to call 'biscuits'); that the sheets and thick, brown blankets were all stacked in a similar way at the foot of the bed on top of the 'biscuits'; and that the beds were side by side and head to toe, this method supposedly being more hygienic and allowing the required amount of fresh air allotted each Waaf!

Their visit to the air raid shelter for Hut Thirty was short, and only to show the girls where it was situated in relation to the rest of the camp in case there should be an unexpected raid.

'There are over two thousand recruits here at the moment,' the runner told them. 'It would never do to have them panicking. I dare say you will have plenty of practice alerts while you are here. And gas drills, too, and everyone has to go through the gas chamber to test respirators. Anyway, it's six o'clock now. You're free to do as you like – to go back to your hut and unpack, or go along to the N.A.A.F.I. – that is our canteen. If you prefer, you can have supper there, but then you have, naturally, to pay for it yourself! The only thing you may not do is leave the camp. You will be given a pass tomorrow or the next day and that will enable you to go anywhere within a five-mile radius of the depôt. For the time being, you will be able to buy more or less anything you should want at the N.A.A.F.I. Well, I'm expecting my posting the day after tomorrow, so in case I don't see you again, good luck to you all.'

'Goodbye, and good luck,' the new recruits said, and dividing up among themselves, they went back towards their hut.

Jonquil, Em and Marion found their future home packed with its seventeen other occupants, most of whom were busy making their beds. One or two were polishing buttons on their new tunics, burning them first over a lighted match to rid them of the hard glaze.

'Overalls are always worn at the depot,' one of the girls explained. 'But tunics if you go out. I expect you'll be issued with both tomorrow.'

The three friends followed the other girls' example and started making their beds, grimacing a little at the bumpy 'biscuits' and the hard, bolster-shaped pillow that was made from straw.

'I'll never sleep on one of those,' Jonquil cried, aghast. But her next-door neighbour reassured her.

'You will!' she said. 'After a day's drill, P.T., games, more drill, marching and parading, and with the thought of getting up next morning at six-thirty, you'll find you can sleep on anything – even these.' And she bounced her rock-like pillow into the air.

The rest of the room laughed appreciatively, and Marion's neighbour explained that Joan was one of the oldest inhabitants of Hut Thirty, having been here nearly three weeks. She was popular with them all for her patience and kindness to them when they had first arrived.

'How long do most people stay?' Marion asked her informant.

'Not more than ten days or a fortnight at the most,' the girl said. 'But Joan, there, thinks they must have mislaid her papers or something. Come on, we're just going to the N.A.A.F.I. for an early supper. Why don't you three join us?'

Marion was reluctant to go, but Em and Jonquil insisted they would not go without her. When they reached the N.A.A.F.I., they wished they had not persuaded her to come. The chattering in the room stopped abruptly when the five girls came into the room, and all eyes were turned with curiosity to poor Marion's face.

'What a sight!' one girl said in a whisper which was nevertheless loud enough to reach Marion's sensitive ears.

A dull flush crept into her cheeks, and with her head held high she turned and walked out of the room.

Jonquil felt a sudden singing sensation in her ears and the same temper which had prompted her to slap Adrian's face, flared into a bright, hot flame. She turned round and faced the silent crowd of girls.

'Just for a minute,' she said loudly and clearly, so that they should all hear her, 'Imagine your face had been marked like that through no fault of your own, but because of a childish illness when you were twelve. Imagine growing up to be stared at, remarked on by everyone, children in the streets, people in hotels; imagine going to a dance and never having a partner. Then think of your reaction to such a thing. You'd want to go and hide somewhere away from everyone, wouldn't you? Hide your face from the staring; shut your ears to the remarks. And you probably would, too! But not Marion. In spite of everything she has suffered, she has been brave enough to join up and face God knows how many new people who are all going to stare and remark as you have just done. And do you know why? So that no more people than is absolutely necessary shall be disfigured by guns and shells and bombs, and have to suffer as she has done. That is courage, and I hope next time you meet her you will remember what I've said and treat her as one of yourselves. Not that she is – she's way above any of us...'

Her voice trailed off and Jonquil was suddenly aware that she, usually so shy and reticent, had just addressed a gathering of several hundred girls. She felt desperately embarrassed, but nevertheless proud that she had had the courage to defend her friend.

The talking started up again, but there was no further discussion about Marion. But she was not forgotten. Somehow word got round the camp and no one was ever seen staring or whispering about her during the rest of her stay at the depot.

'They are all so nice to me,' she said a few days later to Jonquil. 'I feel – well, I don't know how to put it – not as bad as I really am, I suppose.'

'Here, Jonnie,' Em was saying as she elbowed her way through the crowd round the serving hatch. 'I'm treating you after that effort. What are you going to have?'

'Well, it depends what they've got,' Jonquil said.

A few minutes later, they were settling down to large plates of sausages and mash and still larger cups of coffee, very sweet and very hot.

'Tomorrow,' Joan told them between mouthfuls, 'you'll be enrolled. Then you will really be in the W.A.A.F.'

But already the new recruits felt as if they had spent days instead of hours in the Service. And tomorrow seemed a long way off.

Chapter 6

Ten days later Mr and Mrs Mathews sat down to breakfast and opened the day-by-day letter that Jonquil had promised them.

'It's no good my saying I will write every day,' she had said before she left. 'I may not have time for one thing, or I may not like the first few days. So I'll drop you a line my first day just to let you know I've arrived safely, and to give you my address, and then I'll keep a day-by-day diary for you and post it after a week or ten days.'

Robert Mathews slit the envelope carefully with his fish knife, and read the following epistle aloud to his anxious wife:

20 July, 1940
My second day in the W.A.A.F. Was awoken at six-thirty by Sergeant Tate ringing a bell. Surprised to find how well I had slept on the biscuits and pillow I told you about. Em and Marion both say they slept like logs, too, but we've all got stiff necks.

We had early breakfast and had to line up outside our hut and 'parade' before going to the dining-room. When everyone is out of the hut, we are called to attention and marched off in threes. Of course all of us new recruits made a bit of a mess of the drill, but I understand we pass out more or less perfect after ten days. Doesn't seem possible, but we will see!

Breakfast was porridge, rather cold bacon and more of that tea in enamel water-cans. One is 'sweetened' (and how!) and the other isn't. I've got a pretty sweet tooth as you know, but the 'sweetened' is almost too much for me. Em thinks we will get used to it.

We washed our knives, etc., then back to the hut to stack beds. This is a most complicated procedure, but Joan helped us. There is hut inspection by one of the Waaf officers every day, so they have to be done perfectly or else the hut gets what is called 'an adverse report'. We all have to polish our own floor space (about six feet by two) with rags and a bumper thing, and some horrid-smelling floor polish. Wouldn't the staff have giggled to see me on my hands and knees!

Each hut has a runner in charge for the day, and she is last to leave the building. When we were all out, I stood in the door-way and watched her put down pieces of newspaper, and moving them back step by step, polish the floor once more to remove last-minute foot marks left by people going out. What fastidiousness! But it has to be done, and I'm hut runner tomorrow!

We paraded outside the hut in that long asphalt road I told you about in my letter yesterday, to find all the other hut occupants doing likewise. Then there was roll-call and finally we were all marched down the road to a big hangar where we were lined up in long rows. I believe there were more than two thousand of us in that hangar, so you can imagine the size of it.

A Waaf officer then gave out the post, assisted by runners. After that, she read out the postings – there were over a hundred of them. I believe about two hundred recruits come and go each day. When you see how they come and how they go, complete with kit and really well-trained in drill, you realise the terrific organisation behind the scenes. The programme for the day was then given out and it amazed me how well that, also, was organised. Each hut has a set programme consisting of drill, P.T. (physical training) and lectures, and they keep to this unless they require anything from equipment or have to have photographs taken for identity cards and so on. The officer calls out, 'Those for equipment, form up on the right outside,' and the girls concerned leave the ranks for the required group.

Em and Marion and the rest of us were herded into this particular group, together with a large bunch of girls who had not yet got their uniforms, or only part of them. We were marched off to equipment stores in charge of a corporal. We were amazed once more to see how efficient the Waafs were who work in the stores. They take one look at you and say, 'Size thirteen shirt, thirteen-and-a-half collar,' and find these for you, then you move down the bench to another girl who says, 'Bust about thirty-five, hips thirty-seven,' and throws a tunic and skirt at you. And so on. We were given kit-bags, and into these put shirts, collars, shoes, stockings, vests (awful thick things I shall never wear!) suspender belts (not as bad as you might think!), navy woollen knickers (enormous things they call 'blackouts'), brushes for hair, clothes and shoe cleaning. Button-sticks and brushes, respirators, gas capes, ear plugs in case of air-raids – in fact, everything but the kitchen stove!

Needless to say, collecting all this took most of the morning. Having had early breakfast, it follows we have early lunch. This consisted of soup, some shepherd's pie and stewed fruit and custard. Not bad! But not, of course, up to home standard of cooking. From lunch until two-thirty, we were allowed in our huts, and Joan initiated us into the art of button-burning. This not only makes them look whiter, but makes them smoother, and therefore more easy to polish. Did you ever do that, Daddy?

Neither Marion's nor my uniform fits

perfectly, so we have been told to take them on parade in the morning and join the group for the tailor. The camp has one of its own. Em's fits beautifully and she looks awfully nice. We made her try it on.

At two-thirty there was another parade and visit to the big hangar, and we were told to join the enrolment group. We were naturally rather excited and eager for our interviews, but we had such ages to wait that we were pretty fed up by the end. First we were taken into a lecture hut and given a talk by a Waaf officer about Service life, and told that as we were about to be enrolled (which means signing our names agreeing to remain in the W.A.A.F. for the duration) if we didn't think we were going to like it, we had better say so now or for ever hold our peace. She didn't put it quite like that, but that was the gist! Nobody called off, though Em made some caustic remarks about a life sentence in Service gaol, and Marion about sleeping the rest of our natural lives on biscuits and bolsters!

Anyway, the 'talk' over, we had to wait on hard, wooden benches for separate interviews with some fairly high-ranking Waaf officer. We were about fifty odd, and as it was a case of alphabetical order, Marion Phillips and I had to wait for hours. The officer was awfully nice when I did eventually see her. Told me not to be nervous when I went before a selection board for Special Duties and wished me lots of luck. I signed on the dotted line and out I came, really and truly a Waaf, even if my uniform wasn't ready to wear! It was rather an important moment really, and one I suppose I shall always remember and tell my grandchildren about in days to come, if any. (Grandchildren, I mean!)

We joined Em for early tea which is high tea really. There's always cheese on toast or toad-in-the-hole, or something of that sort, as well as bread and jam. After tea we were told to go with the rest of the hut to organised games, and played rounders under the supervision of an R.A.F. corporal who is one of the drill instructors. It was just like being back at school except that we marched to and from the games field and were dismissed at the end.

Six o'clock we were free and Em, Marion and I went for a walk round the games field. Tomorrow we are to get our passes and will be allowed out of camp. We had supper in the N.A.A.F.I. and here I am now, sitting on the hard old biscuits, writing to you. I wonder how you both are and do hope you will write soon. Sergeant Tate takes roll-call at ten and lights are out at ten-thirty, so I'll have to start getting ready for bed. There is a hut next door called 'The Ablution Hut' and is all bathrooms and showers, so at least you can get a hot bath if you want one, even though you have to walk about fifty yards to it!

Em is calling me now to go across with her, so I'll finish for today and write again tomorrow.

21 July, 1940

Middle breakfast and so we stacked beds before we paraded for the meal, and polished the floor afterwards. Em, Marion and I are wearing shirts and collars and ties and navy overalls. We had difficulty with studs and ties and cuff links, but Joan helped us. I'm afraid we're going to be very hot in these things during the summer. They say silk is warmer than anything, but it can't apply to lisle stockings!

Parade at eight, then to the tailor for fittings, followed by photographs for our identity cards which won't, alas! be ready until tomorrow. Lunch, parade again, and this afternoon we went for our first drill lesson. The P.T. instructor shouted at us a bit, but he certainly seemed to know how to teach. It was rather fun and I am looking forward to next time. Second half of the afternoon we had a hygiene lecture. This was most instructive and Em and I agreed that all girls ought to be given a lecture like this on leaving school. I wonder why they don't!

After tea there were more organised games. If it weren't that I eat so much this exercise might take off some weight! Six o'clock Em, Marion, Joan and I went for another walk and told each other the most exciting thing that had ever happened in our lives. It was like school again – in fact, that is the biggest impression I have had so far. Joan told us some stories about the first recruits to come to the station. In the first days of the war before there was time to organise uniforms they had to drill in the pouring rain with no coats, no issue shoes – in fact, nothing but what they arrived in. We have been wonderfully lucky with the weather so far.

We had supper in the dining-room, but it is nicer in the N.A.A.F.I. You can buy almost anything there, cigarettes, chocolate, button-cleaning things, shoe polish, dusters, writing paper, stamps, and so on. In fact it is very like the village shop – only cheaper! Early to bed and to sleep.

22 July, 1940
Late breakfast, so all cleaning had to be done first. (I tell you this so that you can get some idea of the routine here.) Parade and three letters for me, one from each of you and one from Adrian. He says he and Charles are coming over tomorrow in his old Morris, to take us out in the evening. He says they want

to see us in our uniforms. Fortunately our tunics will be ready by then and Sergeant Tate says we are sure to have our identity cards tomorrow. Em is very excited although she pretends not to be. I think she has fallen rather heavily for Charles.

During the morning we had more drill and a gas lecture, and this afternoon we went through the tear-gas chamber to test our respirators (we never call them gas masks for some reason!). I was a bit nervous but it was quite all right once inside. I felt nothing but a prickling round my neck, and my eyes watered a bit when I came out. We also had another hygiene lecture by a Waaf officer whose job it is to keep the depot clean. It sounds easy enough when you think of all the cleaning we do, but what she told us was quite staggering – not really a subject to be discussed, but I think her frankness will do a lot of good and I admire her courage in addressing several hundred girls on such a theme!

After tea, more games and this evening there was an E.N.S.A. show on the camp. It was surprisingly good and I particularly enjoyed the community singing at the end. We sang 'It's a Long Way to Tipperary', Daddy, and I thought of you.

23 July, 1940
This morning we had our interview with

three Waaf officers who were a kind of selection committee for Special Duty candidates. They asked a lot of questions concerning my education and occupation since leaving school. I was worried about this, not having done anything! But it must have been all right because I passed. So did Em and Marion. I was almost as worried about them passing as I was for myself – particularly Marion. I was afraid they might have let themselves be influenced by her face. This took most of the morning.

After lunch we collected tunics, identity cards (you should see my photograph – it's dreadful!) and joined the drill class. We leant saluting on the march and slow marching and are really progressing rapidly. Talking of saluting, we get quite a kick out of giving the officers we meet really wonderful ones. But Em, while showing off the other day, knocked Marion's cap for six. Did we laugh! So did the Waaf officer.

The second half of the afternoon we had a first-aid lecture, then tea and P.T. Six o'clock at last and just time to dash into the hut and change into our uniforms before Adrian and Charles arrived at the guard-room. We were greatly delighted by the smart salute the guard had to give them (they being officers) and weren't quite sure whether or not we should salute them, too. We had decided we would, but Adrian caught hold of my hand before I could raise it, so that settled that!

Both he and Charles were very flattering about our uniforms, and it was nice seeing them. We had a good dinner in a hotel and, deciding against the cinema because it would take up so much time, spent the evening quietly in the lounge talking and smoking. Charles is definitely nice, and Adrian was his usual charming self. He said he had seen you, Mummy, and not had much difficulty wangling our address from you. ('Wangling' is a service word.)

'I'm glad to say we didn't quarrel once – in fact, I found it hard to believe I had once hit him across the face! We left a bit late and only just arrived back in time for roll-call. Wish I hadn't to get up at six-thirty tomorrow. I could just do with one of those long lie-ins!

24 July, 1940
Usual sort of day with P.T., drill and lectures. It is getting a little monotonous now. One or two of the girls in the hut have gone and three news ones came today. We feel like old stagers showing them round. Poor Joan is very depressed. This is her third week here.

Em, Marion and I volunteered for washing-up fatigues, and between us we washed and dried more than a thousand plates. It took several hours and I felt quite whacked afterwards – but triumphant. What a feat! You could tell Molly this next time she grumbles at the amount of washing up to do after a party, though secretly I can sympathise now. I never want to see a plate again!

25 July, 1940

This morning we volunteered for fatigues (not washing-up ones!) and found ourselves cleaning out the officers' rooms – bed-making, floor polishing and everything. I'm sorry for the officer whose bed I made! Anyway, it was a change from the drill and lectures.

This afternoon we had a practice gas attack. We all had to don gas capes, helmets and goggles, and parade outside our air-raid shelters. We looked like a flock of prehistoric birds, vaguely resembling ostriches, in our weird attire. If ever there's an invasion I think the sight of us would turn the invaders back! The gas warning is given by rattling one of those giant 'razzle-razzles', as I call them, that we used to get in Christmas crackers.

The gas 'all clear' had just been given and we were back in the bell-hangar awaiting further orders when they gave the air-raid signal. Another practice. We ran 'at the double' back to our shelters and sat there smoking in complete darkness. It was about the coolest spot on the camp, and Em,

Marion, Joan and a few others and myself pretended not to hear when they gave the 'all clear'. This rather childish prank came to nothing, however, as roll-call was taken outside each shelter and someone came down to find us!

We went down to the village after six, and had supper in a fish and chip shop. It was rather fun.

26 July, 1940
Sunday, so we did not have to get up until lunch time. But Em and I wanted to go to early Communion, so we were up at nine. The 'church' was just a tiny chapel, improvised from a hut. The girl next to me fainted, which was upsetting, as it is the first time I have ever seen anyone pass out completely. Em and I carried her outside and missed half the service. Apparently the girl isn't very strong and the P.T. and drill in hot weather affected her. I must say, I don't feel the worse for it, apart from two blisters from service shoes.

I spent the morning writing letters and bringing this one up to date. After lunch, Em, Marion and I went and saw a good film. Then we had an early supper at the hotel to which we went with Adrian and Charles. Em and I wished they had been there this time, too. But I had a letter from Adrian yesterday and I gather he is very busy at the moment down at the 'drome, and doesn't see his way to coming over again.

We all had an early night, at least, we went to bed early, but lay listening to Joan telling some stories about her sister who has been in the W.A.A.F. ever since it started. It must have been great fun in those days of pioneering. In the end, Sergeant Tate came out of her room (one end of the hut partitioned off) and threatened us all with fatigues if we didn't shut up. Again I felt as if I were back at school with Matron reproving me! We shut up, anyway!

27 July, 1940
The only excitement today was that Joan received her posting at last. She is off to the Midlands tomorrow. We are all sorry she is going, but she is naturally pleased. We shall miss her. Nothing else other than the usual drills and games and lectures.

28 July 1940
This morning we had hoped we might also get our postings, but no such luck. We have been made runners and I spent my day showing a bunch of new recruits round. It seems far more than a week since we came. Oh, well, perhaps we will go tomorrow!

29 July 1940
Today we were posted. What excitement! We

are all heartily sick of the depôt by now, and will be glad to go tomorrow. Twenty-four of us are going for our training, which I understand lasts a fortnight. After lunch, we attended a special lecture given to those about to leave, which was rather like the old 'leaving-school' lecture we had – you know, don't let the service down, sort of thing! But though we laughed a bit among ourselves, I know Em and Marion as well as myself (and no doubt a good many more) are really very proud of our uniforms. We had the afternoon off to pack. It's surprising how everything fits into a kit-bag.

Sergeant Tate seemed sorry to hear we were off. And to be quite truthful, I wish we weren't leaving her behind. She always had time for a few jokes with us before lights out, and I feel so sorry for her stuck here. As she says, as soon as she gets used to one lot of girls, off they go and in come the next. But she never grumbles.

Well, darlings, I don't suppose there will be much time to write any more as we leave immediately after breakfast tomorrow in a large charabanc. But I will write again soon after we arrive, and give you the new address.

So until then, lots of love and a big kiss from your
JONQUIL.

P.S. – Did I tell you that all the girls call me Jonnie? I like it, but I never want to be anything else but Jonquil to you. It keeps home and my W.A.A.F. life on separate plains. So once again, love and a big kiss. J.

Chapter 7

It was nearing tea-time when the large charabanc with its twenty-four Waaf occupants drew up outside the workhouse on the outskirts of a town some few miles north of London. An R.A.F. corporal opened the big gates and the charabanc slid through them into the courtyard beyond.

Em, Jonquil and Marion left their seats eagerly, breathing in the fresh air and stretching their cramped limbs.

'I hope tea is nearly ready,' Em said. 'My throat is as dry as bone.'

Jonquil looked round doubtfully.

'The place seems deserted,' she said, eyeing the long, dark brick buildings on either side of the courtyard.

'Do look!' cried Marion, pointing to a signpost by the gate. 'One points to the "Males" side, and the other to "Females". I wonder what my parents will say when they know I'm living in a workhouse!'

'The end precipitated!' Em retorted cheerfully.

Kitbags and suitcases were unloaded and presently a Waaf officer joined the weary little party.

97

'I'm awfully sorry about this,' she said. 'There has been some misunderstanding. Forty-eight airmen were expected today and twenty-four airwomen tomorrow, so their quarters have been prepared and yours have not. We have only just taken over this building and I'm afraid you will have to get down to the cleaning yourselves, otherwise you won't have anywhere to sleep tonight. I know you are probably all tired and no doubt ready for your tea, and I'm really very sorry, girls.'

'I expect we will survive, M'am,' Em said, speaking for all of us.

The Waaf officer smiled at her gratefully. She herself looked tired.

'What I suggest is this,' she said. 'We will split up into four groups of six. One lot will go and help prepare tea, two groups will dust and thoroughly clean up the rooms you're to sleep in, and the fourth group will collect the bedding and fix the beds.'

She turned to Em.

'What is your name? Charlestone? Well, you divide them up, taking charge of one group yourself. I'll send Sergeant out to collect the two parties for cleaning. Those for the cookhouse come with me, and the others wait here until I get back.'

In a few minutes, Em had the girls organised, Jonquil, Marion and herself joining the cleaning party.

'The workhouse has been empty for some time,' the Waaf sergeant told them as she took her party into what must have once been the laundry room to collect cleaning utensils. 'But they are short of billets here so the R.A.F. have had to commandeer it. Cleaned up it shouldn't be too bad! We've managed to make the men's quarters quite comfortable. There are two showers down here, and two bathrooms upstairs, and plenty of bedrooms. We'll go up now.'

The upstairs rooms could only be reached by an iron staircase leading up from the courtyard. A balcony ran along the length of the workhouse buildings, the doors to the rooms leading off the balcony. It reminded Jonquil a little of the Pension in Switzerland with its wooden verandahs encircling the house.

As the Sergeant had predicted, the whole place was covered with cobwebs and dust, not having been inhabited for so long. It took the twelve girls the best part of two hours to make the place habitable, and even then they were not entirely satisfied.

'We'll have to finish off after tea,' Sergeant said, as someone rang a bell downstairs.

It was nearly six o'clock and Em, Jonquil and Marion dropped exhausted and hungry into their chairs. While they were eating, the officer gave them some idea of what the next fortnight would be like.

'The forty-eight men coming tomorrow are also here for Special Duties training,' she told them. 'They have to live on the other side, but you will all eat together here. You girls will work nine to one and two to five. The men will work five to eight and nine to twelve. The training school is about fifteen minutes walk from here, and you will have to march there and back because there isn't any transport. At the end of the fortnight, we will throw a party, but until then, I advise early nights and plenty of sleep because the training is a concentrated one. I am not making any hard and fast rules as to what you do in your spare time. The only ones I shall make are that your beds are stacked and rooms ready for inspection before you leave in the morning, that lights are out by eleven, that you are punctual for meals, and that the men's side of the courtyard is strictly out of bounds. If anyone wants anything or has any helpful ideas and suggestions to make, go to Sergeant Peale who will pass them on to me if she thinks them practical. Any questions?'

'When do we start work, M'am?' one girl asked.

'I'll try and find out for certain, but I think now you are here it will probably be tomorrow morning. The R.A.F. sergeant who is training you said he wanted you as soon as possible. Anything else? No! Well, I'll see you all later. Oh, I forgot to tell you, there is a small village about two miles away and 'buses go every hour. But you must not go further abroad than that.'

As she left the room, the girls broke into conversation, all talking eagerly and at once. The sudden relaxation of discipline made life seem very pleasant.

'If we had come straight here from home, we would never have appreciated it,' Em said seriously. 'Come on you two, let's go and finish the rooms, then we can go for a walk before supper.'

'I wonder if I could get a dog,' Marion said, following her own train of thought. 'It would be a wonderful companion and...' her voice trailed away. But Em and Jonquil, knowing her well now, could guess the end of that sentence. The dog wouldn't mind her face or be ashamed to be out with her.

'I should wait until we arrive at our station,' Em advised her. 'It would be dreadful if you got one and then had to part with it.'

For the rest of the day, Marion talked of nothing else but the dog. Em, whose thoughts were with Charles, listened with one ear only, wondering as she nodded an occasional 'yes' or 'no' to Marion's questions, just when she would see him again.

'Perhaps we will get a forty-eight hour pass at the end of the course,' she said aloud. She might write to Charles and ask him to come to town to meet her. But she didn't want to do that. It must be he to make the first move.

'I could go to some of the dog kennels and see what puppies they have got,' Marion said happily.

Jonquil alone did not speak. She was thinking about Simon, feeling a little guilty because she had not thought much about him in the last ten days. There had been so little time to think of anything but the W.A.A.F., and this was really the first time he had really penetrated her thoughts.

'It seems so much more than five weeks since I last saw him,' she told herself. 'I ought not to be feeling so – so content with life.'

But 'content' was not quite the right word. She was happy in a mild way, in the excitement and novelty of joining the W.A.A.F. but she was also restless and unsettled. Simon's death had taken away the security of the future, and now she could no longer look ahead, as she had been doing, to a happy married life. The future was uncertain, the past slipping further and further away with every day. The present alone was sure and so it was that she could live from day to day, not ecstatically, but not unhappily either. Em's suggestion that they might have forty-eight hours off, filled her with a warm glow of satisfaction. It would be nice to go home and see her mother and father – to spend a day or two in the old, luxurious surroundings. It would be nice, too, to see Adrian again. He was always so sympathetic and willing to listen to her and offer advice.

'Em, if we do get off, let's go home,' she said suddenly. 'We'll fix up a picnic on the downs with Adrian and Charles.'

'Jonnie, I'd love it!' Em said eagerly. 'But I must go and see the family, too. I tell you what. I'll spend the first day and night at home, then join you, and we can travel back to the station together. Perhaps we could meet Marion somewhere, too.'

'I live further north,' Marion said. 'It would be miles out of my way going down there.'

'Well, that settles that!' Jonquil said, and with a glance at her watch, 'We ought to be getting back, girls, if we are going to be punctual to meals! Besides, I'm hungry.'

They turned back cheerfully towards the workhouse. Everywhere was noise and bustle. The buildings shone a dull red in the sun's late glow and no longer seemed unfriendly and deserted. From the kitchen came the enticing smell of food, and the girls went eagerly into the dining-room.

The following day the twenty-four air-women, in charge of Sergeant Peale, were marched to the building where they were to be trained. It was wired in and had a sentry at the gate, and was also heavily camou-flaged. Sergeant Peale handed them over to

103

Sergeant Miller, a small, dark, severe little man with a surprisingly pleasant smile.

'Before we start work,' he said, 'I want to impress on you all the necessity for utmost secrecy. As yet, the Germans know nothing about the extent of our radio location, and by the time you've completed your training, you will know quite a bit. Talking about your work among yourselves is strictly taboo. You never know who will be listening at the next table, nor who is sitting opposite you on a 'bus or train. As the saying goes, "Walls have ears". You may not think you are giving away anything of importance, but a word from you and a word from the next person and a word from somebody else soon make a sentence. Remember that! You are each going to do a job of the greatest importance and will most probably replace some man, releasing him for more active services. And if you ever reach the stage of getting bored by the job, remember that if you weren't there, he would be. So although you may at the time be doing no work at all, you are still helping the nation. You will have an examination at the end of the fortnight, and I hope no one will fail. If you work with me and are willing to work hard, you'll all pass. Before we begin, you must sign the Official Secrets Act, and Wing Commander Harwood wishes to speak to you first.'

The Wing Commander's talk was much

the same as the Sergeant's, and this finished, they were given typewritten copies of the Official Secrets Act and signed their names to them.

'Now we can start work,' said Sergeant Miller. 'We will divide into two groups...'

The morning went quickly and when the girls were on their way back to lunch, they were excited and animated by what they had learnt.

'I don't understand much of it yet,' Em said, 'but what I have grasped seems every bit as thrilling as Betty told me it was.'

'My goodness! I *am* glad I met you at Victory House that day, Em,' Jonquil said happily. 'I might never have got into Special Duties.'

They were all enthusiastic, eager to finish with lunch and go back to work.

Lunch, however, had its own diversion. The forty-eight airmen had arrived during the morning and were already eating and watching eagerly, for the girls to come in.

They, like the Waafs, had just come from a depot where they had seen nothing but men, men and more men, and they were now delighted to find they were having some female company.

'Eh, but that's a fine wee lass,' a young Scots lad said, with his eye on Jonquil, and he made room for the girls at his table.

'What part t'coountry 've you cum from?'

a Cumberland man asked Em as she sat down.

'I'm from London,' Em said with her quick smile. 'Jonnie, here, is from Kent.'

There was a moment's silence while the two airmen looked at each other. These girls were 'different' – spoke better and were – well, ladies. Class distinction rose in a great barrier between them, and the two men looked abashed and disappointed. They had hoped to get the girls to go dancing of an evening and...

'Where do you come from?' Em persisted, realising their sudden shyness with her quick intuition. 'You've no idea how pleased we are to see some men around after all the girls at the depôt,' she rambled on. 'When the officer told us you were coming we were all very excited.'

This was not strictly true, but it served its purpose nevertheless, and soon the two boys were reassured and chattered away during lunch, the Scots lad even getting a wee bit flirtatious with the silent Jonquil.

'It's no good being high-handed and snobbish,' Em said to her as they marched back to work. 'We're all in the same uniform and hold the same rank, so why should we? Besides, we aren't any better really, if you think about it. We've only got more money to spend on ourselves, and we speak differently. But there are as many bad men in the upper classes as the lower, if not more.'

'Isn't this communism?' Jonquil asked thoughtfully.

'I suppose it is,' Em answered with equal seriousness. 'But honestly, Jonnie, I don't think that class distinction will survive this war. Evacuees alone have done a lot to destroy it. War throws everyone together and together we sink or swim. Look at the girls in our hut – two of them used to be cooks, one was a gardener's daughter, one a cloakroom attendant, one a ladies' maid. Think of the people who hold similar jobs in your own house, and imagine sharing a room with them. You can't. But you didn't complain at having to do so at the depôt, and I dare say you found them good company and charming. I did! No, you took it as a matter of course, force of circumstance, in fact, because it was the approved thing. Because you hold the same rank you are no better or worse in the eyes of the service, than your neighbour, and rightly so. You couldn't favour the rich, make exceptions for them when they were doing the same job. Nor could you promote them above the next girl when they know no more about their work, perhaps less. We've got to work together and we can't do that on different levels. While we're in uniform anyway, we're the same. So it is with these boys. I don't doubt that before the end of the fortnight, we'll be dancing with Jock and Leslie. Leslie said he was a chauffeur till he joined up. Imagine dancing with your father's chauffeur. There's no doubt about it, Jonnie, Service life changes everything, and since all the young people in the Empire will be in the Services, it is bound to affect the post-war world because it is the youth of today who build the world of tomorrow.'

'Why, Em!' Jonquil said, startled at but also admiring her friend's volubility. 'You should have been a Member of Parliament!'

'I often thought I would like to be,' Em replied seriously. Then she smiled. 'But now I'm in the W.A.A.F. instead, so that is that! Wonder what we'll do this afternoon.'

The afternoon's work proved as exciting and enlightening as the morning.

The girls met the airmen again at dinner, but immediately afterwards they went off to work, so they did not meet again until the following morning. Jonquil and Em were wakened from a deep sleep by a chorus of male voices from across the courtyard. Jumping out of bed and going to the balcony they saw Jock and Leslie and a number of the others, lined up in dressing-gowns with bath towels over their shoulders, and they were serenading the Waafs. Jock had a fine baritone and his voice could be heard plainly above the others in his own rendering of 'Early one morning, just as the sun was rising, I heard a Waafie singing in the courtyard below!'

They stopped singing and waved when they caught sight of the two girls and there were several catcalls and whistles at the sight of Jonquil's pale blue dressing-gown.

'Did they issue you with that?' Jock shouted, and Jonquil felt a bubble of laughter rise up inside her.

'Yes, and you should see the nighties that they gave us,' she called back impishly.

There was an answering shout of laughter, and then the singing started again. The noise drew most of the girls on to the balcony, and when the men started 'Little Sir Echo' they joined in the chorus and at the appropriate places.

'Here, we'll be late for breakfast at this rate,' Em cried when the song was over, and there was a sudden rush for the showers and bathrooms. Jonquil, splashing cold water over her face and shoulders, was surprised to find herself wishing that the men were training with them. It would really be quite fun!

When Leslie and Jock suggested that the girls should join a party at the Palais de Dance on Saturday evening when they were off duty, she readily agreed to go.

'Mummy would have a fit!' she thought; but then, 'Mummy need never know.'

So she went to the party and thoroughly enjoyed herself with Jock, who was an amusing companion and a good dancer. But when he tried to kiss her good night, she did put her foot down.

'Why not?' Jock asked. 'There's no harm in kissing, is there? Or have you got a boy?'

'No, not now. But there was someone else,' Jonquil said.

'Then if it is over and done with, what's the harm?' Jock persisted.

'I don't know you well enough,' Jonquil said weakly.

'There's no better way of getting to know one another,' Jock replied in his heavy brogue. 'But no matter, Jonnie. Perhaps you'll be knowing me better by the dance at the end of the week?'

Jonquil thought it more practical not to reply. By the end of the week, however, she could no longer pretend she didn't know him well enough. She had, after all, seen him every meal time, in the mornings, and in the evenings before the men started work. She tried to think of another argument but the only one – the true one – was snobbish and she was ashamed of herself for thinking it. Because of this, she did not draw her hand away when Jock took hold of it, and when he put his arms round her and kissed her with a curious rough tenderness, she surrendered her lips to his.

Jock, aware that this girl was different from the girls he had known, was more thoughtful and reticent in his kissing and unknowingly, he thereby retained her regard and affection. Had he let his passion be known to her, she would have withdrawn from him immediately. As it was, Jonquil remembered him always with an indifferent affection. 'Dear, funny, little Jock,' she used to call him to Em, and she answered every letter he wrote.

When she finally bade him good night, and lay warm and sleepy in her bed next to Em's, she thought over the last fortnight with considerable happiness. It had been fun. They had all passed the examination, and Sergeant Miller had told them he had been greatly encouraged by their enthusiasm and conscientiousness. And the hours at the workhouse, too, had been happy ones with the early morning songs and the admiring, friendly chatter of the boys.

Tomorrow, they had forty-eight hours off as they had hoped, and Em was coming down the second day for a party with Charles and Adrian. Then – to their first R.A.F. station which was in Wiltshire, to begin work in earnest.

Jonquil fell into a deep sleep. Her dreams were a confused muddle of Jock, who, as she was kissing, turned suddenly into Adrian. Simon did not enter into it, and when she awoke in the morning, the dream, too, was forgotten.

Chapter 8

Already the shades of evening were stealing across the clumps of yellow gorse and purple, sweet-smelling heather. The hot breathlessness of the July day was stirred by a light, cool breeze, and the animals, who had lain exhausted and panting in the heat, roused themselves and started to move in the undergrowth.

From where she lay, Jonquil could see half a dozen rabbits sitting on their haunches, nibbling the short green shoots. She watched them drowsily a minute or two before rousing herself sufficiently to roll over on her other side and face Adrian.

'Look!' she said in a whisper. 'Just over there! See them? Three or four baby ones.'

Adrian lifted himself on to one elbow, and followed the line of her pointed finger.

'M'mm! I can see,' he said presently.

He altered the position of his body slightly so that his head rested more comfortably against Jonquil's knees.

'Am I too heavy?' he asked.

She shook her head, and reached out her hand to move a wisp of dried grass from his hair.

'Does it wave naturally?' she asked him, half teasing, 'or do you have it set?'

'I have a Eugène wave once a week,' he answered smiling.

'Idiot!'

She wound a strand of his hair round her finger and coaxed it into a curl.

'Do you mind my playing about with it?' she asked.

'No, I love it!' he said swiftly.

But she drew her hand away, and moved her body slightly so that unconsciously she had slipped his head into the hollow of her waist, and his cheek lay against her soft breasts. He could feel her heart beating steadily, rhythmically, and a shadow crossed his face.

Was he ever to penetrate her consciousness, he asked himself.

Would such proximity as this one day stir and awaken something in her so that her heart would beat wildly and uncontrollably as his was doing now? He sighed a little, unable to find an answer to his own questioning.

Jonquil echoed his sigh.

'What a wonderful, wonderful day it has been,' she said, reliving again the long drive in Adrian's open Morris, Em and Charles in the back seat and the four of them singing at the tops of their voices, and waving to everyone they passed. Lunch, too, had been fun. They had stopped by a wood and found a cool spot among the trees to eat their picnic. Mrs Mathews had provided a wonderful meal of cold roast duck and hard-boiled eggs and potato salad, with chocolate cake and ice creams in cartons to follow, and plenty of beer and ginger beer.

It had been too hot to walk after lunch, so they had driven on to find another place for tea. The downs were voted by everyone in the party as being the ideal spot since they would catch there any breeze that might be blowing in from the sea.

Tea was now over and Em and Charles had gone for a walk, leaving Jonquil alone with Adrian. For a while they had lain side by side in the dry grass, each lost in his own thoughts. But the silence had been a companionable one and Adrian had been content to watch the shadows playing on Jonquil's fair, golden skin; to see the droop of the dark lashes when she closed her eyes; to hear the soft intake of her breathing. She looked delightfully fresh and feminine in a blue, flower-printed frock that matched her eyes, and he liked the style of it, cut low and square at the neck, revealing the creamy column of her throat. He longed to put out his hand and touch her smooth skin, to bury his lips in the cool hollow at the base of her throat. When she moved so that his cheek was against her breasts, he was forced to press his hands against his sides to keep his emotions under control.

Waves of desire swept through him, coursing madly through the veins of his body and throbbing in every pulse. He turned his face from her that she should not see his eyes, reading in them his love for her. Instinctively, he knew she was not yet ready for love. It was too short a while since Simon had laughed into her eyes and touched her lips with his.

'Adrian!' Jonquil said suddenly. 'Do you know how Charles feels about Em?'

'I think he loves her,' Adrian said quietly. 'He has always had an ideal of the woman he wants to marry and Em is the incarnation of that ideal. She is pretty, she has personality and charm, she shares his love of music and art, and from what you tell me, she would be the perfect wife and mother. How about Em, Jonquil? How does she feel?'

'I don't know,' Jonquil said musingly. 'I can only make a guess, and that is that she cares pretty seriously. But she won't ever speak about it because she is afraid it might hurt me … bring back painful memories of – of when Simon and I first met. But I wouldn't mind. I'd like to know. It doesn't hurt me to remember Simon. Adrian, sometimes I feel I don't remember him enough! It's only six weeks or so since – since he was killed, and... Oh, I'm ashamed to say it really, but I find I am forgetting him, his voice, his looks even. It is only when I see his photograph that I can really remember him. Then I have such a feeling of loneliness and unhappiness, such a longing to feel his arms round me again and to hear him tell me he loves me, that I can't bear it. So I don't look at his photograph very often. Of course, there are hundreds of times when I do *think* of him, when I see someone who resembles him, or hear a tune we both loved, and every time Dunkirk is mentioned I have a sick, sinking feeling in my stomach. But I suppose three-quarters of my waking hours I am quite content. Is it wrong of me, Adrian?'

'No, of course not!' he answered firmly. 'Simon loved you and he would be the first to want you to be happy. He'd want you to fall in love again, Jonquil, to get married one day. Not to live in the past, and grow embittered with regrets and self-pity.'

He felt he could have put his point more convincingly had he not had such a personal interest in the issue.

'I suppose I shall marry one day,' Jonquil said thoughtfully. 'But not for a long time, not for ages and ages. I couldn't let anyone fill Simon's place yet. I can't even imagine falling in love again. Adrian, you have never told me how it happened. Was he killed outright? He crashed into the sea, didn't he?'

'He was outnumbered five to one. He shot down two and was attacking the third when the other two Jerries got on to his tail. He was flying very low – too low to jump. He tried to crash land on the beach, but the 'plane was out of control and he hit a cliff and burst into flames.'

'Adrian, he wasn't burnt alive?'

'No! The impact would have killed him outright, and his air-gunner, too. They hit the cliff about four hundred miles an hour. It must have been instantaneous.'

'You're not just trying to be – to be kind?'

'Good God! Jonquil, of course not!' Adrian said, impatient in his desire to convince her of the truth. 'I haven't ever lied to you before. From what you once told me, I believe I was painfully to the point on one or two occasions!'

Her face relaxed into a smile. When she spoke again, she changed the subject.

'Adrian, have you ever been in love?' she asked.

The question caught him unprepared.

'I – yes, I have!' he answered hesitantly.

'Lots of times, or just once?'

'Just once.'

'Do you – do you care for her now?'

'Yes, I do!'

'Does she love you, Adrian? I hope you don't mind my asking you all these questions. I have only just realised how little I know about you. I think perhaps I have been very selfish – always showering my troubles on you and never stopping to think you might have worries of your own. Tell me about her.'

He hesitated, wondering how he could put the matter without her guessing the truth.

'She – she doesn't care for me at the moment,' he said. 'I hope she will – one day.'

'Of course she will!' Jonquil cried. 'She'd be a very stupid girl if she didn't. You would make a wonderful husband, Adrian.'

'Suppose you give me a trial run?' he asked, teasing her.

She looked at him thoughtfully, seeing him now in a different light. To marry Adrian, she was thinking. Well, it wouldn't be such a crazy thing to do. She could imagine him sitting in front of a fire with his pipe in his mouth, or mowing the lawn, and finding taxis for her in the pouring rain after a show in town. Yes, she could imagine him as a husband, but not as a lover. Somehow she could not even visualise him kissing her.

She laughed, surprised at the trend her thoughts had taken.

'I don't think I'd make a very good wife,' she said.

'Well, if neither of us is married by the time I am sixty and you are fifty-five, I'll propose to you again,' he retorted lightly.

'That's a bargain,' said Jonquil.

'Ouch! There's a mosquito on my nose. Please brush it off for me quickly!'

'What's the matter with your own hands?' Jonquil asked puzzled.

'They're paralysed!' he said, jokingly. 'Quick! Take it off!'

She laughed again and ran a finger down the bridge of his nose. He lifted his head suddenly and catching her hand in one of his, pressed the soft palm to his lips.

'Adrian!'

The blood rushed to her cheeks and away again, draining them of colour, and she felt her heart jolt and beat painfully against her ribs. Simon! Simon! she thought silently. That was one of the things you used to do.

Adrian released her hand, and suddenly she started to cry. The tears edged their way out of her eyes and her body shook with deep, painful sobs.

'Oh, Jonquil, don't – please!' Adrian cried aghast that he should have caused such devastation by a kiss he had never meant to give. 'Please – please don't. I'm awfully sorry. I didn't mean to upset you. Really. Jonquil, darling Jonquil, please stop!'

She controlled her tears with an effort, anxious to explain to him that it was not on his account that she was weeping. He had not known it was one of Simon's pet ways of kissing her – dropping a kiss into the palm of her hand, folding her fingers over it and saying, "Don't let it escape. It's very precious!'"

She blew noisily into her handkerchief.

'It's all right,' she said, her voice still shaking a little. 'It wasn't you, Adrian. I'm awfully sorry, I always seem to have these emotional outbursts when you are around.'

He was still considerably shaken to know he had been the indirect cause of hurting her, and he was frightened, too, lest she should have heard the endearment that had slipped out, and guess that he loved her. But she did not seem to have noticed it.

'I'm flattered you should treat me with such confidence,' he said.

She smiled at him and pulled a compact from her handbag, and powdered her nose.

'You're a good friend, Adrian. I'm awfully fond of you. Will you write to me when I go back tomorrow?'

'Of course!' Adrian answered.

He lit his pipe and when it was drawing well, he turned to her again. She had removed all traces of the tears from her face, and was looking composed and utterly charming, he thought.

'You haven't told me where you are going yet,' he said.

'Down to Surdon,' Jonquil told him. 'It's about two or three hours' train journey from London. From what we could gather from Sergeant Miller, they are only just opening the place. Six of us are going there. The other eighteen are off to the north. They asked for volunteers for this place at Surdon, and Em, Marion and I thought it would be fun to "pioneer". I'll write the address down for you.'

She found a scrap of paper and gave him the address.

'I see your parents are quite resigned to your being in the W.A.A.F.,' Adrian said, comfortably, biting the stem of his pipe. It was a relief to talk to Jonquil of mundane affairs.

'When I arrived at the station yesterday they were there to welcome me,' Jonquil was saying. 'Anyone would have thought I'd been away four years instead of four weeks! Mummy was fussing over my uniform and making such a noise that everyone on the platform stared. Daddy, bless him! seemed to guess I wanted to get home quickly, and bundled us into the car and drove off. Oh, the glory of a soft bed! I just sank into it and slept until late this morning. I had breakfast sent up on a tray and how I appreciated the food! That is one thing the W.A.A.F. has done for me anyway – it has made me appreciative of my home. To think how I used to take it all for granted!'

'It must have been quite hard for you at first,' Adrian said thoughtfully. 'Having had everything and then losing it all. What about the discipline. Do you find that irksome?'

'No, it's not too bad. You see, everyone has to do the same thing. It's the same for everyone. It is doing without the little luxuries I used to have, that is the trial. But I'm getting used to it now. You'd laugh to see me on my hands and knees, scrubbing and polishing!'

'I should be extremely admiring,' Adrian said, seriously. 'I have a thorough regard for any woman doing war work – particularly if they have had to leave home and home comforts to do it. It shows a grand patriotism.'

'But I didn't join from patriotic sentiments,' Jonquil cried honestly. 'I joined because I didn't want you to think I was afraid to leave home.'

'I know,' Adrian answered, smiling. 'But that isn't important. It doesn't matter *why* you join. What matters is that you have joined and are now doing the job as well as you can. Tell me, Jonquil, don't you feel some kind of pride in your uniform? In the Service? I don't mean what you look like, but in what you are doing. You are fighting for your country. Does that mean anything?'

'I don't know,' she answered truthfully. 'I have never really thought about it before. I suppose I did have a feeling of satisfaction knowing I was going to replace a man. But pride? I haven't done anything to be proud of, yet.'

Adrian let the argument drop. She didn't quite understand what he meant. Perhaps it was too early yet to expect it of her. After all, she had only been in the Royal Air Force four weeks.

'There are Em and Charles,' Jonquil cried suddenly.

The two came walking towards them, their hands linked lightly, their steps buoyant. Even before they spoke, Adrian and Jonquil knew what it was they were going to say.

'We're engaged!' Em announced happily. 'Oh, Jonnie, Adrian, I'm so happy I could go off pop!'

'Congratulations!' Adrian said. 'As a matter of fact Jonquil and I have been betting this last hour on the odds you would come back with this news!'

'Was it as obvious as all that?' Charles asked, with mock anxiety.

The four laughed happily and Em and Charles threw themselves down on the grass beside the other two, their hands still clasped, their faces shining with an inner glow. Em was transfigured, Where before she had been only attractive, she was now radiantly beautiful. She could not take her eyes from Charles's face.

'When are you planning to get married?' Jonquil asked.

'Oh, not yet awhile,' Em said. 'Charles is

finding it hard enough living on his pay without the addition of a wife.'

'Now, don't put it like that, darling,' Charles reproved her with pretended severity. 'You make it sound as if I couldn't be bothered with the luxury of a wife at the cost of my present amusements!'

'If you want the truth,' Em told Jonquil and Adrian, 'he refuses to let his wife live in what he calls poverty. As if I haven't lived on nothing all my life!'

'That's just it,' Charles argued. 'That is why, Em. I want our life together to be perfect – unmarred by endless washing up and scrubbing floors and pinching and scraping.'

'But, Charles,' Em protested, 'for one thing we wouldn't have a home because I should still be in the W.A.A.F. And even if we had, scrubbing the floors of our own house couldn't be anything else but fun, wonderful fun.'

Charles gave her a look full of love and tenderness.

'You're sweet!' he said simply.

They were so close to each other in spirit now that Adrian and Jonquil felt shut out. In Adrian's heart there was a feeling of jealousy which he quickly rejected, jealousy because of the success of Charles courtship. Life was so short for a pilot and he knew it must be months if not years before he could even mention his love to Jonquil. Tomorrow he might follow in Simon's footsteps, and there would be no one to miss him as Em would miss Charles.

He laughed at himself suddenly for such morbid, self-pitying thoughts, and jumped to his feet, pulling Em and Jonquil up beside him.

'This engagement calls for celebration,' he said, throwing the picnic things into the basket and shaking the old car rug free from crumbs. 'Let's go and dine at the most exclusive restaurant in town.'

'In cotton frocks?' Jonquil said, laughing.

'All right, let's pub-crawl,' Adrian cried, undaunted. 'Let's eat and sing and shout and drink. Let's be gay!'

'Anybody would think *you* were the one to be getting engaged,' Em said, instantly regretting her words. She had some idea of Adrian's feelings for Jonquil and seeing the shadow crossing his face as she spoke, she knew she had divined them correctly, and was mortified at her lack of tact.

But Charles had caught at Adrian's sudden mood of gaiety, and was suggesting all sorts of ridiculous places to which they could go.

'We'll drive to the seaside and put pennies in slot machines on the pier,' he was saying. 'Do you remember, Adrian, that time when...'

'No time for reminiscing now,' Adrian broke in, remembering that Simon had been present on that occasion. 'We'll go into the first cinema we see…'

'Oh, no!' Em interrupted him. 'Not on an evening like this!'

'Let's go home,' Jonquil suggested quietly. 'We can all have a swim, then supper, and afterwards we will dance in the drawing-room or Charles can play the piano.'

So it was agreed upon, and the little party drove back happily towards Jonquil's home. The sky was already turning rosy pink, forecasting a vivid sunset. The air was hushed and seemed pregnant with an uncanny feeling of expectancy.

'I wonder if there is going to be a storm tonight or tomorrow,' Adrian said, sensing this strangeness in the atmosphere.

But the night was clear, and the following day was hot and hazy, and the storm that blew over was a mass of German raiders, carrying their loads of death and destruction. It was the beginning of the Battle of Britain, and Adrian's and Charles's 'drome was the target for the day.

PART II

CROSSROADS

Chapter 9

(To Adrian from Jonquil)

The Yews, Surdon, Wilts.
12 August, 1940

My dear Adrian,
I can't tell you how anxious I was when I
heard the 'drome had been bombed. As
soon as we knew, Em and I dashed to the
telephones. We were both frantic with worry
when she couldn't get through to Charles
and I couldn't get through to home. Then
mercifully Charles 'phoned to say you and
he were all right and shortly after that I had
a call from Mummy and Daddy. I gather a
bomb wrecked the west wing of the house,
but they and all the staff were unhurt. I
suppose you know they have arranged to
put up fifty airmen whose quarters on the
camp were blown to bits? It must have been
a terrifying experience.

I suppose the war is really beginning for us
now. Until the raid I, for one, have hardly

felt it. Even Simon's death seems only remotely connected with it. I'm not frightened for myself, but I can't help being worried for the family and you and Charles and all my friends. I suppose you will be in the thick of it now and won't have much time for letter-writing. But if you do have a spare moment, I should love to hear from you, Adrian.

I am settling down quite happily here. Six of us share a room and we aren't too uncomfortable! I won't pass any other comments yet because I haven't been here long enough to give the place a fair trial. As soon as I am settled in, I will write again.

We start work tomorrow and I am very keen to begin. Incidentally, we are the first airwomen on the camp and definitely pioneers on the job here. It is all rather exciting.

I enjoyed our picnic, Adrian, and I hope it won't be too long before we meet again. You are my dearest friend and I am very fond of you. You know that. You're the brother I should always have liked to have had. I don't mean this in an uncomplimentary fashion. I mean I can be myself with you and know that you don't mind! I feel you would still remain my friend, even if I committed murder!!

It is late now – perhaps that is why I am writing such a lot of nonsense in this letter!

– and I am just going to bed. So I'll say good night – (not goodbye!). Take care of yourself, Adrian.

As always,
JONQUIL.

(From Jonquil to her parents.)

The Yews, Surdon, Wilts.
12 August, 1940

Darling Daddy and Mummy,

I was greatly relieved to know you were safe and unhurt. Em and I were nearly frantic with worry when we heard the news of the raid. I am looking forward to getting a letter from you telling me all the details.

You will be glad to hear both Charles and Adrian are all right, but there were an enormous number of casualties on the station. It is incredible – really unbelievable. The day before on our picnic everything was so marvellously peaceful and unwarlike. Then this!

How are you coping with the fifty airmen? Charles told Em on the 'phone that you had agreed to put them up. Do tell me all about it. Was anyone I know in the village hurt?

Now for some news of my own activities. We arrived here about three o'clock in the afternoon. Once again we weren't expected and only half our bedding had arrived. Our 'hostel' as they call it, is a small, private house which has been taken over by the

129

R.A.F. Unfortunately, they took it over un-furnished!

At the moment we have straw palliasses instead of biscuits – that is to say, large white canvas sacks stuffed with straw, and the same hard old bolsters. But we are allowed our own pillows, so will you send me down one as soon as possible? You had better register it as the posts are most unreliable.

Six of us share the room I am in – Em, Marion and I and three other girls. Two are extremely nice, but the other is very affected and disagreeable, and openly admits she joined up for the fun she would get out of the Service. I think boys are the only things that mean anything in her life.

The black-out had not been done when we arrived, so we had to fix up our own. Em suggested corrugated paper blinds, which work beautifully. The room is small and there are no cupboards, so we have put nails behind the door on which to hang coats and dressing-gowns. The rest of our furniture consists of a tin locker each, about the size of a large suitcase. But Em had another bright suggestion – of using some old orange boxes that were in the garage, as bedtables-cum-cupboards, and yesterday we went to the village and brought some material with which to cover them. They look quite attractive now.

One of our main troubles is that we only

have a small gas jet to light the whole room. It doesn't matter now when it is so light at night, but I don't know how we will manage in winter. Of course, Susan – that's the girl I told you about just now – managed to get the bed nearest the light. But nobody objected as it is an isolated one; the other five are nearer together.

We have put up all our photographs and the place really looks quite homely now. You two are reposing on a converted soap box! Susan has a picture gallery of glamorous young men, but I can't say I particularly like the look of any of them. They are all too film-starish and artificial looking. She is very friendly with Em who thinks it is because she has seen her photographs of all her brothers, and Susan wouldn't miss an opportunity! Miaow! (But she makes you feel catty.)

Another snag to the place is that there is only one bath, and the lavatory and wash-basin are in the same room. As there are thirty girls here altogether, the sanitary facilities are not all they might be. We can use the kitchen sink for washing and an out-side lavatory, but neither are very popular. The kitchen staff are inclined to leave a greasy rim round the sink and I don't like washing my face in that!

However, by getting up a quarter of an hour earlier than most people, one can usually be sure of hot water and a bath, or at any rate, a wash. The boiler was only made to provide hot water for eight people at the most, so it is inclined to run out on you.

We eat in a big room downstairs which must once have been the drawing-room, and the former dining-room is another bed-room. There is also a small corporal's mess. The kitchen staff sleep in a room beside the kitchen. They are all very friendly and let us use the kitchen for washing and ironing, and usually have a kettle on the boil most hours of the day.

The village is a mile away. It is small but quite productive. I bought a nice iron there and am thinking of buying a little portable radio set I saw in one of the shops. All the men hitch-hike but we haven't got into the way of it yet. I suppose we will in time. I always feel so humiliated when someone drives by without stopping. It's like being cut dead in the street by an old friend!

We start work tomorrow and I am looking forward to it. We have to go up to the camp, which is about two miles away, for duty. Transport is provided, and it is a large open lorry, so there is no use in doing your hair before you go. I don't think this method of travelling will be so much fun in the pouring rain or in several degrees of frost. But perhaps everything will have changed by the time winter is here.

Well, darlings, this seems to be all the news for the moment. I will write again in a day or two. Don't be worried or anxious about me. I am really very happy and liking service life. It is full of adventure and interest and I don't have much time to remember even my poor Simon.

Write often and tell me all the little details of home. I don't want to feel a stranger when I come on leave.

A big kiss for each of you,
From your
JONQUIL.

(From Adrian to Jonquil.)

46, Stonefield Ave., Wodecot, Kent
15 August, 1940

My Dear Jonquil,
I was delighted to get your letter and flattered to know you were worried on my behalf. But there is no need to worry, I am quite all right.

For obvious reasons, I cannot give you details of the raid and the extent of the damage to the 'drome. But I can and will say that it was an experience I hope never to repeat.

I went to see your mother and father yesterday, and they are well and bearing up wonderfully. Your father seems more concerned about the damage to his rose garden than to the West Wing! The men are very comfortable and are well looked after. I am sure they won't want to go back when their quarters on the camp are rebuilt.

I am most interested in you and your W.A.A.F. career, Jonquil, so do write often, even if you do not receive many letters from me. I am so busy now that I haven't time to do half the things I *should* do, let alone take time off for pleasures such as writing to you.

My love to you, Jonquil,

Yours ever,

ADRIAN.

(From Mrs Mathews to Jonquil.)

The Manor House, Wodecot, Kent.
15 August, 1940

My darling Child,

I cannot begin to tell you of the *havoc* that has been caused by those *dreadful* Germans. I was terribly frightened at first, but your father kept using such *awful* language every time a bomb dropped near, that I forgot to be frightened while I reprimanded him. I suppose he thought he was back in the trenches. All the same, Germans or no Germans, I *won't* have him swearing in front of the staff, or me.

As I told you on the telephone, the whole of the West Wing has gone. We were *thrown* against the walls of the cellar by the bomb blast, and I must have been temporarily stunned. The first thing I remember is hearing your father swearing again because several of his *precious* bottles of burgundy had been smashed. What extraordinary creatures men are! Robert was within an inch of losing his life and *all* he could think about was his burgundy.

Of course, the whole house was head to foot in dust and broken glass. Most of the windows were smashed and all but a few pieces of crockery and china. I could have *wept* when I saw the mess everywhere. But everything has been cleaned up now and the weather has been *so* fine, we haven't missed the window-panes at all. I only hope we shall get them repaired before it rains, because if they *aren't,* we shall either have to close the shutters and have the lights on, or else be flooded out. Preferably the former, but you know how your father *hates* artificial light.

The East Wing we have given over entirely to the R.A.F. I was *horrified* at first when the billeting officer asked me to accommodate fifty men. But then Adrian came round and explained that the men had *nowhere* else to go, so I agreed to take them in. The poor things are sleeping on mattresses on the floor. Their corporals and sergeants are using the spare room beds, and as you know, there simply aren't any more in the house.

I was afraid the maids would make a *dreadful* fuss, but the men do all their own cleaning, so there really isn't anything to fuss over, is there? They eat at field kitchens on the camp, so we don't see much of them. Helen admitted she rather liked having some young men about the house! So that's *that*. We have stored the billiard table so as to give the men more room.

Last night, Cook asked permission to make some cakes for the men because she had heard them complaining they were *hungry*. So she spent her afternoon off baking and told me afterwards that their gratitude was *ample* reward for her *hard* work.

I do hope *you* get enough to eat, Jonquil. If not, write and tell me *immediately* and I will send you a large hamper of food every week. Now you *must* promise me faithfully to do this, or I shall worry myself *ill*.

As I said, that nice man, Adrian, came round to see us and spent the afternoon helping your father and the two gardeners remove debris from the rose garden, which as you know, is just in front of the West Wing and so received more damage than the *rest* of the garden. But he only had an hour or two off and had to hurry back to the camp *immediately* after tea.

I am very consoled to think of Em being with you, Jonquil. She is such a nice, *reliable* girl and has promised me she would look after you.

There is no more news now, darling. I

have sent your pillow under separate cover, and *hope* it arrived safely.

With *much* love, darling,

from MUMMY.

(From Robert Mathews to Jonquil.)

The Manor House, Wodecot, Kent.
15 August, 1940

Darling Jonquil,

Your mother tells me she has given you the news of the house, so I will not repeat it. But I will tell you how brave she was during the raid. She rallied the staff round her like a hen with her chicks (don't tell her of this metaphor!), and really behaved admirably. If she had shown she was afraid, they would all have panicked and I can imagine nothing worse!

The garden is in a dreadful mess, particularly my rose beds. I was quite heart-broken when I saw them. However, we have managed to tidy it all up a bit now, and Longhurst has put in some late chrysanthemums to fill up the gaps in the herbaceous border.

The West Wing is too badly damaged for there to be any hope of repairing it, I'm afraid. I think I shall have it pulled down completely. We don't need the extra space and the economy will come in handy. Business is not as good as it was a year ago, and income tax is higher. If we wish, we can

137

rebuild the Wing after the war.

No doubt you heard we have fifty airmen billeted on us. We don't see much of them, but the other night I popped in after dinner with a few bottles of beer, and I spent the rest of the evening with them swapping yarns about the last war with one or two old veterans. Among them was a man from my old regiment, so I opened a few bottles of port, too, and your mother says I was roaring drunk when I finally went up to bed! Just between you and me, I was a bit merry, but don't you tell her I said so!

I have decided to let the men use the swimming pool. Now you are away, and as neither Mummy nor I bathe, it is rather wasted. I expect they will make good use of it.

When will you get leave? Let me know in good time and we will kill the fatted duck for you. Would you like me to send you some peaches and nectarines? I dare say they would travel all right if they were packed properly. I gave your friend Adrian a box of fruit to take back to the mess. He is a very nice chap – the sort of son I should have liked to have. Or perhaps a son-in-law, heh?

Be a good girl and write to your mother often. She worries about you although I tell her there isn't any need.

Love and a hug,
from DADDY.

(From Em to Mrs Mathews.)

The Yews, Surdon, Wilts.
18 August, 1940

Dear Mrs Mathews,

As I promised, I am writing to let you know that Jonquil is both well and happy. She is very adaptable and has settled down remarkably well to this new life, considering the luxurious surroundings to which she has always been used.

She is very popular with the girls who find her extremely generous and always very kind-hearted and sympathetic. Marion is devoted to her – you remember we told you about the girl with the pock-marked face when we were home on our forty-eight? Jonnie champions her right and left.

I am afraid I cannot say much about our work. At the moment we are on a watch basis of four hours on duty, eight hours off. We have both found nightwatches a little tiring, but the men say we will get used to it in time, as they have done. Neither of us look the worse for them, anyhow, and we are putting on weight regrettably quickly.

I don't think there is much more for me to say that Jonnie will not already have told you. So I will finish this letter now, and write to you again soon.

Yours very sincerely,
EM.

(From Adrian to Em.)

46 Stonefield Ave., Wodecot, Kent.
20 August, 1940

My dear Em,

No doubt you will be surprised to hear from me, but I need reassurance and you are the only person able to give it.

It concerns Jonquil. Perhaps you have already guessed how I feel about her. At any rate, I am deeply in love with her, and unable to tell her because she still belongs in her mind – if not altogether in her heart – to Simon. I am, therefore, no more than a friend to her and although I have always encouraged her trust and confidence in me, and think she would tell me if she were ever in trouble, I should nevertheless be greatly reassured to know that you would always tell me if anything were wrong, or if she needed me.

You are such an understanding person, Em, that I know you will realise the difficulties that lie in my path, and will help me if you can. Don't be afraid to tell me anything – I fully realise that she might fall in love with someone else. It is her happiness and not my own, that I want above all.

I don't see much of Charles because we are so busy, but when I do see him, he talks of nothing but you, and seems to live in a dream world of his own. So hath the mighty fallen! He used to be anything but absent-minded!

Drop me a line when you can,

Yours,

ADRIAN.

Chapter 10

(From Jonquil to her parents.)

The Yews, Surdon, Wilts.
10 October, 1940

Darling Mummy and Daddy,
It is hard to believe that it is only two
months ago today that we arrived. I feel as if
I have been here years. Summing up these
two months, I must say they have been
extremely happy ones. I love my work and
we all consider ourselves lucky to have been
in at the start of the Battle of Britain. I can
imagine that plotting might be a bit tedious
with nothing to do, but there has certainly
been no lack of work.

I have started a scrapbook of pictures of
bombed London, which should be very
interesting to look back on after the war.
The Londoners are marvellous, aren't they?
I like the slogan 'They Can Take It.' So
could you two last August!

The things I don't like about the W.A.A.F.
are parades – sick parades, church parades,
clothing parades, kit inspections and drill.
They take up so much of one's spare time
and during all that hot weather, we wanted

to swim and swim and go on swimming! But I suppose they are necessary and on the whole I consider myself lucky to have so much time off. People working days, for instance, never see the sun, and we always have either the morning or part of the afternoon off.

Next week, we are starting leave, so we will be on a three-watch basis. That is to say we work eight hours a day instead of six. This obviously isn't so good, but I want my leave, so I can't complain! You can expect me home about the first week in November. Em is getting hers the week after next.

Marion has at last got her dog. I must say it is rather sweet. It is a Welsh Corgi puppy, about four inches square of light brown fluff. Yesterday it was found eating the chocolate pudding we were to have had for lunch! Marion is debating whether to call it 'Blitz' or 'Hurry', short for Hurricane. But as it can only walk about one foot an hour, the name hardly fits. Marion adores it and it can do no wrong in her eyes. Of course, it does do wrong – often! And usually under my bed! But it is so sweet, one forgives it anything.

I told you I had met a rather nice airman at the dance last week? Yesterday we went to the cinema and had supper afterwards. He is a delightful companion and a very good dancer. (You know how I love dancing!)

Tomorrow I am off all afternoon and if the weather is fine we are going picnicking by the waterfall. Bill is stationed about two miles away. He walks over here to fetch me, and then we have to hitch-hike or queue for a 'bus to the town.

Em and Charles are talking of getting married at Christmas, but have not fixed anything definite because her family haven't met him yet. He is also getting leave the week after next, and is spending most of it at her home. He, like Adrian, hasn't a real home of his own, and only has one relation, an aunt, who is living.

I am afraid there isn't much hope of promotion yet awhile, Daddy. There aren't any women N.C.O.s in the job yet, but I believe there might be when the men go overseas. Some of them were in France at the start of the war, and have most interesting stories to tell. Two or three of them had exciting escapes from Dunkirk, but they don't talk about it as a rule. One of them says he remembers seeing a Defiant crashing into a cliff when I told him about Simon. I can't bear to think I was lying idle in the garden while all that was happening. What a selfish, self-centred person I was in those days. I shall always be grateful to Adrian for getting me out of that rut.

I hear from him occasionally and there have been a great number of casualties in his squadron. He is now a squadron leader, you know.

I don't think there is much else to tell you. Every day is much the same as the last unless one goes out in off-duty time. I am really looking forward to my leave and to seeing you both. I shan't want to do anything but eat, sleep and talk! So don't fix up any parties for me.

Lots of love and a kiss for each of you,
from
Your
JONQUIL.

(From Jonquil to Em.)

The Yews, Surdon, Wilts.
23 October, 1940

My dearest Em,

I hope you are having a good leave and that your hopes re Charles and the family are materialising. They can't help but like him, can they?

I miss you dreadfully and particularly need your advice at this moment. How I wish you were here for a good gossip. However, since you are not, I will have to write you my troubles, and I shall begin 'Dear Dorothy Dix,' since it is an *'affaire du cœur!'*

It concerns Bill. He told me last night he was very much in love with me. Now, I don't love him – at least, I love him in a way, but

145

I am not *in love* with him, and the thought of marriage is quite out of the question. As you know, he isn't what you'd call – to use a beastly term – a 'gentleman', and I suppose having been born and bred on class distinction, one can't dispense with it overnight. But because he speaks with an accent ISN'T the reason I am not in love with him. I don't think *that* would matter one scrap to me if I were. After all, if he were a Frenchman in similar circumstances, I shouldn't know the difference. And he has wonderful manners – far better than most 'gentlemen' I know, and is always fastidious in dress and behaviour. I couldn't care as much as I do for him if he were not.

I suppose it was wrong of me to go as far as I have done. But a platonic friendship was doomed from the beginning! To start with, we are both young, and both tolerably attractive, at least I'm told I am! And Bill is definitely very good-looking as you know. He has lovely eyes, and nice teeth and mouth. Secondly, I have been segregated from my own kind and one can't be expected to go through life as a nun. Bill, too, is devoid of female company at his station, and I suppose I have more intellect and *savoire-faire* than most of the girls he meets. Being a person of considerable intelligence, he appreciates that. I think it is his *lack* of intellect that makes me realise I could never marry him. He has no appreciation of good music and although our athletic hobbies are the same, we have no mutual mental interests.

Anyway, I have let him make love to me, and frankly, I have kissed him of my own accord – and liked it! And it isn't just a physical thing. I am very, very fond of him. I know him pretty well by now and he is about the 'goodest' person I have ever known – except, perhaps, Adrian.

But last night he didn't kiss or touch me and just before he left me at the gates of The Yews, he told me he was desperately in love with me, and that he wanted me to know. Then he ran off before I had time to say anything. This morning he 'phoned and left a message for me to say that he was going on leave and would 'phone me when he got back.

So you see, I must decide now what I am going to do about him. Should I refuse to see him any more? I don't want to in the least. He means a lot to me as a companion and a very dear friend. But I don't want to hurt him.

Please write soon, Em, and tell me your views on the whole thing. Marion sends her love, and so do I.

Your loving,
JONNIE.

(From Em to Jonquil.)

Blue Peters, Kings Road, Chelsea.
Darling Jonnie,
I read your letter through twice and as far as I am able, have weighed the pro's and con's of the matter, and this is the conclusion I arrived at. You should leave the decision to Bill. After all, it *is* really his problem, whosoever's fault it was in the first place (and I don't necessarily mean by that that I think it was yours). Tell him outright how you feel about him and say quite frankly that you would like to go on seeing him, but only if he realises there isn't a chance of your marrying him. Then if he wishes to go on seeing you, it is his own lookout. But you must state definitely that you will never change your mind, otherwise he might continue seeing you in the hopes you would one day grow to care his way.

I suppose you are sure, Jonnie, aren't you? I have always been a bit communistic at heart and I think that if you do love him, it would surmount all the petty difficulties of choosing a husband from a different class. But then you can't be in love with him, because you would have no doubts about it if you felt for Bill as I feel for Charles. Oh, Jonnie, I love him! I love him! I love him! And the family love him too. Isn't it all wonderful?

Both Pete and Mark are on forty-eight hours, and Joe comes on leave two days before I go. The girls are home for half term, so Charles has met most of them, and they all get on together like a house on fire. I don't know what I should have done if they hadn't liked each other. I love both him and the family so much, it would have been frightful.

Sometimes I am a little afraid that this happiness cannot last. I am *too* lucky. But I am refusing to worry about something which may never happen such as losing Charles or one of the boys, and am living the present to the full and letting the future take care of itself. Charles says happiness is one of those things you should take while you can (as long as it isn't anyone else's!) and I think he is right. Perhaps this will be Bill's attitude to you.

I shall be back Thursday, Jonnie, and we will have a long talk about Bill then. Don't worry about it. It will all work itself out.

Give my love to Marion and the puppy, and keep plenty for yourself.

Your affectionate,
EM.

P.S. – Charles and the family send their love, too.

(From Bill to Jonquil.)

Sandiways, Torquay.
25 October, 1940

Darling Jonnie,

While I've been home, I have realised what a silly fool you must be thinking me for my behaviour the other night. I don't know why I was so silly as to tell you that I care for you because I've known ever since I first met you – and I liked you then – that you would never marry me. We just aren't the same sort. I was quite determined to keep my feelings to myself, but suddenly they were out before I knew they was coming. Perhaps it was because you looked so lovely standing there in the moonlight. Honest, Jonnie, I haven't ever met anyone as lovely as you are – not just to look at but right through. You're the tops, and I shall always be ever so glad I met you.

I know it would be more sensible not to see you again, but I am rather expecting my overseas posting to come through when I get back from leave, and I'd like just to say goodbye. Let's have one of our special after-noons together – a picnic by the waterfall if it is fine and the flies and some dancing if it isn't. Let's make it be just like it always was. Don't let's what I said change anything, even our good night kiss.

Guess I must be a sentimental old fool,

Jonnie, so I'll stop talking tripe. You're a grand girl!
    Your loving
    BILL.

(From Jonquil to Bill.)

The Yews, Surdon, Wilts.
1 November, 1940

Darling Bill,
I can't tell you how utterly wretched I felt saying goodbye to you yesterday. I wanted to tell you all sorts of things about the way I felt, but you kept so determinedly off the subject that I couldn't get started. So I will tell you in this letter.

Bill, dear, the fact that we belong to different worlds means nothing, absolutely nothing to me. If I were in love with you, I would marry you like a shot. That is the honest truth. Love is a funny thing really. I am not very sure I do know what it is. I thought I was in love with Simon, but I think perhaps I was more in love with love itself than with him. I feel it is a very definite emotion and that when I do fall in love I shall know it quite surely and it will be for always, and I shall know that there can never be anyone else. Fond as I am of you, Bill dear (and that is no small amount), this is not my feeling towards you.

But I do want you to know you have

meant a good deal more to me than just a flirtation. In fact the word is an insult used in connection with our friendship. I admire, respect, and am deeply fond of you, and shall never forget you or the wonderful days we have had together. All those days by the waterfall, for instance, and the evenings at the Palais. You were always the best dancer in the room. And our cinemas together and the late suppers at *our* fish and chip shop, as we liked to call it. And not least, the kisses we gave one another and the great comradeship that has always existed between us.

I hope this letter reaches you before you leave England, Bill. I want you to know I shall be thinking of you often, and that, if you would like me to, I will write as well. I shall pray for your safe return and for your ultimate happiness. I think you're 'the tops', too, Bill, and I shall always be glad I have had the privilege of knowing you and of being loved by you.

Always your sincere and grateful friend,
JONNIE.

(From Bill to Jonquil.)

Sandiways, Torquay.
3 November, 1940

Darling Jonnie,
Thank you for your letter, which I shall treasure always. I don't know how long I shall be

here, but I don't think it will be much longer.

Please do write as often as you can. I will send you my A.P.O. number when I know it.

I shall always remember that you cried when I kissed you goodbye.

BILL.

(From Jonquil to Adrian.)

The Yews, Surdon, Wilts.
3 November, 1940

My dear Adrian,

I am going on leave on 7th and do hope you will manage to find time to come over. I am really looking forward more than I can say to seeing you again. I have so much to talk to you about. Quite a lot has happened in the last few weeks and I am anxious to hear your views on it all.

I have no plans and shall spend my entire leave at home, so come when you can. There is no need to telephone first.

As ever,
JONQUIL.

(From Em to Adrian.)

The Yews, Surdon, Wilts.
3 November, 1940

Dear Adrian,

Jonquil has just told me she is writing to you to ask you over while she is at home.

Remembering my promise to write and tell you if ever she were in trouble or difficulty, I feel I should tell you now that there *has* been a bit of a problem on hand.

She has been having a light affair – nothing serious – with one of the airmen from a neighbouring camp. It is all over now and he is on his way overseas. I think Jonquil was very upset by his going and I know she will miss his cheerful company. He was always around to take her out dancing or swimming or something.

I expect she will tell you all about it, but I thought I had better let you know how the land lies in case you decided to take steps forward yourself. She wasn't in love with him, but she was exceedingly fond of him and I don't feel this would be a propitious moment for you.

My very best wishes to you, Adrian, and I don't mind telling you that Charles and I both hope it will end up all right with you and Jonnie. She is very young – not twenty-one yet, so you must be patient.

Yours ever,
EM.

(To Em from Adrian.)

R.A.F. Station, Wodecot, Kent.
5 November, 1940
Thank you for your letter, Em, and it's

154

timely warning. As it happens, I am due to go away on a course tomorrow. I had thought of trying to get it postponed so that I could see Jonquil, but now I think perhaps it is a good thing if I am away.

I don't think I can keep up this 'brotherly' attitude towards her much longer, Em. Perhaps there is something in the saying 'Absence makes the heart grow fonder', so that if I am not there, she may miss me!

Anyway, thanks for the letter, and your good wishes.

ADRIAN.

P.S. – I am finding it hard to be patient. If I were only confident of ultimate victory, it would be easier. That goes for the war, too! P.P.S. – Go on taking care of her for me, Em.

A.H.

Chapter 11

(From Jonquil to her parents.)

The Yews, Surdon, Wilts.
10 December, 1940

Darling Mummy and Daddy,

Thank you for your letters and the hot-water bottle. I have nearly died of cold since mine burst. If only we could have a hot bath before going to bed, we wouldn't be so cold all night. But the pipes have frozen up and burst, and apart from leaking all over the house, have ceased to produce either hot or cold water. Every drop we do get has to be carried in from the garden tap and boiled before use.

To give you some picture of my life at the moment, if I am on duty at eight o'clock in the morning, I rise at six, put on a dressing-gown and a great coat over it, and gum boots over my bedroom slippers. I go downstairs threading my way past the tin cans, jugs, bowls, buckets, etc., that have been put on each step to catch the water that is leaking through the roof; I go into the kitchen and find a bucket, then walk about fifty yards in the pitch dark to the garden tap. I find the drips have frozen into an icicle, but I manage to break this with a stone, and fill my bucket with icy-cold water.

I stumble back to the house, the water slopping over the edge of the bucket into my gum boots. I squelch indoors and fill three saucepans, light all the gas rings and wait for the water to boil. While I am waiting, I find a teapot and as soon as possible brew a cup of tea and take the pot and some mugs up to the girls in my room. I come downstairs, drink my own tea and feel a little better!

I carry two of the saucepans upstairs to the bathroom to find somebody else in it for other reasons! I wait on the stairs keeping my hands warm by cuddling the saucepans. Presently the girl comes out and I attempt a strip bath in a basin full of water. The plug doesn't fit tightly, so I have to hurry before the water drains out.

It is now about a quarter to seven. There is a queue outside the bathroom waiting for me to come out. I put on all the clothes I can find and feel a little warmer. I make my bed and dust my floor space and tidy up. Breakfast is at seven-thirty and I still have five minutes to spare, so I try to stick the wallpaper that is peeling off in strips with the damp, back to the wall! But without much success.

I go down to breakfast and eat plenty of

hot porridge and sausages and bacon. Some of us make toast in front of the gas fire, and eat a lot of that. At a quarter to eight, the lorry arrives and tonks its horn. I swallow a last cup of tea, grab a slice of bread and marmalade and follow the others out to the lorry. It is pouring with rain now and although they have fixed up a tarpaulin covering, the wind blows the rain in at us in great gusts and we arrive at the camp soaking wet and very cold.

The plotting room is well heated. The warmth makes me sleepy and I write letters or read a book to keep awake. There is no work to do on days like this. Em is busy darning stockings. I wish she would send her mending home with mine, but she is too proud and refuses every time I suggest it.

The morning passes and at twelve o'clock we come off duty and go regretfully out into the rain again and are driven back to our hostel in the lorry. The kitchen staff have lit all the fires and have a hot lunch waiting for us. We are all very hungry. During lunch I debate with Em whether to brave the storm and take a 'bus into town to see a flick, or else stay in. We decide to stay in. Susan is going out but we are all glad she won't be in, and spend the afternoon in our room.

We have the gas fire on and Em sews. She is busy making undies for her trousseau. The wireless is on and I curl up on my bed with a rug round my shoulders and read *David Copperfield*. Marion is playing with Hurry, who has grown enormous. She keeps drawing our attention to him because one ear is half pricked, or to show us how clever he is at some trick she has taught him. The wireless is playing a selection of 'Strauss melodies' and so the other two girls who sleep in our room have gone down to the mess where they have on the Forces programme with plenty of jazz.

Outside the wind is sending sheets of rain against the window and the sky is dark and stormy. At tea-time we draw the curtains and light the gas and the two oil lamps I bought in the village. It is warm and cheerful and friendly, and we are glad we did not go to the cinema.

We fetch tea from the mess and bring it up to our room. Marion shares everything she eats with Hurry – even her slice of chocolate cake, although it is the last of the cake you sent me. Em and I are fond of Hurry, but we are not so generous, because we are fond of cake, too! We make our beds before going down again for early supper. We are on duty at eight.

It is still raining when the lorry tonks its horn announcing its arrival. Hurry is shut up in the greenhouse and his howls can be heard through the wind as we run down the drive towards the transport. Marion's face is white with misery at having to part from him. Em and I are hating the wind for the discomfort it causes us, but Marion hates it for the fear it gives her dog. She will not be happy again until she returns and finds he is neither hurt, drowned, burnt, stolen, nor dead from a sudden heart attack! She is not allowed to have him in the bedroom, but will manage to smuggle him up when the N.C.O.s have gone to sleep.

It is cold on duty now, and because it is night, we are allowed to bring blankets. We sit round the plotting table huddled in greatcoats and scarves and mittens, with rugs round our legs and feet. The wind whistles through the slates and occasionally a mouse scuttles across the stone-flagged floor. We all grumble a lot about the conditions in this temporary place of work, but we will all be very sad when we do eventually move into the new block.

The men smoke and read; the girls knit and sew and gossip among themselves or to the men. Tea and cocoa is made every half hour or so with the aid of an electric kettle. There are only two cups, so these are washed and refilled in relays. Sometimes the electric light cable is blown down and the room is plunged in darkness. Then large flashlights are switched on until the candles are lit. Candlelight is soft and mysterious and the harsh lines of the room are softened and shadows leap and dance on the walls.

The wind has dropped and the rain is pattering softly on the roof. There is a spirit of friendliness and comradeship among the plotters and I am reminded of the things Daddy said to me about the spirit of the men in the trenches. Now I understand.

Em is writing to Charles. In ten days' time they will be married and she glows with some inner light that makes her outstanding and turns her from an attractive girl into a beautiful woman. I think of Simon and the fact that I should have been married four months had he lived. I wonder what you are doing at home, and where Adrian is. It is a long time since I heard from him and I must write and let him know I have managed to coincide my forty-eight with the wedding so that I shall see him there. He is to be Charles's best man.

The clock is ticking by the minutes and soon it is midnight. The door opens and the relieving watch burst in with a rush of cold air. The electric light comes on suddenly and the candles are snuffed and put away for another emergency. There is a lot of noise and chatter, and we rouse ourselves and go sleepily out to the waiting transport. On the way home somebody starts to sing. We all join in and I feel tired but happy.

The kitchen staff have filled every available kettle and saucepan with water and several of these are on the boil. Those in first grab them and fill their hot-water bottles. The queue for the bathroom gathers on the stairs. There is a lot of talking and noise. At one o'clock it has all ceased, and I am snuggled down in my bed, very nearly asleep. Marion is talking quietly to Hurry, who is wide awake and playing games with the blanket. He falls asleep suddenly like a baby, and the room is quiet. Em rolls up the blackout and opens the windows. It has stopped raining and the air is fresh with the smell of damp earth and leaves. The clouds have left the sky and it is bright with a hundred million twinkling stars.

'Good night, Marion! Good night, Jonnie!' Em says as she climbs into bed.

'Good night, Em,' I murmur, sleepily.

It is the end of another day.

Well, darlings, this letter is far too long, so I won't add any more to it now.

A kiss for you both from your,
JONQUIL.

(From Jonquil to her parents.)

The Yews, Surdon, Wilts.
22 December, 1940

Darlings,

I can't tell you how disappointed I was not to be able to come down and see you yesterday, but as I explained on the 'phone, my

162

forty-eight was cut to twenty-four because one of the girls' fiancés has just been killed in the Middle East and she could not have gone home had I not returned. Never mind! I shall be home for leave over the New Year and that is in ten days' time.

Em and Charles were very disappointed you couldn't come to the wedding, but I explained that you had both had a bad attack of 'flu and they quite understood you didn't feel up to rushing to town for the day. I expect you were sorry to miss it, too, so I will give you a detailed account.

Em managed to get fourteen days' leave. We left The Yews first thing in the morning (that was on the 20th) and arrived in town about ten o'clock. We went straight to her home and spent the rest of the morning helping her mother and two sisters cut sandwiches and decorate the big studio which was to be used for the reception. They couldn't afford a caterer, and I must say the result of their own toils was far prettier than anything one of the big firms could have produced. Instead of flowers, they had holly and mistletoe, and all Mr Charlestone's paintings were propped up round the walls. The effect was delightful and most original.

Mrs Charlestone had made all the patties and cheese straws, etc., herself and a wonderful three-tiered wedding cake. Em's eldest brother, Pete, had carved a tiny model Defiant and painted it silver for the top of the cake, and Mrs Charlestone had made some most realistic Air Force wings in icing sugar.

Em's two sisters were home for the Christmas holidays and all the boys managed to get leave. So there was a large family gathering at lunch and I thoroughly enjoyed myself. It must be fun to be one of a large family like that! But, as Em says, if you're poor it has its snags – cast-off clothes, for instance. Only the eldest wears anything new.

The wedding was held at St Mary's at three. Betty and Jean and I were the bridesmaids and we all wore pale blue net dresses that Mrs Charlestone had made for us, and tiny bluebirds in our hair. Em's dress was a dream! It was her mother's wedding-gown and her grandmother's before that, and was made of the most beautiful Belgian lace. Em was very pale and looked ethereal in the creamy white gown and veil. Mr Charlestone made a quick sketch of her before we left the house and is going to paint her from memory with the sketch to help him.

We arrived at the church punctually at three. As I went up the aisle holding Em's train, I could see Charles looking very handsome in his uniform and Adrian standing beside him. I don't think Em was a bit nervous. She walked quite steadily with her hand resting on her father's arm and her head held proudly erect. I have always felt brides should look like this and not as if they were going to their doom! Charles came forward to take her and they smiled at one another and clasped hands, and the service began.

I think my mind wandered a bit then. Once I caught Adrian's glance and noticed he was looking very pale and tired, and somehow a little lost. Until this moment I had always imagined he was quite self-contained and independent. But this was another side of him, and for once I felt older and stronger and wanted to 'mother' him. (Usually he is the one to 'father' me!)

I recovered my thoughts in time to hand Em her bouquet of white lilies, and then I was following her down the aisle out into the wintry sunshine to the waiting, beribboned cars. Adrian came with the two ushers and Betty and Jean and myself. The rest of the family drove home in another car, and the guests in taxis.

The reception was a great success. Em and Charles cut the cake and made speeches; then the bride went upstairs to change into her going-away clothes. I left her with her mother and stayed in the studio talking to Adrian and the other guests. He says he thinks he can get a forty-eight over the New Year, and wants me to go with him to the

R.A.F. dance at the 'drome.

At five o'clock, Em and Charles left and the guests departed shortly afterwards. Adrian and I helped the family clear up the débris. We all felt rather deflated and miserable suddenly, but Adrian suggested we should go out to dinner and a cinema and took us to an amusing little restaurant called 'Old Black Joe's' in some remote corner of Chelsea, where we sat at a large communal table and ate spaghetti and mushrooms. He told us a lot of amusing stories about Charles and himself and the R.A.F., and the evening's end found us all in high spirits again, thanks to him.

When we reached home, or rather the Charlestone's home – the family retired to bed, and Adrian and I sat in the kitchen by ourselves talking for half an hour before he left.

The next morning (that is to say, yesterday) I came back here. It is hard to believe that when Em returns in two weeks' time she will be a married woman! She and Charles are spending their honeymoon near Oxford. Charles used to go to one of the colleges there and Em wanted to see where he passed his childhood days!

I should be home on the twenty-eighth or ninth, but will let you know definitely in a day or two. I am still waiting for my leave forms to be signed.

Lots and lots of love to you both, and take care of yourselves after that 'flu!
Your own,
JONQUIL.

(From Jonquil to Em.)

The Yews, Surdon, Wilts.
22 December, 1940

Darling Em,

As you see, I can't do without you even for a day! But before I inundate you with my troubles, I will tell you what a wonderful wedding it was and how much we all enjoyed it. I hope you and Charles will go on being happy all your lives and that you will not have to be separated too often or for any great length of time. But I feel that you love each other so much that distance will never part you. I am so happy for you, Em darling.

Now for my woes! After you left and the last of the guests had gone, we cleaned up the studio and Adrian took us all out to dinner and a cinema. We were all in very good spirits when we returned, although a bit tired. Your family went straight to bed, but Adrian and I went into the kitchen to drink a last cup of tea before he left. I washed up the cups and put them away and dropped into the old wicker chair beside the stove. Adrian curled up on the rug at my feet and rested his head against my knees. He had taken one of my hands in his and his cheek was against it, and suddenly I was aware of something warm and wet dripping on to my hand, and I realised that Adrian was crying. My insides turned over completely and I felt physically sick for a minute. (Wasn't this an odd reaction?) Then I slipped down to the floor beside him and took him in my arms and let him cry.

Oh, Em! They were such painful, difficult tears. He did not cry as I have done, flowing, easy tears that bring relief. His sobs seemed to be dragged from the very depth of him and his whole body was shaken by them. He seemed to have no control over them at all. Do men always cry like this? It was the first time I had ever seen a man weep and I was horrified. And that it should be Adrian – *Adrian* weeping in my arms...

'Tell me what is the matter, Adrian, dear,' I said, when he seemed to be feeling a little better. 'Let me help you, please do. I can't bear to see you like this. Tell me what is the matter.'

But he wouldn't. He said he *couldn't*. I told him he could tell me anything, anything at all, but all he answered was, 'No, not this, not this!' Later, he apologised, and said he was tired and overworked and needed leave, all of which I think was true. But there was something else, too, that I could not understand.

I comforted him and kissed him good night as if he were a little boy, and he seemed happier when he left. But now *I* am thoroughly unhappy. I can't bear to think of him being miserable and do wish he had told me what was the matter. Perhaps I could have helped. But when I suggested it, all he said was, 'No, not yet!'

I shan't be happy again until I know he is all right. Perhaps you would write to him, Em? He may confide in you now you are a married woman. If it has anything to do with this girl he loves, he may feel I am too young and inexperienced to know about it. So do write, Em, *please.*

There is a rumour going round the camp that some of us are to be chosen as officers to replace the R.A.F. officers in our jobs. If this were true, we would put in for our commissions, wouldn't we?

Marion sends her love, and says, 'So does Hurry!' She is really crazy about that animal. I can't bear to think what she would do if anything happened to him.

I shall be eagerly waiting your reply and to hear what you think about Adrian. I am really awfully fond of him.

Love to you and Charles,

Your,

JONQUIL.

The Three Swans,
Newdicote Lane, Oxford.
24 December, 1940

Darling, Jonnie,

This is a perfectly adorable little pub on one of the backwaters of the Oxon. It would be quite perfect in summer and is really very lovely now. I am deliriously happy and love Charles more every day, if this is possible. I did not read him your letter, because I know you wrote to me privately, but this is the first and the only thing (I hope!) that I shall ever *not* share with him.

I was so sorry to hear about Adrian, Jonnie, but I do not think you need worry too much. From what you tell me, I should imagine he has been under considerable strain, and what with overwork and tiredness and the day's emotions and activities (a wedding *is* an emotional thing, even somebody else's!) and perhaps some temporary worry or longing for this girl he loves, things were suddenly too much for him and he broke down. After all, Jonnie, if you love someone and can't have them, it does put you under a certain amount of strain, and then, seeing your friends being married... It all seems accountable and unless you insist, I don't think I will write to him. I expect he is ashamed of his lack of control (not that it

170

is anything to be ashamed of) and is worrying now that even you should know of it. He certainly wouldn't like to know I did, too.

Just keep on writing as if nothing had happened, but write more often if you like and when you next see him, pretend you have forgotten about it. That is the way he would want it, I feel sure.

Now, cheer up, and enjoy your Christmas, darling, as well as you are able at The Yews! Charles and I are going home just for Christmas Day. He says it is years and years and years since he had a family party. He sends his love to you, and we are posting your Christmas present under separate cover.

All my best wishes, Jonnie, for a good leave and a very Happy New Year.

Your loving,
EM.

Chapter 12

(From Jonquil to Bill.)

The Yews, Surdon, Wilts.
8 January, 1941

My dear Bill,

Your letter from the Middle East arrived the day after Christmas. What timing! I was so glad to know you had arrived safely and that you had such pleasant company on the boat. Sheila sounds awfully nice and it will be grand for you to have someone to take dancing if ever you get leave and can go to Cairo. I suppose I can't ask how many V.A.D.s went on the boat with you, but I bet they had fun!

I have heaps of news stored up for you. As you know, I have been waiting for you to send your A.P.O. address, or I would have written sooner.

Firstly, Em was married before Christmas and is wonderfully happy with her Charles. She doesn't see much of him, but they write to each other every day, and are hoping to get leave together early in February. She sends her love to you.

Soon after the wedding came Christmas at

The Yews. It is the first time I have been away from home and I missed Mummy and Daddy a lot. But we really had grand fun at the hostel and on duty on Christmas Day. We decorated everything with holly and mistletoe and paper chains, and hung up stockings on Christmas Eve! Then we all went round after lights out, putting little things in each other's stockings, having previously arranged that no one must spend more than sixpence on each gift. We had great fun in the morning, undoing our parcels, and I'm afraid we all behaved like a bunch of schoolchildren.

Breakfast was specially good, fried eggs and bacon and coffee instead of tea. We then went to church and, of course, Hurry had to go, too, and sat shivering on a tombstone throughout the service. We had early lunch as we were on at mid-day, and kept our Christmas dinner for our late meal.

We had no work to do all afternoon, and one of the officers had brought a small portable wireless set down with him and we listened to a B.B.C. recording of *The Babes in the Wood*. It was most amusing and made the watch pass surprisingly quickly.

Tea was a gala affair with the W.A.A.F. officers dishing out tea and passing sandwiches since they hadn't served lunch as is the custom. Afterwards, we put on mackintoshes and gum boots and took Hurry for a long walk.

The kitchen staff excelled themselves in the cooking of our turkey and Christmas pudding. After dinner we helped them wash up as they were all anxious to get to the special dance on the camp. I missed your company, Bill, and would have given a lot to have you there. Nobody seems to dance as well as you do!

We were on duty again at midnight and I can't tell you what fun it was – more fun than the dance, in fact. The officers were downstairs doing our job, and we joined the off-going watch who were standing on the balcony upstairs singing community songs. They left about one a.m. but we went on singing until we were relieved at four. We had all the old part songs – *'Frère Jacques'* and *'Three Blind Mice'*, etc. It was such fun! One or two of the R.A.F. officers sang solo and the girls persuaded me to do the same. I sang a selection from *'Maid of the Mountains'*.

We were exhausted when we finally got to bed. The last thing I remember before dropping asleep was Marion's voice asking Hurry if he had had a good Christmas! I was so tired I shouldn't have been surprised to hear him say he had. I know I had, anyway!

I went home on leave on the 28th and had a quiet time with the exception of a New

Year's Dance at the neighbouring R.A.F. station. We still have our fifty billetees. Their quarters were rebuilt some time ago, but they were almost immediately occupied by the W.A.A.F. who came to do A.C.H. and M.T. duties.

We also have six small evacuees. Mummy says I wouldn't believe what they were like when they arrived. They couldn't use a knife and fork and ate with either a spoon or their fingers – usually the latter! The eldest child was thirteen. She was the only one who *could* speak, but what she said was quite unintelligible. The others, whose ages range from seven to eleven, could only grunt and behaved just like little animals. They had never seen a bath and were frightened to death of it and of running tap water. They had never eaten cake or seen a biscuit and it took a long time to persuade them that apples and plums were eatables. Their meals at home seemed to consist entirely of fish and chips when they were lucky, and bread and dripping when they were not.

They didn't like sleeping alone or in sheets and as soon as the lights were out, crawled into one bed together between the blankets! Nor did they like sleeping in the nighties Mummy bought for them. For weeks they used to put their clothes on again as soon as she left the room.

It is unbelievable that such squalor as they

have obviously lived in still exists in what we call a civilised Christian country. I never imagined such a thing possible. But the children have improved enormously now, and their thin little legs and arms are quite chubby, and the sores have gone, I hope for good. Daddy says the evacuation scheme will do a lot towards helping the abolition of the dirt and filth in the slums. For one thing, many people (including myself) never realised before what it was like the poorest districts. For another, these children at least know now what cleanliness is, and even although they will return to their homes after the war, Daddy thinks they will have the grounding of decent living too firmly embedded in them to dispense with it completely.

I feel that before we start improving things in Europe (the papers are already full of plans to do so) we should improve conditions such as these in our own country. If I'm not too old after the war (!) I'd like to help in this work.

Mummy is a changed person. She is devoted to the children and looks after them herself as she never cared for me. I was always handed over to a nurse! She is tireless where working or sewing for them is concerned and will probably end up by being a second Silver Lady – you know, like the patroness of the Silver Lady canteens in

London for down and outs!

Em and I have both put in for our commissions and if we pass our board, we will be off to Lincoln for our training next month. Marion was given the offer but refused it. She is quite happy where she is.

I don't think there is any more news, Bill. This letter is already over-weight, I'm sure, but I will try sending it by air mail and see what happens.

Write when you have nothing better to do. And I'll hold thumbs for you about Sheila. She sounds sweet.

All the best, Bill,
from JONNIE.

(From Jonquil to Adrian.)

The Yews, Surdon, Wilts.
10 January, 1941

My Dear Adrian,

It seems a good deal longer than ten days since I went to your New Year dance at the camp. I really did have a lovely time and you were a grand host. I think it was the most impressive evening I have ever spent – hearing all the men in the squadrons singing *'Should auld acquaintance be forgot...'* The room was filled with ghosts and although I think they were happy ghosts, I was nevertheless glad you were holding my hand. Maybe I was too fanciful, but the flickering

177

candlelight plays weird tricks on one's imagination, I find. And the steam rising from the cauldron of boiling punch – oh, it was all most eerie and fascinating! How did you feel?

I am really writing to tell you that I shall not be able to get home on my next forty-eight after all. Em and I are having our selection board interviews next week and all being well, we go off to Lincoln the following week for our training. I believe it lasts about a month. If we pass, we will be the first W.A.A.F. officers in this particular job and it is in the form of an experiment. If we do well, there will be a grand substitution of W.A.A.F for R.A.F. personnel. So a lot will depend on us and we are determined to do well.

Some time ago, you asked me if I were proud of being in the R.A.F. and I didn't quite understand what you meant. But the other day there was a kind of review of the Battle of Britain at one of the local cinemas and the audience cheered and clapped at the end, and some of them were crying. I looked down at my uniform and realised suddenly that it was the same as yours, and that I was part of the R.A.F. and had contributed in an indirect way, therefore, to their glorious effort. Then I did feel proud and I thanked you silently, Adrian, for pushing me into this uniform rather than the others. Not that they aren't doing good work, too, but I wouldn't change now for anything in the world.

I suppose now you are instructing, you will be in comparative safety. No doubt you are horrified at the thought of being grounded, even if it is only temporarily, but it relieves my mind somewhat. Do you know how long you will be down? Em is naturally thrilled that Charles should be out of it. You knew, didn't you, that Pete was reported missing in action the other day? She took the news with her usual calm, but I know she is terribly worried because she has talked about it in her sleep several times lately. I think the intensive training (if we pass our board!) will take her mind off him and be very good for her.

And now I must clean shoes and buttons ready for the morning watch. So I will say 'good night' Adrian, my dear, and I hope to hear from you before too long.

Your affectionate,
JONQUIL.

(From Mrs Mathews to her daughter.)

The Manor House, Wodecot, Kent.
16 January, 1941

My Darling Jonquil,
I am *so* glad to hear you have passed your board. Daddy and I *knew* you would. You

must write and tell us all you can about your course.

Daddy is *very* busy at the moment with his office work and fire-watching and Home Guard duties; so he has asked me to give you his love and to tell you that he was stationed at the same place in Lincoln at the start of the Great War. Now *isn't* that a coincidence!

The children are all very well and growing fast. Bobbie's mother came down to see him the other day and was *very* pleased with his progress. Annie's father came to see her, but she hid in the garage loft all day because she thought he had come to take her home, and she didn't want to go. *Poor* little thing! Her home life was never very happy. Few days went by without a kick or a blow from her father and mother, and often as not she went to bed hungry because there simply *wasn't* anything to eat. Imagine that! However, her father is in the army now and earning quite good pay, and he must be a changed man because I found him very courteous and gentle and sensitive to his small daughter's fear of him. There is *no doubt* but that this war is doing us *all* good.

Your father is working terribly hard, and when I do see something of him, he is always too tired from the previous night's fire-watching in town, or his Home Guard exercises in the village, to say more than 'good night' or 'good morning', and drop into bed! He seemed upset because Long-hurst couldn't keep the garden looking nice now that the other gardeners have been called up. The rose beds were badly in need of attention and he hadn't time to do it him-self. So I set the children on to weeding it at sixpence a bucketful of weeds. It gives them something to do and sets your father's mind at rest. He says it is bribery and corruption! But I think it encourages a working spirit.

This seems to be all my news at the moment, darling. Daddy and I are *longing* to hear how you get on.

Annie loved the golliwog you sent her for her birthday and is going to write you a letter. It makes me quite *proud* when I think she couldn't even speak a few months ago.

Take care of yourself, darling.

Ever your fond

MUMMY.

(From Jonquil to her parents.)

Langdon Hall, Lincoln.
24 January, 1941

Darling Mummy and Daddy,

Here is my news and this is Cadet Mathews reading it! I now wear a white band in my cap and have a certain number of privileges due to an officer. We still salute commis-sioned ranks and we make our own beds, but no longer have to clean the floors. Nor do we have to have late passes if we wish to be out until midnight. I can see that being an officer will have distinct advantages especially in the comforts line.

Em has had no word yet of Pete, but I keep telling her no news is good news, and I think the hard work is taking her mind off him to a certain extent. Charles telephones her every night and she receives one, if not two, letters from him every day. Such is love! I think Charles would have liked her to have a baby and get out of the W.A.A.F., but Em says she has started one job of work and she is going to finish it before she starts another!

We work long hours, starting at eight-thirty a.m. and going on until seven-thirty p.m., with an hour's break for lunch, and half an hour each for elevenses and for tea. Sunday we have the day off, thank goodness! and we are spending the morning in bed and in the afternoon we are going to town to hear Beethoven's Fifth, which is being played by the London Philharmonic, with Sir Thomas Beecham conducting. Won't it be wonderful!

Em and I had a letter from Marion today. She is distraught because Hurry has distemper. If anything happens to that dog, I think Marion would kill herself. What a good thing she decided not to take her commission just yet! She would never have had time to cope with him here. I believe she has a good vet, visiting him every day, so if he does die, it certainly won't be through lack of attention.

I had a letter from Adrian who thinks he will be instructing for the next three months anyway, maybe more. He says he is feeling much better in health, although naturally he is a bit fed up not to be flying. He doesn't talk about it much, but it means an awful lot to him. It meant a good deal to Simon, too, but in a different way. *He* loved the thrill and excitement of flying. Adrian loves the perfection and beauty of an aircraft in motion, the symmetry of a squadron in formation, the unison of the men and their machines, as if they were part of each other. He has a certain fighting spirit, too, with which one doesn't credit him at first. A lot of the boys in his squadron have gone and when he fights, he fights back for each one of them. Charles told Em that the C.O. had recommended him (Adrian) for a D.F.C. and that he is pretty sure to get it.

Give my love to the children, Mummy, particularly to little Bobbie, for whom I have fallen in no small way! And don't you go over-working, Daddy. Your health may have been A.1. in the last war, but you're nearing fifty now!

I wish I could tell you more about my work, but I can't. I will say, though, that I still find it both exciting and interesting.

Em sends her love to you both (what she can spare, which isn't much!) and I send all mine.
Your own,
JONQUIL.

(From Jonquil to her parents.)

Langdon Hall, Lincoln.
16 February, 1941

Darling Parents,
I have four important items of news for you. Firstly, I have passed the examinations and within a day or two I shall be a fully fledged officer... Secondly, we are to get forty-eight hours between now and when we go to our next R.A.F. station, mainly to get our uniforms. We are given a £30 grant and have to buy uniforms, greatcoats, mackintoshes, hats and shirts, but we are allowed to keep issue shoes and underclothes and respirators and gas equipment and the like. So you can expect me home on Friday. I shall shop all day and catch the train down in the evening, Daddy, and hope to goodness you don't choose that night for fire-watching or H.G. exercises. If you can leave the children, Mummy, why don't you come up to town and help me choose my uniform? I am so excited I feel I could pop! This last month has been a very nerve-trying one, and the reaction, now that it is all over, is making us

light-headed.

Third on the list of good news items, is that Adrian has got his D.F.C. Did you notice it in the papers? He went to Buckingham Palace to receive it a few days ago. I had a letter from him this morning, telling me about it.

Lastly, and not 'leastly', Em's brother Pete has been reported a prisoner of war in German hands. Em is naturally thrilled and we are feeling so exuberant between us that I am sure something will get broken.

Oh, yes! Hurry is out of danger, so Marion is happy too. In fact we are all happy, and I am too excited to write sensibly, so I will finish this off. I must sober down in time to write my congratulations to Adrian, and to see if he can get over when I come on my forty-eight.

Lots of love, darlings, and you had better wire me, Mummy, if you can meet me in town. Otherwise I will be on the 4.30, Daddy.

Longing to see you both,

Your own,

JONQUIL.

(From Jonquil to Adrian.)

Langdon Hall, Lincoln.
16 February, 1941

My dear Adrian,

Congratulations! It is wonderful news and I

am feeling proud for you! In fact, I would say I am proud to know you, but then I always have been. The King sounds charming, and I shall look forward to shaking his hand when I get the G.M. or the M.B.E. or whatever it is Waafs get! Don't laugh! It's not impossible, although I will admit it is not very probable, either!

I have passed my exam and should be an Assistant Section Officer in a day or two. The day after tomorrow I have forty-eight hours and shall be home by the evening. Is there any hope of your getting over then or the following day? I should so like to see you.

I suppose Charles told you Em's brother, Pete, was a prisoner of war? It is such a relief to her to know he is safe and the fact he is a prisoner of war hardly bothers her.

I am not going to write any more because I hope to see you the day after tomorrow and I'll give you all the 'gen' then. Do try and come, Adrian. It must be months since I last saw you – not since New Year's Eve, in fact.

As ever,
Your affectionate,
JONQUIL.

Chapter 13

(From Jonquil to Adrian.)

> Officers' Mess, R.A.F. Station,
> Worsley, Cheshire.
> *21 February, 1941*

Darling Adrian,

What a heavenly day that was! Even among all the excitement of arriving here and being saluted for the first time by the guard at the gate (!), the memory of it fills me with a warm glow of pleasure.

To start with, we were so lucky with the weather. It might have been blowing gales and raining squalls, or even April showering! But instead it was the most glorious spring day.

I think the children loved every minute of it. I know I did. You never told me where you managed to get the horse and cart, nor what gave you the idea of camping out for the day. How did you guess I was so fond of frying sausages over a camp fire and baking potatoes in the embers? You are truly a marvellous man! And our evening alone together afterwards, listening to *La Bohème* … I felt inexplicably happy and content with life. Thank you, Adrian, for the happiest day I have ever spent.

This camp is very different from our last station. For one thing, the officers mess together. There are only twenty W.A.A.F. here to two hundred R.A.F. officers, so we are assured we will have a good time. Em and I still feel a little shy and new to it all, but everyone is awfully nice and helpful.

I still feel a bit shaken when I am saluted, and the inclination to salute myself whenever I see an officer is somewhat overpowering! I feel sure I shall forget one of these days and give some equally new pilot officer a really smart one!

As far as work is concerned, Em and I both find it more interesting here, although we are not quite so busy. We still get forty-eight hour stand-offs, so I hope to come home again next week and tell you how I am liking it.

Em sends her love and I will send a kiss in return for the one you gave me the other night!

Always your affectionate,
JONQUIL.

(From Em to Adrian.)

Officers' Mess, R.A.F. Station,
Worsley, Cheshire.
22 February, 1941

My Dear Adrian,

I know you will be happy to hear that Jonquil has talked of nothing else for the last few days but your day out together with the children. I do hope this may be the beginning for you two and that your patience is at last being rewarded. Jonquil is a darling and I am as fond of her as of my two sisters, and there is no one I would rather see her married to than you. Besides, it would be such fun after the war if you two and Charles and I lived close to each other.

But perhaps this is looking too far ahead. I don't want to raise your hopes unduly, Adrian, because I know what a bitter disappointment it would be if things were not as I believe them to be. So you must not count on anything and do take what I have said at its reading worth. There is no more or less to it that I know of than I told you at the beginning of my letter.

I expect Jonquil and Charles between them have given you all my news, so I won't elucidate now.

Good luck to you. I'm holding thumbs!
Yours ever,
EM.

(From Jonquil to her parents.)

Officers' Mess, R.A.F. Station,
Worsley, Cheshire.
1 March, 1941

My Darling Mummy and Daddy,

I know you will be surprised to hear that I have at last fallen in love. This is the most serious thing that has ever happened in my life. I realise now that Simon was a childhood affair and that what I felt for him was only a kind of calf love with no depth of feeling to it. But this – oh, this is different! I am so happy, so wildly crazy that I can't eat, drink or sleep. At least, not much!

I had better tell you how it all began. To start with, I have only spoken to him once! His name is Wing Commander Brian Lee, and he is a regular – that is to say, he was in the R.A.F. before the war. He has his wings and a D.F.C., D.S.O. and Bar, but has been grounded now and can't get back to flying because he is over age. He is thirty-five.

Now don't go saying 'He's much too old!' I am nearly twenty-one so that makes him only fourteen years older than I am, which isn't so much really. Anyway, I am definitely counting my chickens before they hatch because, as I say, I have only met him once!

To give you some idea of what he is like – he is about five foot eleven, of slight build.

He is very dark, but has surprisingly blue eyes with a detached, aloof, rather sad expression in them. I think it was this look that first attached me to him. When he speaks about anything that is of interest to him, his whole face lights up and he seems to come alive. I don't think a lot of things do interest him, but if you mention flying, or the R.A.F. ... and music, too! It was through a Beethoven piano concerto that I came to meet him. I had noticed in the *Radio Times* that it was to be broadcast after the news on the Home Service. Usually the wireless in the big ante-room is switched to the Forces, or else turned off altogether. So when the time came for it to begin, I went into the card room and found the programme on the little radiogram in there.

Em had gone to her room to write to Charles and I was quite alone. The door opened quietly and someone sat down beside me. I only gave him a quick glance, and that without really seeing him. You know how engrossed I get when I listen to some music I am particularly fond of! When it was over I turned round and said: 'Wasn't that absolutely perfect!' and realised for the first time as I said it that I was addressing a Wing Commander. In the mess one isn't supposed to address a senior officer unless he speaks to you first.

But he wasn't a bit cross and before we

knew where we were, we were having a heated debate on whether Beecham is a better conductor than Adrian Boult! Then he asked me how long I had been here, and how I liked the Service, and seemed very pleased that I felt some attachment for it. It means so much to him. He told me about his own career, and we stayed talking until eleven o'clock. I found him a delightful, sympathetic, amusing person. But when we joined the others in the big anteroom, he changed completely. He was lost in his own thoughts most of the while. I went to bed quite thrilled to realise that he had allowed me to see his real self while to other people he wore an armour of aloofness which I think has earned for him the reputation of being rather stand-offish. But he isn't.

Today he has not yet been to the mess, but I am hoping to see him again this evening. I wish he were not so high-ranked. If he were a pilot officer, I could go up and speak to him, but as it is, I must wait until he notices me.

No doubt you think I am quite mad, and I suppose I am, but I have never felt like this in my life before about any one. The only thing that matters to me is that I should see him again, and I can think of nothing else. Don't write to me about him yet. I will write another letter to you in a day or two when I hope I shall know him better.

Em says I am quite crazy, and I think I am – crazily in love.

Your own,
JONQUIL.

(From Jonquil to her parents.)

Officers' Mess, R.A.F. Station,
Worsley, Cheshire.
3 March, 1941

Darling Parents,

Here is the letter I promised you and I am afraid my news isn't too good. Brian is married. I might as well tell you the whole story, so I'll begin where my last letter ended.

I had supper with Em and waited in the ante-room until news time. I had almost given up hope of seeing him, when suddenly he appeared with the C.O. He looked round the room quickly and when he saw me he smiled, and I knew he had been searching for me. He went in to a late supper with the C.O. and returned to the ante-room just as the news finished, and came straight over to me.

'I have brought some of my good records up to the mess with me,' he said. 'Would you care to come and listen to them? I'm going to play them on the radiogram in the card room.'

Would I care!

As usual, the card room was empty and we had a wonderful evening playing his records. We have practically the same choice as regards piano concertos, but his choice of opera is more sober than mine. I like Verdi as against his love of Wagner. At midnight I had to go on duty, but he asked me if I would be free the following afternoon to go to a concert in Chester.

Yesterday we went to the concert and it was truly magnificent. It was so wonderful to share it with someone you liked and who appreciated it as well. Brian is a wonderful person. He has all the older man's courtesy and *savoir faire*. Everything we did he had planned beforehand, so that our table for dinner was booked for after the show and there were flowers on it for me from him. (Can you imagine a young man of today doing this?) And he ordered just the right meal and seemed to attract waiters like honey fetches bees.

When we came home in the car, he asked me if I had been happy. I said I thought it was the happiest day of my life, and asked him if he had enjoyed himself, too.

'I have been happier these last few days, Jonnie, since I have known you than in all the last six years put together ... though I have no right to say so,' he answered.

'But why not?' I asked. 'Why shouldn't

you say so if it is true?'

'Didn't you know I was married?' he asked me quietly. 'I thought you must have known, Jonnie. I don't know why. I'm so very sorry...'

I couldn't speak for a minute or two. The idea that he might be married was one which simply had not occurred to me. I felt as if I had received a really hard blow in the regions of my heart. It could all have been so marvellous, so perfect if we could have fallen in love and become engaged in the usual way.

'Does it mean so much to you, Jonnie?' he asked me. 'Can't we still be friends?'

'Of course,' I forced myself to say. 'I was just – just surprised...'

'Let's be honest with each other, my dear,' Brian said suddenly. 'I hate lies. When I first saw you, I knew I was going to care. I knew, too, that I ought not to make a point of seeing you more than I could help, but it was too much for me. I tried to persuade myself that it was just your interest in music that attracted me, but I knew it wasn't in my heart. It was *you,* your sweetness, your charm, your loveliness. I didn't mean to tell you all this, Jonnie, I have no right. But when I saw your face just now... Oh, Jonnie, my dearest, your expression gave you away. You do like me, don't you?'

I nodded my head, unable to speak for the

tears and the lump in the back of my throat.

'Darling,' he said, putting his arms round me and holding me tightly. 'I'm so sorry, so very sorry!'

Presently, when I asked him, he told me about his wife. She married him for his money – he had large private means in those days and his flying pay as well – and it wasn't until after he had married her, that she showed up in her real colours. Then she told him outright that if he wanted a divorce, she would either give him grounds – at a price – or let him give her grounds and the alimony. Brian was so cross, so disgusted, that he refused to do either. Often enough he has been tempted to do so. She is always running up large bills in his name and nagging at him to give her a bigger allowance. She threatened to disgrace him in front of his senior officers if he didn't. She knew his career meant more to him than anything and she made his life hell. He told me that now he had met me, he had known the two extremes of happiness and misery through a woman, and that if I decided when I knew him better, that I loved him and was not just infatuated, he would let his wife divorce him and ask me to marry him.

This has all happened so quickly that I hardly know where I am. Brian says there is no need to rush into anything and that the best thing for us to do is to see as much as we can of each other and really get to know one another properly. Then if we still find our feelings unchanged, we can talk again about divorce.

He is very sensible and honest about the whole affair. He says I must realise he is fourteen years older than me and that although this doesn't seem much now, it *will* do when he is fifty and I am only thirty-six, for instance. But I don't think I would mind that. I don't think anything like that would matter. He has been so wretched in his home life I want nothing more than to make him happy and help him regain some of his ideals.

I shall eagerly await your letters, darlings, and do beg you not to judge too quickly or severely. If you once met him, you would like him, I know.

With love from

Your bewildered and intoxicated!

JONQUIL.

(From Mrs Mathews to Jonquil.)

The Manor House, Wodecot, Kent.
6 March, 1941

My darling child,

I must admit your last two letters have caused me *considerable* worry and anxiety. It seems to me that this man has *deliberately* misled you, waiting until he was sure of your feelings towards him before telling you he was married. I think it is *very* wicked of him and do trust you will come to your senses before it is too late. You are just infatuated by this man and flattered because he is *somebody* in the Air Force and a man of the world as well. It is all very well for him to point out the discrepancy in your ages when he knows you are too infatuated to *care*. But do you realise what a lot fourteen years is?

I cannot think, Jonquil, that you are *really* serious about this man. You know your father's views on divorce and I think it would break his heart if ever you brought the family name near the divorce courts. Besides, how do you know *his* story about his married life is the *true* one? Naturally he would tell it in his favour, but I wonder what kind of story his wife would have to tell. You know *nothing* about him and I am inclined to believe he is a thorough bounder.

Now, Jonquil dear, *do* be advised by me. I am a *good* deal older than you and you should try and benefit by my experience of the world. Forget this man, and if you still have to see him, be *sure* you are not alone with him. I am not suggesting he might try to harm you, but infatuation is a *dangerous* thing.

Your father is writing to you separately,

and I feel sure is counsel will be well worth taking.
From
Your fond but anxious
MOTHER.

(From Robert Mathews to his daughter)

The Manor House, Wodecot, Kent.
6 March, 1941

Darling Jonquil,
I have read your last two letters very carefully and I must say I am a little disturbed. You know the views I hold on divorce.

On the other hand, I trust you implicitly and I feel sure you would not like this man if he were at all dishonourable or false. Instincts are all-important and if you trust and believe in him, I shall go by your decision. But do be sure, Jonquil. Marriage is (or should be) for always, and that is a long time. I respect him for not trying to rush you into anything and feel this is the correct attitude to the whole affair. There *is* no hurry, so don't make up your mind now. Wait a bit and think it out carefully.

Your mother has never been a very easy woman to live with, but at heart she is as sound and solid as gold and I know she has never looked at another man since the day she married me. Had we not loved one another really deeply, we would never have weathered the storms of our married life and retained our present devotion and respect for one another. Marriage is made up of more than just attraction. It must have true friendship and understanding, respect and patience in its roots. Then it will be enduring. If you think this man can be all this to you, then I shall not oppose your marriage to him when he is divorced.

Always your loving
DADDY

(From Jonquil to her mother.)

Officers' Mess, R.A.F. Station,
Worsley, Cheshire.
8 March, 1941

Darling Mummy,

Your letter made me extremely angry. You write of Brian as if he were the proverbial villain trying to seduce the innocent young girl. You also assume that I am completely without experience of the world and am silly enough to be humbugged by flattery.

To start with, how can you judge someone you don't even know? Why, because he says he is innocent, do you immediately jump to the conclusion that it is he and not his wife who is the culprit? You have taken such an old-fashioned view of it all, Mummy. You have been shut away in the country so long with Daddy that you haven't the least idea what is going on in the present-day world. I am not a child any longer. I am nearly of age, and I am a woman, and old enough to recognise the truth when I hear it, and I know Brian is good all through. As to him rushing me into an affair, it is absolute nonsense! I told you I fell for him the first time I saw him and that was long before I knew he felt the same way about me.

And do you suppose every man goes round saying: 'I must tell you, I am married!' to each girl he is introduced to? There was no question of his purposely not telling me. He simply assumed I already knew. Most people know each others' private affairs here and it can only have been chance that I did not hear some gossip to that effect.

You obviously don't understand one little bit, Mummy. Even Daddy with all his conventional ideas, has taken a more reasonable attitude towards the whole affair. I'm sorry if you are worried and anxious. But there is no need to be. I think Brian would rather kill himself than hurt me.

Your loving
JONQUIL.

Officers' Mess, R.A.F. Station,
Worsley, Cheshire.
8 March, 1941

Darling Daddy,

Thank you for your letter which made me realise for the hundredth time what a wonderful person you are. Mummy wrote a silly letter and I'm afraid I've just let off steam in my reply to her. She doesn't understand and writes to me as if I were still seventeen.

I will take your advice, Daddy, and think very carefully before I make up my mind. I see Brian every free moment we have and even if I am not absolutely certain whether my love for him is all that it should be, I *am* sure that he loves me truly and deeply, and it is this that is making me doubly cautious. If I let him down or hurt him in any way, his faith in women would disappear altogether.

If ever we should manage to get leave together, I will bring him home so that you can meet him, Daddy. But at the present moment, he is terribly busy and he doesn't see any hope of leave for quite a time ahead. I am due for seven days fairly soon, probably the week after next.

I am longing to see you, Daddy, and to speak to you in person about Brian.

Always your own
JONQUIL.

Chapter 14

> Officers' Mess, R.A.F. Station,
> Worsley, Cheshire.
> *10 March, 1941*

My Dear Adrian,

I hardly know how to tell you this, but it must be done before Jonnie goes on leave. Adrian, this time it is far more serious – she thinks she is in love with a married man. It all happened very suddenly and I was quite convinced when I last wrote to you that you meant a good deal more to her than you had ever done before. I would never have mentioned it if I had *not* been sure... And now everything is changed.

Quite honestly, I don't know what to think about it. To do him justice, he is charming, and he *is* in love with Jonnie, and is only too ready to divorce his wife and marry her. He is even being decent enough to refuse to make any decisions until Jonnie is more sure of herself and her feelings. Not only this, but a divorce at the moment would seriously jeopardize his career. He is a regular and there is an important job in the air for him, meaning a big step up. The slightest breath of scandal might mean the loss of this job, but he is willing to risk it if Jonnie says she will marry him. If you had met him and knew how much the Service and his career in the R.A.F. mean to him, you would understand the extent of his selflessness in the affair.

I find I am quite unable to make up my mind as to what will be best for her. If she *does* love him, I think he would make her happy. But I feel it is partly hero-worship – that it may just be the stage most girls go through of thinking they are in love with an older man. Brian is certainly very attractive and I've nothing at all against him, but somehow I cannot see Jonnie married to him.

This must all come as a great shock to you, Adrian, and I would far rather have let Jonnie tell you herself. But following the encouragement in my last letter, I felt I ought to prepare you. I am very worried and more upset than I let Jonnie realise. Why – *why* couldn't she have fallen in love with you...?

Yours with deepest sympathy,
EM.

(From Adrian to Em.)

47, Stonefield Ave., Wodecot, Kent.
22 March, 1941

My Dear Em,
Unfortunately your second letter went astray

and I did not receive it until too late. Jonquil had asked me over for supper the second day of her leave. Mr Mathews was fire-watching in town, and Mrs Mathews retired to bed early, leaving Jonquil and me alone together. She was looking radiantly beautiful and remembering the contents of your first letter, I was foolish enough to mistake the animation and excitement in her eyes for pleasure in seeing me again. Fool that I was! I took one of her hands in mine and said: 'I am glad to have you alone at last, Jonquil. There is so much I have to tell you...' But before I could begin, she turned to me and cried: 'And I have so much to tell you, too, Adrian. I need your advice. You have always been my greatest friend and I feel I can confide in you...' And she told me the story of Brian.

To use a piece of Air Force slang, was I shaken? My breath was completely taken away and for a moment I was quite stunned. 'It isn't possible!' I kept telling myself. 'Not after all this time, after all my patience! She is teasing me.' But I could see plain enough with my own eyes how deadly serious she was, and with a great effort, I pulled myself together and listened to her.

But Em, how could I help her or give advice? I have far too much at stake, to start with. Secondly, it is a thing only she can decide. She seemed chiefly concerned with the effect of the divorce upon this fellow's Service career, and seemed afraid to let him risk anything in case she didn't remain in love with him. I stress this because it is the one straw at which I, the drowning man, can grasp. If she can imagine she might one day change her mind, she cannot yet be fully in love with him.

She was also worried about her father, who, as you probably know, has very strong feelings against divorce. But I do not feel he would really withhold his consent to their marriage if Jonquil's heart were set on it.

All I could do, and what I did, was to tell her to make up her own mind, and in the meantime, if she should ever need me, I would always be waiting.

And that is just about it, Em. I *shall* always be waiting. There will never be anyone else and I shall love her all my life, whichever road she takes now.

You once told me to be patient. I am the model of patience and control, but it is wearing me out. Oh, Em, I love her so...

Thank you for your letter, and write and tell me when things make a move one way or another. I doubt if Jonquil will have much time to spare for letter-writing now.

My love to you and Charles,
ADRIAN.

Officers' Mess, R.A.F. Station,
Worsley, Cheshire.
1 April, 1941

Darling Daddy and Mummy,

There is a new regulation out that we shall all go to an Officers' Training Unit and I am off to a place called Bulberry Park, Dorset, next week. I shall be there about two weeks.

Quite honestly, I think I shall be glad to get away. I want to try and come to some decision about Brian. When I am with him, nothing and nobody but he counts. When I am away from him, I begin to doubt my own feelings. This frightens me because it means it is his physical presence that is holding me. Em once said: 'If ever you do fall in love, you will be quite, quite sure,' and deep in my heart, I think she is right. Yet at the same time, the thought of never seeing Brian again is intolerable. I just couldn't bear it. I do love him ... oh, I don't know. *I don't know.*

If only he were to try and persuade me one way or another. But he doesn't. He is always quite calm and refuses to discuss the problem with me.

'When you've made up your mind, Jonquil, you must tell me,' he said. 'Until then, we will go on seeing each other as friends.'

But I want more than his friendship. I want his arms round me and his lips on mine. I want to hear him call me 'dearest' and to hear him say he cannot live without me; that he loves me more than anything in the world. I know he does, but I want him to say it, to stop this farce of trying to turn a love affair into a platonic relationship. It is unnatural. It is wrong by the laws of nature, and yet I realise it is right conventionally. Oh, damn conventions! Sometimes I wish I had never met Brian. But *that* isn't true. He means everything to me.

I'll stop talking nonsense and will try to write you a decent letter tomorrow. Good night, darlings. Do please try to think kindly of Brian. He is too good to be true, really. I wish he weren't!

Your loving, distracted daughter,
JONQUIL.

(From Jonquil to Brian.)

Bulberry Park, Larkspur, Dorset.
9 April, 1941

My darling Brian,
This is the first opportunity I have had of writing to you. I have been travelling most of the day, and until now have been un-packing and finding my way about.

I have never seen so many women in my life – except at the depôt! The only consolation is that practically everyone is an A.S.O., so I do not feel too strange. There are one or two

Flight Officers about who give the lectures. Tomorrow we are scheduled to have lectures on 'Hygiene', 'Gas' and 'The R.A.F.' and some drill and P.T. thrown in. Fortunately the weather isn't too bad, so I shan't mind the exercise. But my mind is always apt to wander during lectures.

Oh, Brian, it's no good! I can't go on writing to you as if you were an aunt or something! I am only human. I must tell you I miss you dreadfully and I can't even work off steam on Em. If only she had come, too!

Darling, I wish I could make up my mind. It seems so horribly unflattering to you to go on wavering like this. It isn't that I don't love you. I do. I know I do. I think if you hadn't been married before I should have said 'yes' days – weeks ago. But now I am afraid. What if I should change my mind when I am older. I have changed so unbelievably in my views since I was engaged to Simon, and that is only a year ago. What if next year when the decree *nisi* for the divorce came through I should have changed again? I would never forgive myself, Brian. And this job you're hoping to get... Suppose you lost it because of me? I know how much the R.A.F. means to you. It is the one ideal that you still retain, isn't it? It is the one thing that hasn't let you down.

Brian, my darling, I will try not to take too long over my decision. I know the effect it has on a man if he loves a girl. A friend of mine called Adrian Hepworth has been in love with a girl ever since I first met him, and he is still waiting for her. (I wonder if her reason for keeping him waiting is the same as mine!) You'd like him, Brian. He is a little like you in one or two ways, although I never thought of it before now. I hope you will meet him one day. He is the best friend I have.

We are due in to supper in five minutes, so I must go and tidy up now. Write to me soon, darling, please. I shall be watching the post most anxiously.

Your loving
JONQUIL.

(From Brian to Jonquil.)

Officers' Mess, R.A.F. Station,
Worsley, Cheshire.
11 April, 1941

Darling Jonquil,
It was sweet of you to write so soon and I am glad really, that you broached the subject which for all my silence has been foremost in my mind. I do want you to realise, my dear, that my future job has nothing to do with it. It would not be the R.A.F. who let me down if I did lose the job (which I very much doubt on this account). So my ideal, as you call it, would still be whole. You

may rest your mind on that score, darling.

As to your changing your mind when you are older – it is a possibility I have considered most carefully, and that is why I do not wish you to hurry over your decision. You may rest assured, Jonquil dear, that I am not under great strain. I have become fatalistic to a degree these last few years and I feel that in the end it will all work out for the best. We have not discussed religion much, have we? I believe God watches over each one of us and guides our ways – that if we trust in Him, He will show us the right path. I do not blame Him for the mistake of my first marriage. I was young and impulsive in those days, and if nothing else, I have learned my lesson. If everything had gone right for me always, I may never have appreciated it. As it is I have dedicated myself to the R.A.F. and attained peace of mind and realised myself through my work.

So, Jonquil, if you do decide you do not want to go through with it, I shall not be left entirely destitute. If you do decide to marry me, I shall be the happiest man on this earth.

Until then – and for always, you have all my love, my darling,

Your

BRIAN.

(From Jonquil to Em.)

Em darling,

I am in such a dreadful muddle in my mind over Brian. It seems to get worse instead of better. In my last letter to him, I said that if I did agree to marry him and he lost his job through me, I should never forgive myself because I knew that his career in the R.A.F. was the one ideal in his life which had remained untarnished. His answer to me was – literally, 'It would not be the R.A.F. who let me down.' In other words, it would be he who let down the R.A.F. And that is the last thing I want him to feel.

Oh, if only the divorce could be got through decently and quietly. But he is so well known. All the papers would be full of it. 'Famous air-ace divorced'. 'Wing Commander breaks another record'. 'Wife sues well-known flyer' ... I don't think I could bear it – for myself, yes, but for him, no. He was happy before I came into his life. If I went out of it quickly now, I wonder if it would leave him happy. Oh, I don't know, Em. If only I could be sure what was best for both of us.

Brian says he doesn't mind how long he waits for me to make up my mind. But if he does get this job, it means an immediate

212

posting overseas, and unless he starts the divorce proceedings before he goes, we couldn't get married until after the war ends, and that may be years and years ahead. If I decided to marry him, I would want him now, today, not years and years ahead. It would be too awful if he did go abroad and when he came back I found I no longer loved him.

My mind is just going round in circles. Em what *shall* I do? What shall I *do?* The question keeps drumming in my head and I have to use all my powers of concentration to take in the lectures with any degree of sense. I think I shall fail all the exams at the end of the course at this rate. I wish Adrian had been more helpful. But I suppose he was right, really, when he said no one but I can decide the question. And I can't!

Em, didn't you feel any doubts *at all* about Charles? Not even at the beginning?

Please write,
Your loving
JONNIE.

(From Em to Jonquil.)

Officers' Mess, R.A.F. Station,
Worsley, Cheshire.
14 April, 1941

Darling old Jonnie,
I do wish I could help you more, but I agree

213

with Adrian. No one but you *can* make up your mind! I never had any doubts about Charles, but that doesn't necessarily mean to say you can't fall in love with someone after you have known them some little time. For instance you might suddenly realise you loved Adrian who you've known for years. It is possible.

Personally, I don't think you would always be happy with Brian. I can give you no reason for this, so the opinion is worth nothing whatever. It is just a feeling and I can't explain it. I *do* think that if he loves you, Brian would quite willingly lose ten careers if he gained you in the end. On the other hand, if you dropped out of his life now, I don't think he would commit suicide! Too big a part of him belongs to the R.A.F.

Incidentally, you would have this fact to contend with if you *did* marry him. His Service life would always come first. You couldn't arrange when you had your holidays; you would just take them when he had leave. And you wouldn't be able to decide where you wanted to live; you'd go where he was stationed. Your friends would, of necessity, be his R.A.F. friends and their wives, and you'd have to like the wives, or pretend you did, for his sake. Your life would in no way be your own. You would probably have to let your son fly and risk all the dangers thereof! At night, you would have

Air Force talk, and you would never be alone much because when Brian wasn't busy, he would want to entertain important people. It wouldn't be fish and chips cooked together and shared over the kitchen table! It would be Group Captain So-and-So and his wife eating a well-served six-course dinner. And the day you planned to go to the concert, if Brian had to go away suddenly on duty, it would mean you going alone to the concert or cancelling it. He couldn't cancel his trip for you.

I have painted the worst possible side because you are an incurable romanticist at heart, Jonnie, and far too idealistic and impracticable when it comes to your emotions. You have plenty of commonsense, but you don't always apply it to yourself when your heart is involved. You are, in fact, a dear, sentimental old thing, and I am more than just fond of you.

In your next letter, do tell me more about the course. Are the lectures interesting and how strenuous are the P.T. classes and the drill? Do you remember the P.T. instructor at the depôt? Those days seem a long way off now, don't they? I can hardly believe that this time last year I hadn't even met my darling Charles.

Have you heard from Adrian lately? Charles says he (Adrian) is doing his best to get back to operational flying, but without much success.

Well, darling, write again soon, and don't worry too much about Brian. It will all work itself out. I am sure there is no need to point out to you that emotions all run much higher in war time. It is the insecurity of our present existence that makes us all doubly desirous of security and we are apt to cling to anything firm and dependable. So do be sure your love for Brian isn't really a longing to settle down. The material side won't affect you of course, but do be certain, too, that your love isn't only a protective instinct. It wouldn't satisfy him in the long run.

I must stop preaching and go and do some work. I am on duty in a few minutes and still have two pairs of stockings to wash!

All my love to you, Jonnie,

Your EM.

(From Brian to Jonquil.)

Officers' Mess, R.A.F. Station,
Worsley, Cheshire.
18 April, 1941

My Dearest,

I am afraid what I have to tell you may come as a bit of a shock to you. I admit it surprised me. I had to go to the Air Ministry for an interview yesterday, and was told there that the job I've been after is all mine, and that I had better take some embarkation leave quickly while I can get it.

My first thought, my darling, was of you, and although I knew there was a certain amount of tropical kit I would have to get, I decided to come down to Dorset for at least three or four of my seven days. But my second thought was entirely different, and I have decided quite irrevocably, Jonquil, that I shall not see you again before I go. You are so impulsive, so sweet and generous always, that I could not answer for my actions if I were to see you again. In other words, I dare not. I know you well enough to realise your reaction to all this will probably make you decide you want to marry me, and I am not going to allow this to happen. It will be far better if there are no ties of any sort between us. You are far too young to be tied down by any agreement, however unofficial.

Believe me, my dearest, I have thought this all out very carefully and I am certain it will be best in the long run for us both. We will write to each other as often as you wish, and always with complete frankness. If by the time the war is over and I come home you should still be unmarried and unattached, then we will meet again. If you really love me, as I love you, nothing but a little time will have been lost, and we will pick up the threads of our friendship where we have been forced to lay them down.

I am going to spend my leave with my mother and father. It is a long while since I was at home and I have a sudden yearning to go back there. For some reason, I feel I may never see them again ... not that they are ill or very old, but this indiscriminate bombing of civilians has frightened me, I suppose. My mother is one of those wonderful old ladies who has grown old gracefully. I know she would love you, Jonquil, just as I do. I wish you could have met her. Perhaps you would go and see them sometime after I have gone? Cynthia never went near my home and mother and father were bitterly hurt and disappointed. At first when I went to see them by myself, I made excuses for my wife, but it grew gradually more and more apparent that she wasn't interested in them – or me, and ended by my not going home at all. My address is Sedwick, Burtonfields, Cumberland. I should appreciate news of them from you if you should ever visit them.

Please do not think me heartless or unfeeling for not coming to see you. You must know by now that I would like to spend every second of my life with you, my very dearest.

When you write, give me your telephone number and I will ring you one evening if you will be in. If I cannot see you, I can at

least hear your voice once more.
  All my love, my darling,
  Ever your devoted
  BRIAN.

Chapter 15

(From Jonquil to Brian.)

Bulberry Park, Larkspur, Dorset.
21 April, 1941

Darling, darling Brian,

You can't mean it! Please write and say it isn't true. And yet I know it must be so because deep inside me I have already resigned myself to the thought of not seeing you again ... at least, not until after the war.

But Brian, I want to see you. I want you to kiss me goodbye and to hear you say you love me just once before you go. Do you realise we have only kissed once since we met? I should certainly never have been so strong-minded, but you were always so determined to be good! Perhaps it is true, after all, that women are the weaker sex. Do you remember our debate on the subject?

Brian, I can't bear to think about it. All last night I lay awake imagining every conceivable kind of horror awaiting you overseas. You *will* take care of yourself, won't you? Promise me you will. It is only the thought of our reunion one day that makes this parting bearable for me.

Looking at it sanely, I can see that it is perhaps a good thing insomuch as that I don't have to come to any immediate decision. But I am afraid, Brian ... afraid that I shall forget what you look like. You must find me a photograph or have one taken and send it to me before you go. You won't refuse me this, darling, will you?

My telephone number is Wirral 266, and I shall be in every evening waiting for you to call. Brian, *must* you go? But of course you must! I am so selfish. I want you all to myself. Take me with you! I could be your batwoman or secretary or something, couldn't I? Oh, how I wish I *could!*

I am afraid this letter is very disjointed, but I am distracted by the suddenness of your going. You didn't expect to get the job until June or July, did you? Darling Brian, I am pleased for you. I should have said that first in my letter instead of being so selfish. But I *am* happy for you, darling, and I know you are bound to make a great success of it.

Of course I will go and see your mother and father. I should love to. I will make them tell me all about you when you were a little boy, and I shall ask to see all the family photographs. Shall you tell them about us?

Oh, darling, dearest Brian! (You *are* dearer to me than anyone else, you know.) I want to take the next train to Cumberland and catch hold of you and keep you from going.

I shall be so terribly alone. You will write often, won't you?

I shall be waiting for you to ring, and until then, my love and as many kisses as you want, my darling,
From Your
JONQUIL.

(From Brian to Jonquil.)

Sedgwick, Burtonfields, Cumberland.
23 April, 1941

I know you will like these recordings, darling. It is one of the many symphonies we have played so happily together. Music means so much to us both that I feel sure you would rather have this as a parting gift than a cigarette case, or something of that sort.

Let me know if you receive them safely.

All my love, my dearest,
BRIAN.

(From Jonquil to Brian.)

Bulberry Park, Larkspur, Dorset.
25 April, 1941

Brian darling,
How marvellous of you! You know how passionately fond of Beethoven I am, and the 'Pastoral' is my favourite of all his symphonies. Thank you a million times.

Whenever I play it, I shall close my eyes and think of you – not that I need close my eyes to do that! It seems as if I can't stop thinking of you. I *am* so thrilled with the records. Thank you, again and again.

It was wonderful hearing your voice on the 'phone last night. For how long did we talk? It must have been quite fifteen minutes, and I think we would have gone on longer if they hadn't kept interrupting us. Will you 'phone again before you leave? And darling, don't forget the photograph, and your A.P.O. number so that I can write immediately you go.

I have no news for you other than what I told you on the 'phone last night. Only to repeat that I am constantly thinking of you – more than is good for me, in fact. I shall have to do some hard 'swotting' at my notes before the exams!'

Write to me, darling.
Here are three XXXs for luck,
JONQUIL.

(From Jonquil to Adrian.)

Bulberry Park, Larkspur, Dorset.
25 April, 1941

My dear Adrian,
Once again I need your advice, but this time it should be easy enough to give. Brian is going overseas any minute and has given me

Beethoven's 'Pastoral' as a parting present. Now, I want to give him something, too, and I thought you could help me decide what it should be. Daddy's ideas would undoubtedly be impracticable, and, being in the Service, you should know exactly what Brian would like.

Expense is unimportant. I don't mind what it costs so long as it is nice – something personal for him to remember me by.

How are you, Adrian? And how is the instructing going? Do write and give me all your news. It seems ages since I last heard from you.

Your affectionate
JONQUIL.

P.S. – Time is short, so write soon. – J.

(From Adrian to Jonquil.)

47, Stonefield Ave., Wodecote, Kent.
25 April, 1941

My dear Jonquil,

If I were Brian I should want a small leather-framed photograph of yourself, one side of you in uniform, the other side of you in civvies.

If you are not anxious to give him this, a cigarette lighter or an identity wristlet might come in useful. But I should prefer my first suggestion.

Am fed up with instructing, but can't get back to flying (real flying!) yet awhile.

Sorry this is so short, but have a lot of work to do and no news anyway.

Yours in haste,
ADRIAN.

(From Brian to Jonquil.)

Sedgewick, Burtonfields, Dorset.
28 April, 1941

My dearest,

I cannot begin to tell you how pleased I am with the photographs. There is absolutely nothing I would rather have had. You will always have the most prominent position on my desk as you know you already have in my heart.

My A.P.O. number is 263, and letters should be addressed to me at that number, Middle East Forces.

Yes, I have told mother and father about us, and as I expected they are extremely pleased I should have found happiness after all this time. They had realised how unhappy and wretched I had been in the past, and are longing to see you.

Now that I have your picture, you will always be near me – not that you are ever very far from my thoughts, my dear.

I am glad you like the 'Pastoral' so much. I was wondering if you would care to have

225

all my good records while I am away? I can leave them at the camp for you and if you should be posted somewhere else where it would not be possible to keep them, you could either send them to your home or to mine.

You must not expect to hear from me again for a little while. For security reasons I cannot give you the date of sailing or announce my whereabouts by post. I will write at the first opportunity and cable you on my arrival in the Middle East. I had hoped to fly over, but it is quite impossible at the moment. So don't be anxious if it is some weeks before you receive news of me.

There is no need to tell you how much I shall look forward to your letters. Tell me every little detail of yourself (not Service matters, of course) so that I can picture you in my imagination.

I have had a wonderful leave, quiet, but extremely enjoyable. I managed to get some fishing and golf, and I spent a good many hours playing chess with father. I had almost forgotten how; it was such a long time since last I played. Mother made me all my favourite dishes and I should think I have put on a good deal of weight.

Look after yourself, darling, and think of me sometimes. Don't forget me.

All my love, always your
BRIAN.

Officers' Mess, R.A.F. Station,
Worsley, Cheshire.
30 April, 1941

Dear Mrs Lee,

Now that Brian has gone, I felt I would like just to write to you because it somehow brings him closer. He has told me quite a bit about you and I am hoping to be able to come and see you soon. We get forty-eight hours off every now and again and if it would be convenient for you, I would love to come down and meet you, and see where Brian lived as a little boy.

He said he had told you all about me, so I will not repeat my life history. I hope it won't be too long before we hear from him. I will let you know immediately I have word and would be grateful if you would do the same. He has promised to cable on his arrival.

I hope you will not mind my writing like this.

Yours very sincerely,
JONQUIL MATHEWS.

(From Jonquil to Em.)

Officers' Mess, R.A.F. Station,
Worsley, Cheshire.
8 May, 1941

Darling Em,

How are you liking the course? It was all rather a nightmare for me with so many other things on my mind, but I feel sure you will like it there. It is nice having a full night's sleep each day of the week, isn't it? Night watches are all very well, but I'd rather fight this war without them if it were possible. Needless to say, I am writing on watch now and the time is 3 a.m. Doesn't that shake you? It is very quiet and I am beginning to feel sleepy, so if this letter gets incoherent you will know why...

It is ten days now since I last heard from Brian and I suppose much too soon to expect news. All the same, I'm a little worried. I had a short note from his mother thanking me for my letter and saying I could go down any time I liked. She's had no news of him either.

Are you coming back here before you go on leave or will you go straight from Dorset? If you let me know in time I will have your pass, railway warrant and ration card sent on to you.

Good luck to the exams, Em.

Lots of love from
JONQUIL.

(From Em to Jonquil.)

> Bulberry Park, Larkspur, Dorset.
> *10 May, 1941*

Darling Jonnie,

Thanks for your letter and the suggestion re-forwarding my pass, etc. This would save me a good deal of time because Charles and I have definitely decided to spend our leave in Edinburgh and I can go straight up from here when the course finishes. You might ask the C.O. if this is all right next time you are on duty, would you? My leave passes have gone in, but he might not realise when he signs them that my seven days will follow the course. I don't fancy being recalled at the last minute!

Hope you have news of Brian soon, darling.

Excuse this short note, but have some shoe and button cleaning to do ready for tomorrow.

Yours with love,
EM.

(From Jonquil to Em.)

> Officers' Mess, R.A.F. Station,
> Worsley, Cheshire.
> *14 May, 1941*

Darling Em,

Here are your pass, railway warrant and

229

ration card. I hope you will have a wonderful leave, but of course you will! Give
Charles my love. The C.O. says it is quite
O.K. for you to go straight off from Dorset,
and says have a good time!

Still no news of Brian. Em, I am so
worried. It is over two weeks now. Surely
some word should have come through.

But I mustn't worry you with my troubles.
You no doubt have enough on your mind
with the exams about to take place any
moment. Best of luck to them, anyway.

Send me your Edinburgh address so that I
can forward any post and write to you there.

Always your devoted
JONNIE.

(From Em to Jonquil.)

The North British Hotel, Edinburgh.
17 May, 1941

Darling Jonnie,
Thanks for yours, plus the enclosures.
Above is my address and if you are going to
write, you had better make it snappy, Miss
Mathews! We leave on the twenty-third.

You mustn't worry about Brian. I am sure
you will hear soon, Jonnie. After all, you did
say he warned you that you would not hear
from him for some time. He was obviously
trying to infer it would take him a good
while to get out there.

I passed the exams all right, and weathered the drill parade at the end without any blunders. But my nerves were extremely strained and I felt slightly hysterical when saluting on the march. I kept thinking of those early days when you and I imitated our depôt P.T. instructor in pyjamas and dressing-gowns at 'The Yews'. Which reminds me, have you written to Marion recently? I have been meaning to answer her last letter for a week now. It would be rather fun to see her and Hurry again one day. I wonder how she likes being a sergeant! Much better pay than ours, anyway! Let's fix a reunion on our next forty-eight. We'll make her treat us!!

Charles sends his love, and so do I.

As ever,

Your

EM.

(Telegram from Mrs Lee to Jonquil.)

Time handed in: 2.30
Date: 19 May, 1941

REGRET TO TELL YOU TROOPSHIP IN WHICH BRIAN SAILING TORPEDOED STOP NO SURVIVORS STOP LETTER FOLLOWING STOP
ROSALIND LEE

(From Mrs Lee to Jonquil.)

Sedgwick, Burtonfields, Cumberland.
19 May, 1941

My dear little Jonquil,

I have just telegraphed you the dreadful news, and although I would rather have written first so that I could in some measure have spared you the shock, I promised Brian I would send you a wire. He knew that being his next-of-kin we should hear if anything should happen to him and made me promise to let you know immediately. Had he anticipated this sort of news, I am sure he would have preferred me to break it more gently.

The Air Ministry reported him as missing, presumed killed, and stated just that the ship in which he had been sailing was torpedoed on the eighth of this month and that there were no survivors. There is, therefore, no hope for him.

Both father and I are stunned by the shock and cannot believe we shall never see him again. It is so hard for us to lose him just when he had come back to us after all these years.

My thoughts are with you, even although we have never met, my dear. More than before I should love to meet you. We have no other child but Brian and we always wanted a little girl. The house has been empty for many years of young voices and young laughter and now, alas, it is full of ghosts.

I have some nice photographs of Brian as a little boy, as a schoolboy and as a young man when he first joined the Air Force. You must come and see them.

Do not be too unhappy, Jonquil dear. At least he is out of danger and the horrors of the war. I like to remember this. He is in Good Hands now.

Write to me as soon as you feel like it, my dear.

Yours with deepest sympathy,
ROSALIND LEE.

(From Jonquil to Em.)

Officers' Mess, R.A.F. Station,
Worsley, Cheshire.
21 May, 1941

Darling Em,

Brian is dead. The ship in which he was sailing was torpedoed and sunk and there were no survivors. I just can't believe it. His mother wired me the news and I had a letter the next day giving more details.

It doesn't seem possible ... to think that I shall never see him again, or hear his voice again. To think I caused him so much worry and anxiety. If only I could have foreseen this! I would have told him I'd marry him and at least have made him happy for a while. Poor Brian. Poor, darling Brian. He was so pleased to get this job and so terribly keen to make a go of it. Now he hasn't even the chance to try.

He seems very near to me still in spite of everything, and if there are such things as ghosts, then I am sure his spirit is with me. I am going to throw myself into my work and try in some measure to produce results of which he would be proud. I shall take up his love and devotion to the Service where he was forced to leave it off. He shall live on through me. In this way only can I bear to think of him.

If I was selfish and spoilt and bad when I was a child, I have certainly paid for it now, Em. I am beginning to be afraid of myself. The only two people I have really cared for (Simon and Brian) have both come up against it. I shan't let myself fall in love again. It is too painful, too worrying, too heart-breaking a process, and I seem to be a sort of hoo-doo to those I love.

I must try and write to Brian's mother now. She wrote me such a sweet letter. But I don't know what to say. Oh, Brian, Brian...

Come back soon, Em. I am feeling so wretched, so desperate. I can see no happiness in the future, unless it is in the realisation of my work. For Brian's sake I shall make an effort and it shall be as untiring and complete as his would have been.

Remembering our motto, Em, *Per Ardua Ad Astra* ... I am certainly going through Adversity all right now. But shall I ever reach the stars?

Always your loving
JONNIE.

Chapter 16

Em wanted Jonquil to take compassionate leave and go home to her parents. But Jonquil refused to stop work and was adamant in her decision.

'Brian wouldn't want me to,' she said with conviction. 'If you had heard him, Em ... talking as he so often did to me, about shirkers and how badly they let down the rest of the team...'

'Yes, but this is different,' Em argued. 'Take a short rest, Jonnie dear. Your nerves are like violin strings.'

Jonquil smiled but without mirth.

'My nerves are perfectly all right!' she said finally, and then she caught her friend's hand in a sudden quick grasp which reminded Em of a small, frightened child.

'Don't you understand?' she cried urgently. 'I must work, work, WORK. If I stop for a moment, I think about... No, Em, I shall stay.'

And for four weeks, she worked without sparing herself, daily growing more ringed beneath her large hazel eyes, more drawn about her pale cheeks.

'You MUST ease up a bit,' Em told her.

'Go to bed early tonight for a change, and sleep a good ten hours.'

'Sleep?' Jonquil echoed bitterly. 'Do you suppose I can sleep? If I shut my eyes I see that troopship and – and Brian in the water... Oh, Em, Em, it's dreadful, horrible! I feel haunted...'

But she never relaxed and Em was not surprised when six weeks after Brian's death, Jonquil was forced to retire to sick bay with a high temperature and a relaxed throat, which soon developed into tonsillitis. For a week, she could neither eat nor drink nor swallow in comfort and lay in a state of semi-consciousness, too drugged with M and B to think very carefully about anything.

Em went to see her once or twice, taking flowers and magazines, and a letter from Adrian among several anxious ones from her parents. But Jonquil could not rouse herself from the dreadful feeling of apathy that had replaced her furious energy and will to work, and Em went away disheartened and unhappy about her friend.

The drug had its effect eventually and Jonquil's temperature dropped to below normal and her spirits even lower. Her throat became less painful and the M.O. advised that she should have her tonsils removed as soon as the swelling had completely subsided.

'You had better take a week's leave first

and try to put on a little weight before the operation,' he told her. 'You're too thin and very run down.'

'Must I have leave?' Jonquil asked. 'Couldn't I go into hospital right away?'

'No!' the M.O. said firmly. He had had a chat with Em and knew the circumstances, but he was not going to be responsible for letting this child – she was only twenty-two – to take any unnecessary risks. Removing tonsils was a common enough operation, but not always without complications, and the patient always stands a better chance of recovery, and quicker recovery, if he is in the best possible health.

'You will take leave a week from tomorrow,' he told her. 'Then into hospital you go!'

Jonquil went home and tried not to mope, or let her mother's solicitude get on her overworked nerves. She understood Mrs Mathews well enough to know that in her heart, she was glad Brian had 'been removed' from Jonquil's life, so solving a difficult problem, and although she never actually put such thoughts into words, Jonquil was very conscious of them.

Robert Mathews tactfully refrained from offering sympathy where it was so obviously not wanted, but as all Jonquil's thoughts were centred round Brian or her work of which he knew so little, they were unable to find any mutual ground for companionship, and Jonquil was not sorry when the week came to an end and she returned to camp prior to her operation.

'I have arranged for you to go to the R.A.F. Officers' hospital at Worsley,' the M.O. told her. 'It's really a convalescent home, but you need two weeks' convalescing. You go in on Saturday. I'll arrange transport.'

Jonquil was operated on first thing Sunday morning. There were no complications, and apart from an extremely sore throat, she felt no worse for it. Within three days she was sitting up in an easy chair and begging the young V.A.D. to find her something to do.

'I'll go crazy sitting here!' she told the girl restlessly. 'How long before I shall be allowed out?'

'About seven or ten days from now, I expect,' the young nurse said. 'Haven't you any books to read?'

'Yes, but other people's love stories don't interest me!' Jonquil replied bitterly.

The girl looked at her curiously and Jonquil felt some explanation was owing, but that she was not equal to giving it.

'What's your name?' she asked to change the subject.

'Connie Worth!' the V.A.D. told her. 'Constance, really, but I can't bear that!'

'Then I'll call you Connie, if I may,' Jonquil said, suddenly liking the girl. 'Are you

married? No, I see you aren't! Nor engaged?'

'No!' the girl said quietly.

Jonquil looked at her with a sudden
quickening interest.

'I didn't mean to pry into your affairs,' she
said apologetically.

The girl smiled and said, without rancour:

'I thought you weren't interested in other
people's love stories!'

'I meant 'in books', I suppose,' Jonquil
amended with a smile. 'They always end so
happily and in real life, it just doesn't work
out that way.'

'No!' Connie said again in her quiet voice.

There was a short, awkward silence; then
Jonquil asked suddenly:

'Are you happy?'

The girl thought a moment before she
replied:

'Yes, I think so!' she said. 'You see, I am at
least near him, serving him!'

'Do tell me about him!' Jonquil pleaded.
'Unless of course, you would rather not...'

'I'd like to!' Connie said simply. 'It has all
been bottled up inside me so long, it would
be a relief to tell someone.'

'Sit down here!' Jonquil said, patting the
edge of the bed beside her.

'I shouldn't!' the girl said with a laugh. 'If
Matron or Sister walked in...'

'I'll take the blame!' Jonquil said. 'Now tell

me all about him.'

'His name is John!' Connie said, and the way she said it he might have been the only John in the world. 'He's a pilot, a patient here at the home. He crashed about ten months ago and was terribly injured. He's better now, but still paralysed in both his legs. His fiancée came to see him soon after he arrived here, but when the doctor told her about his legs – that he would never walk again – she went away without seeing him. And he had been looking forward to her visit so much...'

'How dreadful!' Jonquil whispered.

'She left a note to say she was breaking the engagement,' Connie went on, 'and asked me to give it him personally and explain why. She hadn't even the courage to tell him herself. That was the first time I ever saw him...'

'Did he know he was paralysed?' Jonquil asked.

'Oh, yes! He knew!' Connie answered bitterly. 'At first I thought I just pitied him. He was so young, so attractive and so very unhappy – and brave about it. But when I talked to him once or twice, I found out that he didn't pity himself. He didn't want pity from other people either. Then I knew I – I loved him. Of course, *he* doesn't know; he never will, I suppose. Not unless one day he should look on me in a different light. I'm just "Nurse" to him now.'

'Perhaps one day...' Jonquil suggested.

'Perhaps!' Connie said with a smile. 'In the meantime, I am happy just to be here. There is so much I can do for him, to help him. But he is very lonely and gets rather bored with his own company. I suppose you wouldn't care to visit him?'

'I'd love to!' Jonquil said. 'He sounds a grand person.'

'He is!' Connie said, and by the light in her eyes and the tone of her voice, Jonquil knew that the girl really did love him.

'Suppose he did come to love you?' Jonquil said quietly. 'Had you thought what it means to be married to a man who can't walk – who is bedridden maybe and...'

'If you could have back the man you loved – without his legs, wouldn't you want him?' Connie asked.

Jonquil thought of Brian – of how little his life would mean to him if he had to leave the Air Force, and instead of the quick retort that had first sprung to her lips, she said:

'Not unless I was sure he wanted to live.'

'But John does want to live!' Connie said quickly. 'He has often told me so.'

'But to have lost so much...' Jonquil said, more to herself than to her companion. Why, she herself, had no desire to prolong these days which seemed so full of misery and futility...

'You must meet him!' Connie was saying. 'Please will you?'

Jonquil looked into the girl's eager face and found herself unable to disappoint her, even if she had wanted to avoid meeting this pilot.

'I'll go this afternoon, if Sister will let me,' she promised.

John Seele was twenty-three years of age, but he looked a good deal older. Jonquil, when she was introduced to him, put his age at twenty-seven or eight. She liked him immensely and immediately, and in particular his large, frank eyes with their dual expression of sadness and humour; his long sensitive hands and the expressive way he moved them to illustrate his words.

'Connie suggested I should come!' she said to break the silence which had fallen when Sister left them alone together.

'Connie?'

'Yes, the young V.A.D. with the dark wavy hair and grey-blue eyes.'

'Good Lord!' the boy said, the humour momentarily ousting the sadness in his eyes and mouth. 'Is her name Connie? I've got an aunt called that!'

'Well, at least *she* doesn't look like someone's aunt,' Jonquil said with a smile. The boy looked at her for a moment, then his eyes smiled again and he said half-apologetically.

'Do you know, I don't think I ever really noticed what she looked like. You women are always so much more observant.'

'Some men are, too!' Jonquil replied.

John laughed outright, then as suddenly, was serious again.

'Did she tell you about me?' he asked.

'She said you were paralysed in both legs!' Jonquil said.

The boy nodded his head.

'I thought ... I'm glad you spoke about it so frankly,' he said. 'People who come to see me usually avoid the subject like hot cakes. I suppose they are afraid to hurt me, or something. But I don't mind a bit. I'm used to it now – the idea, I mean.'

He changed the subject abruptly.

'The V.A.D. – Connie – told me about you. You're the girl with tonsils, aren't you?'

'Without tonsils!' Jonquil corrected smiling.

'*She* said *you* were pretty, too!'

'Compliments flying!' Jonquil laughed, and was glad to see the humour return to his eyes.

'I'll have to take a careful squint at her next time she comes in,' he went on. 'I never noticed how a woman looked since – since...'

'Does it matter what she looks like?' Jonquil filled in the gap quickly. 'Surely it is what she *is* that counts.'

'Yes!' said the boy and his voice held a note of bitterness. 'I found that out myself – that a pretty face doesn't always conceal a pretty heart. Not that I blame her…'

'You're speaking of your fiancée, aren't you?' Jonquil said quickly. 'Connie told me about her, too. If I were you, I just wouldn't want to go on living … I don't!'

John Seele turned and stared at her aghast.

'Say that again!' he told her. 'You can't mean it! You, who have everything, a lovely face, your youth, your whole life before you!'

'To spend without the person I love?' Jonquil finished harshly.

'That's sentimentalising!' the boy cried swiftly. 'No one is indispensable to anyone. I have found that out. You get over anything in time. I don't say you ever love anyone else the same way, but you can live without them.'

He stopped for a moment and stared out of the window at the blue sky. Then he turned again in Jonquil.

'I thought I wanted to die!' he went on quietly. 'I thought I couldn't live without her – and without my legs. I wanted to die and prayed every night that I'd pass out in the next op I had. Then one morning I woke up and heard the birds singing and saw the sunshine on my bed and I felt – gosh! I don't know how to explain – but as if I was reborn and I was so darn glad to find myself alive that I wanted to shout at the top of my voice. She didn't matter any more. There were other things in the world as lovely and not so changeable – things which I could appreciate without the use of my legs – with my eyes and my ears and my sense of smell. Have you ever smelt gorse bushes on a hot summer's afternoon? Just like apricot jam…'

Jonquil remained silent, but her eyes never left his face.

'Have you ever heard Beethoven's Pastoral Symphony?' John went on. 'Well I can still listen to that. I can still touch a peach, or a velvet dress. (My mother had many velvet evening dresses when I was little and I used to love to run my fingers down the folds when she came to tuck me in.) I can still see the blue sky and the sunlight and enjoy bacon and eggs for breakfast!'

He broke off and looked at her half shyly, half eagerly.

'Do you understand?' he asked. 'You will one day, you know. This man you've lost … was he killed?'

Jonquil nodded her head.

'He'll be less and less in your thoughts every day,' John said. 'Time is the greatest healer of all. Do you know, I think that one is more alone when one is in love than when one isn't.'

'Oh, no!' Jonquil broke in quickly. 'Brian

and I shared so much – our mutual love of music for one thing…'

'Yes, but that's a small thing really,' John said thoughtfully. 'In the really big things, no matter how much you love someone, you still have your thoughts, your desires, your free will, however much you may be trying to adapt it to fit in with that person, to share everything with him. We are always alone, and love shuts out everyone but the dearest, so making one more lonely than ever…'

He broke off as Connie came in with two tea-trays. She stayed a moment to straighten the coverlet and tidy a few magazines, then went quietly out of the room again.

'You know, you're right!' John said to Jonquil with a laugh. 'She *is* pretty. And I've been here nine – no, ten months, and never noticed it!'

'There must be something wrong with your eyesight!' Jonquil said with a smile.

'Dare I ring the bell and ask for another look?' he asked boyishly.

Jonquil got up and rang the bell for him. When Connie came hurrying in to see what it was they wanted, she found them both laughing and obviously sharing a secret she knew nothing about.

'Turn sideways, Connie!' John ordered.

'What *is* the matter?' Connie asked breathlessly, her heart hammering as she heard him call her by her Christian name.

'Have I a smut on my nose, or something?'

'No, I just wanted to take a really good look at a really good looker!' John said calmly.

Connie blushed and went quickly out of the room. John was delighted.

'I do believe I made her blush!' he said with an infectious smile. 'Had I better ring and ask her pardon?'

But Sister came in at that moment and bustled Jonquil back to her own room, ready for the doctor's evening visit, and Jonquil was left once more to her own reflections.

She was surprised to find how carefree, how much happier she felt. There was no real reason for it, she thought. It was just that John's good spirits and his courage were infectious and in her desire to bring him and the little V.A.D. together, she had found a corner of life she still wished to hold on to.

'Come to think of it, there are other things I want to live for,' she thought seriously. 'Em's baby, for instance. Charles keeps saying he wants a child and perhaps soon Em will agree to leave the W.A.A.F. ... and Adrian. I'd like to see him happily married to that girl who has kept him waiting so long.'

She wondered idly where he was, and decided to spend the evening writing to him. He would like John, she thought. And John would like him, too.

She settled down to a long, newsy letter to Adrian, and Connie posted it for her on her way back to the billet that evening.

Two days later, Adrian came down for a very fleeting visit. He thought Jonquil looked very drawn and white but did not say so to her. He liked John and when Jonquil told him privately about Connie, agreed that it would be a good show if it all worked out right for them both.

'John's really quite interested!' Jonquil assured him. 'But it will take time for him to fall in love again, and I am so afraid that when he does he won't ask Connie to marry him because of his legs.'

Adrian lit his pipe and puffed away at it for a minute or two before he replied.

'Connie will probably propose to him!' he said then. And seeing the look of doubt on Jonquil's face, he laughed outright, and called her a precious little match-maker.

'Why not?' Jonquil retaliated. 'I shall also find you a wife, Adrian.'

A shadow crossed his face, and seeing it, Jonquil remembered the girl he loved and wondered again who she might be. But already he was teasing her, saying:

'Yourself, Jonquil?'

And when she taxed him with making her a proposal which she might have taken seriously in 1820, he twirled an imaginary moustache and said:

'But at least my proposal was honourable, dear lady!'

Brian was not mentioned by either of them, but when Adrian rose to go he held her hand for a moment in his own and said:

'Do you remember my saying once before, Jonquil, that in the Air Force no one really dies?'

And he kissed her lightly on top of her topmost curl and went quietly out of the room. Jonquil did not see him again for some time, though occasionally she had an odd note from him from different parts of the country.

Her remaining two days at the home, she spent almost entirely in John's company. They seemed to have so much to discuss and Jonquil felt as if with his philosophy of life he was re-equipping her for the outside world. He didn't belittle Brian, but he put a different proportion on her emotions so that he no longer seemed so essential to her happiness.

She thought a trifle guiltily that she had spent some very happy hours with him and with Connie, in which they had discussed their views on the war and the re-organisation of the post-war world which had never been of interest to Brian. They became very heated over their politics and John closed the argument by saying that the war was still a long way from finished, and the most important thing to discuss was the quickest way to victory.

When Jonquil left the hospital she had this thought foremost in her thoughts and in her heart. First finish the war. It gave her a definite stable aim in life, something to work for, and she was going all out for it.

'Em!' she announced when she returned to camp. 'I am heaps better mentally and physically, and my nerves are no longer violin strings! Now I want to work and work and then do some more work, and I shall be quite content.'

Em did not ask her how long this feeling would last. She was happy just to have her friend back and to know that for the time being, anyway, Jonquil was happy.

Exactly one month later Jonquil had a letter from Connie to say that she and John were unofficially engaged, and that as she felt she owed their coming together to Jonquil, she wanted her to be the first to know. So did John.

She wrote back, congratulating them, and then posted a short note to Adrian, thinking he, also, might be interested. But she did not have a reply and wondered for a day or two whether she had been tactless to refer to other people's happiness when his own was still so uncertain.

But, as Em said, you could never tell with Adrian. He might just be exceptionally busy.

'Poor Adrian!' Jonquil thought, and then forgot him in a new rush of work. But he had not forgotten her.

PART III

ADRIAN

Chapter 17

It was more than a year ago now since Brian had been killed. It was, in fact, 31 May, 1942, the day following the thousand-bomber raid on Cologne, and Jonquil and Em were discussing the news with unconcealed excitement.

'It's wonderful! It's marvellous!' Jonquil was saying. 'To think that this time last year we were only sending an occasional two-fifty to bomb Brest...'

'I wonder if we'll be able to keep it up,' Em remarked thoughtfully. 'Did they give the number missing, Jonnie?'

'Oh, about forty or fifty, I think. I don't exactly remember,' Jonquil answered her friend.

'That's a lot!'

'It's only about five per cent, Em,' Jonquil protested.

'It's still a lot,' Em insisted, 'when you count the number of men in a bomber crew.'

She's remembering Joe, Jonquil thought

compassionately. He had been killed six months earlier and Em had felt his death far more than most people realised. But Jonquil, who knew her so well, understood the extent of her suffering beneath her outward calm and apparent indifference. Even Charles who possessed the greater part of her heart, could never quite replace that corner held by the companions of her childhood, of whom Joe had been the most constant, the most affectionate.

Jonquil directed the conversation into happier channels.

'I'm so glad Marion has at last got her commission,' she remarked. 'She'll make an awfully good admin. officer with her patience and understanding.'

'We'll see plenty of her now she is stationed so near to us,' Em said. 'I don't suppose we'll recognise Hurry.'

They walked slowly and in companionable silence. Em was thinking back over the past few years. She and Charles had been married nearly eighteen months now. It was hard to believe. They had had so very little time together – only two weeks' honeymoon and since then five seven-day leaves and an occasional forty-eight hours. It seemed to her that their married life had consisted of a series of partings, each one growing more difficult, more painful than the last. Now Charles was on operational flying again and she lived from day to day in an agony of fear for him, lest he should follow in Joe's footsteps. She hid her feelings well beneath a calm indifferent exterior, and many people considered her hard and unfeeling. Only Jonquil really understood the extent of her anxiety and suffering.

Charles still wanted her to have a baby. At their last meeting they had discussed the subject again and Em had been half-persuaded to his point of view. The country wanted a higher birth-rate and would she not be doing her duty as much in helping to build up the future as in her present job in the W.A.A.F.? And suppose she lost Charles … Em asked herself. Suppose she faced up to this all too-existent possibility and if Charles was killed … then wouldn't a baby be her one comfort and compensation?

Suddenly Em made up her mind. A deep heady excitement swept through her and she wanted to run to the nearest telephone and ring Charles. She toyed with the idea for a minute or two, then she laughed a little breathlessly and turned to Jonquil.

'Jonnie, I'm going to that 'phone box over there to ring Charles,' she said. 'I've just decided I want a baby and I must tell him!'

'Oh, Em darling, what a crazy woman you are!' Jonquil said smiling. 'I'll wait for you outside. Tell Charles to give my love to Adrian if he sees him. He owes me a letter.'

Jonquil sat on the stone wall swinging her long slim legs while Em fought with the operator. She wondered idly if Em would be able to contact Charles at the camp, and thought with affection of her friend and how much she would miss her if she did have a child. Em meant so much to her, particularly when she had first joined the W.A.A.F. – and when Brian had been killed, it was Em's affection and silent understanding that had kept her at her work and sustained her through those days when depression settled over her in a dull, damp cloud, and in spite of John Seele's philosophies the future seemed to hold no happiness for her. Gradually she had become more and more absorbed in her work and Brian slipped into the back of her mind, not forgotten, but not so often remembered. He had become part of the past and the present was the only thing that she allowed herself to dwell on. The future she did not even attempt to visualise.

Her mother and father she saw only on her leaves, and lately she had grown to love and respect them both in a way she had never imagined possible. Mrs Mathews was working at full pressure for her voluntary service committees, her evacuees, her knitting for the troops and the Red Cross. Her days were long, tiring, full of aggravating little set-backs and difficulties. But she was selfless and tireless and she forgot her own worries in the greater need of others. There seemed, too, to be a renewed feeling of affection between her and her husband. It was as if they had fallen in love with each other all over again.

'Perhaps it is seeing Robert in his khaki Home Guard Uniform!' she had tried to explain to Jonquil. 'It does remind me so of the last war... Or perhaps it is because we see so much less of one another nowadays, that when we do have a moment together we value it too much to spoil it with petty arguments and quarrels. And I think Robert feels younger, too. I know I do!'

It was extraordinary, Jonquil thought, that anyone should feel younger since this war had started. She, herself, felt so much – so very much older. It was as if she had lived through ten years in the last two. The Jonquil of today was so far removed from the Jonquil whom Simon had known and loved, that they might not have been the same person.

But there was no doubt about the fact that her parents did seem younger, happier. Her father had ceased to worry about business. Prices were controlled and no amount of worrying would alter them. So he wisely threw his energy and interest into his Home Guard activities, and felt physically much fitter for the exercise and training. The mixed company of his fellow-soldiers broadened his outlook and made him feel a schoolboy again. The men played practical jokes on each other and it wasn't long before Robert Mathews for all his forty-five years was one of the worst offenders. He joined wholeheartedly in the work and in the fun and he felt ten years younger. When Jonquil went home, she found him thinner, more energetic and full of humour, and theories about Hitler and rationing and the black-out and the war in general. They went for several long walks together and Jonquil found him sympathetic and interested when she told him all about Brian. In return for her confidence he told his daughter about the 'other woman' in his life.

'You were about six or seven years old when I first met her,' he said reminiscently. 'Your mother was nervy and emotional and difficult at the time – nothing like the woman she is today – and I went off for a week's shooting with a man friend. I had thought it was to be a twosome, or a foursome, perhaps, but I found instead a whole party of men and women. We all went to stay at my friend's shooting-box in Devon.

'The women were wonderful. They came out with the guns all day and then cooked and washed up in the evening. This girl I am going to tell you about, was one of them. I couldn't help comparing her with your mother, who had everything money could buy (we were rich even in those days, you know), and yet spent most of her time grumbling about this and that. Ursula was to my mind the perfect woman. In the day she was a gay, spirited companion. In the evening a delightful feminine creature who would sit and listen to a man talk and who could say something intelligent when it was wanted.

'I suppose it was natural that we should all pair off as we did. Ursula and I were together. Within three days I knew she was in love with me. I was about thirty at the time – in my prime. She was twenty-four.'

'Did you love her, Daddy?'

'I don't know. I thought I did then, anyway,' Robert Mathews said quietly. 'It was the most difficult week I have ever spent. I wanted to tell Ursula I would ask my wife for a divorce, but something kept me from doing so. I don't know what it was – perhaps the memory of your funny little face as I had seen it the day I left home. It was all red and puckered from crying and you were saying, "I want to go sooting wiv' my Daddy!" You couldn't say your "sh's" in those days. I picked you up in my arms and told you I'd be back soon, and you said, "And you'll stay till happily ever after like the stories? Promise?" – and I did.

'All through that week I remembered my promise. I told Ursula all about you and she understood. That was the most marvellous thing about her. She always understood.

'"Go back to her, Robert," she said. "And if ever you change your mind, or if one day she should leave you, write and let me know. I'll always be waiting."'

'Did you – did you ever write?' Jonquil asked breathlessly.

'When I arrived home Mummy was very ill. She was rushed into hospital and was operated on for appendicitis and peritonitis. She nearly died. Whenever she was conscious she called for me. She suffered a great deal but she never complained. I knew then that I could never leave her.'

'And Ursula?'

'We wrote occasionally. I still hear from her. She is head of some A.R.P. organisation in London.'

'Is she married?' Jonquil asked, curiously.

'No! No, she never married,' Robert said slowly.

Jonquil caught his hand and pressed it tightly in her own.

'Daddy, you have been – happily ever after, haven't you?' she asked childishly, impulsively.

He smiled down at her and squeezed the small hand in his own affectionately.

'How could I help it with a daughter like you!' he answered, half laughing – half seriously.

'Shall I meet Ursula one day?' Jonquil asked him.

'I haven't seen her since that week's shooting,' her father said slowly. 'We didn't want to spoil it.'

'Daddy, you romantic old thing!' Jonquil teased him. 'Now I know where I get it from. Em is always accusing me of being a hopeless romanticist. Don't you ever wonder what Ursula looks like now?'

'Oh, I expect she is older, a little grey, perhaps, and fatter,' Robert said whimsically. 'I've changed, too. But at heart she will still be the same.'

'Daddy, you *did* love her!'

'Did I?'

'Didn't you? Don't you?' Jonquil persisted.

'I may have. I don't now,' her father answered firmly. 'I've fallen in love with your mother.'

'Daddy, you're wonderful!' Jonquil said. It was her way of telling him how much she loved and appreciated him, and he understood. Father and daughter exchanged confidences and became the greatest friends.

Jonquil jumped to her feet and went to meet Em as she came out of the telephone box. Her face was drawn and anxious.

'I managed to get through to the camp,' she told Jonquil. 'But Charles wasn't about.

I tried the mess and dispersal and the briefing rooms – in fact everywhere. Adrian wasn't there either, nor any of the squadron. I think they must be on ops. I left a message for Charles to 'phone me as soon as he returns. Let's go back to the mess.'

Unconsciously, Em hurried her pace, indicating to Jonquil how worried she was about Charles. How dreadful, how unimaginably awful it would be if anything should happen to him. Em loved him so much. Every day seemed to bring them closer together and their lives were so bound up in each other that it was impossible to imagine one without the other.

'Would it have been like that with Brian and me if we'd been married?' Jonquil wondered. Perhaps. But deep inside her she did not really think so. Charles and Em were contemporaries, friends and companions in everything they did, as well as lovers. With Brian there would always have been a certain number of differences which fourteen years between their ages would automatically have created. As Em had once pointed out, it would not have meant a unity of their two lives, but of herself sharing Brian's Service life.

And with Simon? Jonquil mused. But no! With Simon they had been lovers only, knowing nothing of the other's deeper, inner feelings.

'I was just in love with the idea of being in love,' she told herself with a smile. 'Anyone with Simon's charm would have filled the bill.'

Supposing … supposing she had met Adrian first; would she have imagined herself in love with him?

But Adrian was in love with another girl, she told herself quickly. So the question would never have arisen. But just suppose he weren't, some inner self insisted. Adrian is understanding; he is good-looking; he loves music; he shares your interests in the more artistic things of this world and yet he can be as much fun on a picnic, for instance, as Bill used to be. Why not Adrian?

'Oh, I don't know,' she exclaimed aloud.

'Don't know what?' Em asked.

Jonquil laughed self-consciously.

'Did I speak aloud?' she asked. 'I was just thinking.'

'Share your girlish dreams with me, oh beauteous maiden!' Em teased her friend.

But Jonquil shook her head. There were some things she could not discuss even with Em.

'I'm glad Bill is so happy,' she said, changing the subject. 'His wife sounds sweet.'

'He deserves the best,' Em agreed. 'Was she the Wren he met on the boat going out?'

Jonquil nodded her head.

'Romance with a capital R!' Em remarked

with a smile, and added more seriously: 'You know, Jonnie, for all its horrors, this damned old war has done some good. Take Bill, for instance. In peace time he would never have travelled further than from Land's End to John o' Groats, if as far. As it is, he has seen Jerusalem, Bethlehem, Cairo, Alexandria, and a dozen other famous places. He has bathed in the Mediterranean; ridden a camel round the Pyramids; spent a week in South Africa; two months in Iraq. He has, in fact, joined the Air Force and seen the world! *And* he has met the one and only girl!'

'Lucky Bill!' Jonquil agreed laughing.

But Em was persistently serious.

'Look at the difference in your own home, Jonnie!' she said. 'You say your mother is a changed woman, and there's no doubt about the change being for the better. And study the British people as a whole. We've had to mix in together because of the Blitz and the common fear of invasion, and we've done it and liked it. We're far less selfish, far more hospitable, far more thoughtful and tolerant and understanding than ever before. We're poorer, but nicer!'

'Definitely poorer!' Jonquil said ruefully. 'Daddy has lost thousands since the war broke out. But I can't say he seems unduly worried about it. No amount of hard work can alter things, so I suppose with the lack of responsibility and worry, he feels ten years younger. How sensible it was of him to have been saving during those years of luxury. Mummy, I know, spent every penny she had, and, of course, I did! I think if I hadn't been promoted when I was I should have felt it badly when Daddy cut my allowance so drastically. But a Flight Officer's pay is well worth having.'

'You work for it, Jonnie,' Em said. 'I've never known any one slave at it the way you do. I always think I am doing my bit until I look round and see you doing twice as much! Tell me, Jonnie, is it still for Brian? To forget him, I mean?'

'No, not any more,' Jonquil answered after a pause. 'At first, just after he died, work seemed to be my only salvation. Now it has become a habit – and I have a good deal of pride in it, too. I'm happiest when I'm working. It takes up all my time and interest, and I haven't the opportunity to worry about anything else.'

'Well, I have enough to do bothering about Charles,' Em said with a smile. 'Come on, Jonnie. Let's hurry. He may ring the mess while we are still on our way. I'd hate to miss him.'

The two girls quickened their pace and were soon entering the large combined R.A.F. and W.A.A.F. officers' mess. Tea was laid out in the ante-room and the girls were helping themselves when the 'phone bell rang. Em said slowly:

'That's for me, Jonnie, I'm sure.'

An orderly came into the room and went straight across to Em.

'Telephone for you, Ma'am,' she said.

Em's face had gone a chalky white, but she shook her head when Jonquil made as if to go with her.

The minutes while she waited, seemed interminable to Jonquil. She tried to eat one of the sandwiches, but the bread stuck in her throat.

'This is quite absurd!' she told herself. 'There is no reason to suppose anything should have happened to Charles...'

At last Em reappeared, and if it were possible her face was whiter, more strained than before. Jonquil felt her heart throbbing painfully in her throat and she had to force the words through her lips.

'Em, it's not Charles...?'

'It was Charles on the telephone,' Em said quietly. 'Jonnie, Adrian has crashed. He is severely hurt, and they don't expect him to live. He is asking for you.'

'For me?' Jonquil repeated dully.

'Yes,' Em said gently. 'You'll go, won't you, Jonnie?'

Jonquil nodded her head.

'Yes, of course I'll go.'

'He's at St George's Hospital, Exmouth,'

Em went on. 'Charles said every minute was precious.'

'Is he conscious?' Jonquil heard herself question.

'Yes, at times.'

'And you're sure he asked for *me?*'

'Yes, of course I'm sure,' Em said impatiently. 'Oh, Jonnie, do please hurry. You don't realise how important it is. He – he loves you.'

'Loves me? But… Oh, I don't understand. I thought… Em, how long do they give him?'

'I don't know. Charles said not long. Jonnie, please hurry. Go and see the Wing Commander and get compassionate leave. You could catch the seven-thirty which gets you down soon after midnight. I 'phoned the orderly room for train times as soon as Charles rang off. I'll ask corporal to make you up some sandwiches. You won't have time for supper.'

Somehow or other Jonquil caught the seven-thirty, and soon she was speeding on her way to Cornwall, and the wheels of the train were going round and round and saying over and over again:

'Hurry, hurry, hurry – hurry – hurry.'

The sandwiches lay on the seat beside her, untouched, unopened, and every now and again she said to herself:

'Oh, no! Not Adrian. It can't be true.

Please God, let it not be true!'

But when at last she found her way to the hospital and the door was opened by the night porter, it was only to be told that they were expecting her – that Wing Commander Hepworth had been asking for her continually.

'He was brought in this morning at twelve,' the old porter told her kindly as he led her towards Matron's room. 'Operated on for severe internal injuries. But don't you worry too much, Miss. I've known people pull through much worse than that afore now.'

Jonquil clutched his arm desperately.

'But they told me every minute was precious,' she said.

The old porter looked at her thoughtfully.

'Might want to change his mind now you've come,' he said with a wink. 'You sweethearts?'

'No – yes. Oh, I love him,' Jonquil whispered, the tears coming suddenly in a rush to her eyes.

'There, Miss. Don't take on so. He'll be all right,' the old man said again. 'See if he don't! I'll be praying for him.'

And then there was Charles ... and Matron in a white, starched apron, and she was being marched down endless long corridors between them both. They came to a stop outside one of the doors and Charles said brokenly:

'I hope to God it isn't too late!'

Matron turned the handle of the door, and Jonquil dug her fingers into the palms of her hands and prayed feverishly.

'Please, God– Oh, please don't let it be too late.'

Charles took one of her hands and drew her gently into the dimly lit room.

Chapter 18

The doctor, who had been standing with his back to them, turned as they came into the room, his eyes taking them in quickly and returning again to his patient. His fingers were feeling for the weakening pulse while his mind sought through past years of experience for something more that he could do to save this man's life. They had done what they could – an emergency operation during the afternoon – but the patient had not rallied as he should have done. He seemed to lack the will to live, which was half the battle in cases like this.

He turned again to the visitors and his eyes widened a little as they came to rest on Jonquil's face. Maybe the girl could help. The patient had been asking for some girl during his periods of delirium...

'You are...?'

'Jonquil Mathews! May I go to him?'

The doctor nodded his head. Jonquil with a glance at the white immobile face lying so still against the pillow, dropped on to the floor beside the high hospital bed, and buried her face against one of Adrian's hands.

For a moment, the room was quite silent,

then the sick man gave a deep, long-drawn sigh, and his eyes opened and consciousness returned to them.

'Jonquil!'

The word was almost inaudible, but the girl heard it. The blood rushed to her cheek and her arms went around him as she pressed her cheek to his. Matron made as if to stop her, but the doctor laid a restraining hand on her arm. Jonquil was unaware of anything but the urgent, overwhelming desire to keep Adrian alive; to make him want to live.

'Darling, darling, I love you. You mustn't leave me,' she cried in a soft undertone. 'I love you, Adrian. I love you!'

His eyes crinkled a little at the corners in an attempt to smile. His lips formed the words.

'And – I – love – you...'

Then the dark lashes closed over his eyes and it seemed to Jonquil as if he were drifting slowly away from her. She turned to the doctor in an agony of fear.

'Don't let him die! Oh, please don't let him leave me,' she cried. 'How can you stand there doing nothing while he is...'

'He is sleeping, my dear,' the doctor interrupted gently. 'It is the best possible thing for him. Now I think we can begin to hope for recovery.'

'Then here *is* hope?' Jonquil cried.

'There is always hope,' the doctor answered her gently. 'But until now it has been only the faintest glimmer. He seemed not to want to live. Your presence has made all the difference. He will fight for his life now, and that is half the battle.'

'I shall make him live,' Jonquil said fiercely, 'because I love him and he loves me, and I cannot live without him.'

She turned suddenly to Charles and tears of fatigue and thankfulness, of almost every emotion, filled her eyes and flowed unheeded down her cheeks.

'To think I never realised it before,' she whispered. 'That he should have had to wait so long...'

Charles put his arm round her and said with rough tenderness:

'There, there, it's all going to be all right now. You must go and rest, Jonnie, like a good girl. You must be terribly tired!'

'Give her a sedative, Matron,' the doctor said. 'She can sleep in one of the beds in the empty ward.'

'No, no! I'll stay here,' Jonquil protested quickly, 'I can't leave Adrian.'

'He'll sleep until morning without waking,' the doctor told her. 'Probably until the morning after if he knows what's good for him!'

'But he might wake,' Jonquil insisted. 'He mustn't wake to find me gone.'

'He won't wake,' the doctor repeated. 'But in case he should, you shall have the next-door room which I believe is empty. If he stirs, the night-nurse can call you.'

'You must sleep, Jonnie,' Charles said persuasively. 'Otherwise you'll never be fit to cope with tomorrow when Adrian really will need you.'

Jonquil gave in and with a last look at Adrian, she followed Matron out of the room.

Charles turned to the doctor and said quietly:

'Is there really hope, Doctor? Or were you ... well, were you just being kind?'

'No, he stands every chance now,' the doctor said. 'The nervous system has suffered a tremendous shock and sleep is the best possible cure. To be frank with you, I was afraid the operation hadn't been a success. It was very tricky and had un-expected complications – added to which, the patient made no effort himself. But if he can sleep like that ... I think you can rest assured your friend will live, sir. The girl – Miss Mathews, is she his fiancée?'

'No, just a friend,' Charles said. 'But I have hopes'

'Very good!' the doctor broke in. 'The girl can do more good than any amount of medicines. She'll be a tonic. Now I must be getting along. You staying here?'

'I have a room at the hotel down the road,' Charles said. 'Matron has my telephone number and has promised to call me in an emergency.'

'Trust you'll have an undisturbed night,' the older man said courteously.

'Thank you, sir. Good night!'

As Charles walked back to his hotel, he ruminated on the oddities of this life. All these years Adrian had meant no more to Jonquil than a very good friend. And now, realising she might lose him, she had found she loved him.

For a moment, he wondered if Jonquil could have been playing a part – pretending for Adrian's sake that she cared. But he thrust the thought from him immediately. There could be no doubt when he remembered her voice, her expression, when she had turned to him and said, 'Charles, to think I never realised before!'

Em will be pleased, he reflected. His last thought before he fell asleep was, as always, for his wife.

Jonquil undressed and had a bath. The hot water relaxed her taut nerves and she felt suddenly immensely tired. She climbed between the white hospital sheets and smiled thankfully at the little nurse who hung up her uniform for her and brought her a glass of hot milk with two tablets to make her sleep.

'I don't think I need them,' she protested.

But the nurse put them into her hand.

'Doctor's orders!' she said.

Too tired to argue, Jonquil swallowed the tablets and the milk and when nurse tiptoed out of the room, she was already sleeping peacefully. In the next room, the ever-watchful nurse sewed by Adrian's bedside and saw him safely through the night.

When Jonquil awoke, the sun was streaming in through the windows and a different nurse – a V.A.D., who reminded her of Connie Worth, was clattering round the room with a tray.

'Breakfast?' Jonquil asked sleepily.

'Lunch!' the V.A.D. corrected her, with a smile.

Jonquil sat up suddenly, now wide awake.

'Adrian!' she said. 'Oh, why did they let me sleep so long?'

'Wing Commander Hepworth hasn't woken yet,' the girl told her kindly. 'Matron said there was no point in disturbing you. Now you must eat some lunch. You must be hungry.'

Jonquil was. It was almost twenty-four hours since she had eaten. Tea yesterday had been a farce – both she and Em far too worried to touch any food, and the sandwiches for her supper she had left unopened in the train, in case some hungry traveller should want them.

While she was eating her lunch, Matron

came in to see her. Jonquil found her both sympathetic and charming and soon she was telling her all about Adrian and Em and how they had all met.

'The doctor suggests you should go in and sit with the Wing Commander after you have had lunch, if you'd like to,' Matron said. 'He may wake for a minute or two.'

'Of course,' Jonquil said eagerly. 'Oh, Matron, he will live, won't he?'

The older woman patted her hand sympathetically.

'We're doing our best,' was the most comforting thing she would say.

Adrian did not wake during the afternoon. Jonquil sat by his bedside, content just to watch the rise and fall of his breathing and to know that he was all right. When the day-nurse left the room for a few minutes, she slipped her fingers round his wrist and tested the pulse. It seemed too slow to her, but reassuringly steady.

Through the long hours, Jonquil thought back over the years she had known Adrian, remembering all the details of the days they had spent together. She was surprised to find how much she *could* remember.

'I have loved him always without knowing it,' she thought. Em was right when she said it was possible. Strangely enough, Jonquil could remember her very words.

'I never had any doubts about Charles,'

she had written, 'but that doesn't mean you can't fall in love with someone after some little time. For instance, you might suddenly realise you loved Adrian whom you've known for years...'

Had Em known all along then? Jonquil wondered. Had Adrian confided in her? It was quite probable.

With a sudden rush of blood to her cheeks, Jonquil recalled the evening of Em's wedding when she and Adrian had stayed up late in the kitchen.

'Tell me what's the matter,' she had said when Adrian had given way to his feelings and cried against her heart. And Adrian had refused. Oh, how could she have been so blind – so senseless all this while?

'I've been too wrapt up in myself and my own affairs,' she thought regretfully. 'But I'll make it up to him as soon as he is better.'

Charles came in for a few minutes, but did not stay long. He told Jonquil he had telephoned Em during the morning and she had asked him to tell Jonnie she was holding thumbs! A simple, childish message but it conveyed to Jonquil all Em's sympathy, and the knowledge that she was thinking and praying for her and Adrian.

The doctor called in at tea-time, took Adrian's pulse and studied the temperature chart, then hurried out again. He was a busy man. The whole hospital was understaffed and Jonquil suggested to Matron that the day-nurse should go if she were needed elsewhere.

'I've had first-aid training,' she said. 'And if he moved or stirred or if his pulse changed or anything, I could easily ring the bell.'

After consultation with the Doctor, Matron gave her consent and Jonquil was left alone with Adrian and her thoughts and the large golden bumble bees who flew in through the open window in a steady procession, attracted by the heady scent of the June roses Charles had brought for Adrian at Jonquil's request.

At tea-time, the day nurse brought in a tray and cast a half curious, half sympathetic look at Jonquil as she gave it to her. The whole hospital was buzzing with the story of the good-looking young Wing Commander's crash and the tall, slim W.A.A.F. officer who had arrived in the dead of night and saved his life. From the newest probationer up the scale of importance to Matron, they were all interested in the romance surrounding the new patient.

Jonquil drank her tea, put the tray outside the door, and resumed her watch by Adrian's bedside. Her eyes never left his face and she noted every feature in detail, the exceptionally long lashes, the straight, firm mouth and square chin. She allowed her fingers to trace the outline of his forehead, travel lightly down across his cheeks. A great tenderness seemed to flow through her into her fingertips as she did so, and she was aware of a feeling almost of physical sickness yet strangely ecstatic stabbing her heart and running in little electric shocks down to the pit of her stomach.

'Adrian, Adrian!' she whispered softly, and leaning over him, touched his lips gently with her own.

'That – was – nice!'

Jonquil stared back and the tell-tale colour rushed to her cheeks.

'I didn't know you were awake,' she said breathlessly. 'I must ring for your nurse.'

'Don't – just yet!' Adrian said softly but clearly. One of his hands stole out from beneath the sheets and caught hold of hers.

'Hullo!' he murmured, his eyes crinkling at the corners in a half-smile.

She smiled back at him.

'Hullo – darling!'

Adrian watched her eyes for a few minutes before he spoke again. He had not much strength to his voice, but although he spoke so hesitantly, his words were clear and precise.

'It wasn't a dream ... then? That you...'

'No!' Jonquil broke in quickly. 'I did tell you last night that I loved you and I meant it then and now, and for always, with all my heart. But Adrian, you mustn't talk. You mustn't exert yourself.'

He smiled at her again, his eyes never leaving her face.

'Darling?' he whispered presently.

'Yes, darling?'

'Nothing, darling!... Only ... darling, darling!'

'Oh, Adrian!'

She lent forward and kissed him again and this time she could feel a faint answering pressure of his lips.

'You're putting my temperature ... up!' Adrian said presently. To Jonquil he appeared frighteningly pale and tired.

'I'm going to ring for nurse now,' she said firmly. 'Matron would never forgive me...'

'No, please... Not just yet!' he pleaded with her.

'If I were responsible for setting you back I should never forgive myself,' Jonquil told him.

'You're the ... best cure ... for me!' Adrian said. 'Please Jonquil darling...'

She gave in weakly and let him retake possession of her hand. He laid it against his cheek and covered it with his own, and for a minute or two he lay quietly without speaking. Then he asked:

'How long ... have you been here?'

'Since lunch time,' Jonquil told him. 'I arrived at the hospital about midnight last night.'

280

'I remember now,' Adrian said slowly. 'We were on a train-busting outing and got shot up over Cherbourg. Thought we could make home but we lost too much height and hit a tree as we came in for a forced landing...'

'You mustn't talk so much, darling,' Jonquil said gently. 'I think I must call the nurse now.'

'No, please! I'll lie still. Please don't go.'

'I won't leave you, darling.'

'Ever?'

'Ever!'

The sun dipped behind the trees and the shadows in the room deepened. Jonquil and Adrian did not break the silence for it had become more eloquent than words and the clasp of the other's hand told them everything they wanted to know. But Jonquil's conscience refused to allow her to sit there without calling nurse any longer, and presently she got up and rang the bell.

Within a minute or two, the doctor and Matron and the day nurse came bustling into the room and with a hasty promise to return and say good night later, she hurried out of Adrian's private ward.

'Why don't you go for a walk?' the day nurse suggested kindly, following her out. 'The fresh air will do you a lot of good and give you an appetite for supper. We can't have you ill, too!'

Jonquil readily accepted the suggestion.

She called in for a moment at Charles's hotel and told him how much better Adrian was.

'If he's really on the road to recovery, I think I'd better get back to camp,' Charles said with considerable relief. 'This was a compassionate forty-eight and if I overstay it, it'll have to come out of my annual leave.'

'Will you be telephoning Em this evening?' Jonquil asked him.

'Yes, just after seven. Any message?'

'Give her my love and tell her – tell her everything is going to be all right.'

'A masterpiece of understatement from what I can gather of the situation,' Charles said laughing. 'I'll give her my uncensored version, Jonquil. It will be far more enlightening.'

'Pig!'

Jonquil thanked him for everything he had done and let him reserve a room in the hotel for her for a day or two hence.

'If Adrian is really out of danger now,' Charles said, 'there will be no need to stay in the hospital any longer. You'll be far more comfortable here.'

Jonquil thanked him for all his trouble and promising to keep him informed of Adrian's progress, said goodbye. She set out towards the Beacon. The climb up the hundreds of steps to the top of the cliff exhilarated even while it tired her. She felt exhausted but triumphant when at last she reached the summit. She stood on the cliff edge staring across the bay where the river Ex runs into the sea, a slight sea breeze sending her skirt flapping against her knees. She pulled off her W.A.A.F. cap and ran her fingers through her hair, shaking her head so that her curls were loosed and were blown across her face by the light wind.

High above her, the seagulls wheeled and cried and the salt taste of the sea stung her lips and cheeks. Far below, the sea, blood-red in the setting sun, lapped gently against the rocks and it seemed to Jonquil to be the emblem of her spirit.

So had she come through difficult waters to this calm, peaceful harbour which glowed nevertheless with all the fire and passion of her love for Adrian. She did not feel dwarfed but rather magnified by the glory and splendour of her surroundings. She felt her heart was large enough to embrace the world, and unconsciously she stretched out her arms to the horizon as if to welcome every stranger; as if to comfort every sorrower; as if to shield all the troubled.

As she raised her eyes to the blue sky above her, she paid tribute to those two she had so nearly loved and so truly lost, and thanked them for all they had given her. She thanked God, too, for His mercy and His goodness to her and prayed for His blessing on her love for Adrian.

When at last she turned her back on the sea and set her steps towards the hospital, she felt purified and uplifted by her earthly and spiritual communion. In those few minutes she had dedicated herself to her God and her country, and above all to the man she loved.

Chapter 19

Adrian's journey was slow but steady. Within a few days of Jonquil's arrival at the hospital, he was considered strong enough to stand up to another operation, and this successfully completed, he made sure progress.

Jonquil, sitting by his bedside on the last day of her leave, found it hard to believe that this Adrian so cheerful and talkative, could be the same person whom she had visited only a week ago when he was believed to be dying.

'I shall be able to leave you tomorrow with my mind quite at rest,' she said smiling.

Adrian caught hold of one of her hands and squeezed it playfully.

'Aren't you afraid I might get off with one of the pretty V.A.D.s, once you're safely out of the way?' he teased.

Jonquil smiled down at him.

'Silly!' she said softly. 'I meant I wouldn't be worrying about your health.'

'Not at all?' Adrian asked, his eyes belying the seriousness of his voice.

'Not at all!' Jonquil announced firmly.

'Then I shall have to have a relapse,' Adrian countered. 'I like you to worry about me. It satisfies my ego!'

'I'll be thinking of you, every hour of every day,' Jonquil told him, seriously.

Adrian lifted her hand and dropped a kiss into the upturned palm.

'I love you!' he said irrelevantly.

'Darling!'

'Yes, darling!'

'Nothing, darling – only darling, darling!'

They smiled at one another in perfect understanding. It was one of their own private conversations that for all it might sound silly to an outside listener, was nevertheless precious to them.

'What time is your train?' Adrian asked presently.

'Three-thirty! But don't let's think about it yet. It's only midday.'

'They've been frightfully decent, letting you in to see me so often,' Adrian said thoughtfully. 'There are supposed to be certain visiting hours and those only.'

'I think Matron has a soft spot for you, darling,' Jonquil said smiling.

'You do?'

'How could she help it?' she countered swiftly.

'It was quite a long while before you succumbed to my charms!' Adrian said without rancour.

'Oh, Adrian, no! Not really!' Jonquil cried. 'I've always been terribly fond of you. I think deep down inside me I have always loved you. That is why I was so angry when you spoke to me as you did the day after Simon was killed. And why I cried when you kissed me that day on the picnic with Charles and Em. Do you remember?'

Adrian nodded his head.

'Oh, and why that New Year's Eve was so perfect, and the day Em was married ... Adrian, I can't bear to think about that. If only I had known...'

'Don't have any regrets, sweetheart,' Adrian said gently. 'The more difficult a thing is to get, the more marvellous it is when at last you have won it. The fact that you love me now wipes out all the past.'

'I'll make it up to you,' Jonquil vowed. 'I'll love you twice as much for every year I have wasted.'

He smiled up at her with great tenderness and pulled her head down so that her lips touched his.

'Kiss me!' he whispered softly.

As the pressure of her lips hardened against his mouth, his arms tightened round her and passion sprung between them like an electric shock. Adrian released her suddenly and his face was white.

'Not at all good for the patient!' he said shakily. 'But beautiful all the same!'

Jonquil resisted the impulse to repeat the little incident, and sat silently while each controlled their emotions.

'Kissing you is rather like being on a scenic railway,' she said presently. 'You know – when the car goes over the top but your stomach gets left behind!'

Adrian laughed.

'Mine hasn't caught up with the car yet!' he said.

'Must be awfully bad for the digestion,' Jonquil remarked naïvely. 'And yet married and engaged couples don't seem to suffer from it!'

'We haven't talked about getting engaged yet,' Adrian said eagerly. 'You are – you will marry me, Jonquil?'

'Of course, of course,' Jonquil cried.

'Then we are engaged,' Adrian said simply. 'Darling, what sort of ring would you like?'

'I don't mind as long as it's yours!'

He smiled at her tenderly.

'But haven't you any preference for stones?' he insisted.

'I – well, I like pearls.'

'Pearls mean tears!' Adrian said thoughtfully.

'That is only superstition,' Jonquil chided him.

'Yes!' Adrian agreed. 'All right, darling. You shall have your pearls. And there will never be any tears in our life.'

'*Our* life!' she echoed, almost inaudibly.

'How soon shall we be married?' Adrian asked. 'I shall be fit again in three months at the most. That brings us to September. Or would you rather wait until the following Spring?'

'No, I don't want to wait,' Jonquil told him definitely. 'Anyway, I like the Autumn. It is my favourite season.'

'Yes, mine, too!' Adrian agreed. 'But some people think it is a sad season. Spring is all promise; summer the realisation of that promise; winter is full of hope for the coming spring, but autumn, they say, is the slow decaying of the summer's glory.'

'Adrian, how poetic!'

He smiled, a trifle embarrassed by his own outspokenness.

'Pearls for our engagement and autumn for our wedding,' he mused. 'Can we overcome all this superstition, my darling?'

'Yes, a thousand times yes!' Jonquil said confidently. 'There will never be a cross word, a second of unhappiness between us. Not as long as we love each other.'

'I shall love you as long as I live,' Adrian said.

'And I shall love you beyond this life,' Jonquil returned. 'When we are dead and nothing more than spirits, my ghost will go on loving yours into eternity.'

'You'll be tired of me long before then!'

'No, never!'

'Wait until I am old and grey and really have got indigestion, and have to put my false teeth into a glass before we go to bed!'

'Oh, darling, you idiot!' Jonquil cried, laughing. 'By then I shall be just as old and just as grey and I shall love you just as much as ever – even if you are bald and have got false teeth.'

'I shall keep you to those words,' Adrian said with mock seriousness. 'Then when we are both ninety and you don't love me any more, I shall sue you for breach of promise!'

The entry of the pretty V.A.D. with their lunch put an end to their conversation, but only temporarily. Adrian was supposed to sleep after lunch, but as Jonquil had to leave at three, Matron gave her permission to stay in the room while Adrian rested. She knew it might be a long while before Jonquil could get leave again.

'You're a darling,' Jonquil cried, putting her arms round her and hugging her. 'Let's tell her our news, Adrian. She shall be the first to know. Matron, we're engaged to be married.'

'Well, what a surprise!' the older woman said, although she wasn't in the least bit surprised. 'Let me congratulate you both.'

Adrian beckoned to Matron to come over to the far side of the bed.

'I'd far rather have got engaged to you!' he said in a stage whisper.

Matron laughed coyly and fussed round the bed like a ruffled hen.

'Now you lie still and behave yourself, Wing Commander Hepworth,' she said, and bustled out of the room.

'You lie down beside me,' Adrian said to Jonquil when it was all quiet again.

'Oh, no! I couldn't, Adrian,' Jonquil protested. 'Supposing someone came in!'

'Suppose they did,' Adrian replied. 'The only complaint would be that your shoes were marking my counterpane.'

'Then I'll take them off!' Jonquil said with a laugh. 'After all, we are engaged, so you are hardly putting me in a compromising situation!'

'And my intentions are strictly honourable!' Adrian finished, smiling.

Jonquil took off her regulation shoes and her W.A.A.F. jacket and climbed on to the bed beside him, moving very carefully so that he should not be jolted. He put his arm round her and she curled up against him, her head settling comfortably against his shoulder.

'When we're married we will always be like this,' Jonquil thought aloud.

'We'll have such fun!' Adrian said happily. 'We'll have one of those low-down-to-the-floor-beds...'

'A divan...' Jonquil put in for him.

'Yes, a divan. And lots and lots of pillows

and cushions on it.'

'And one night we'll sleep one end and the next night the other,' Jonquil suggested with a smile.

'And some mornings I shan't let you get up. You shall stay in bed and I will make the breakfast and bring it up to you.'

'Oh, Adrian!'

'And then I'll go back to bed and we will sleep until lunch time.'

'When do we work?' Jonquil asked.

'When we feel like it!' Adrian said. 'Anyway, when we are on leave we won't have to work.'

'But after the war...' Jonquil insisted.

'After the war I shall do what I have always wanted and become an aircraft designer.'

'Oh, Adrian, that would be wonderful. Then you will be able to work at home.'

'We will probably be dreadfully poor!' Adrian warned her.

'Oh, I don't mind!' Jonquil cried eagerly. 'It might have mattered before I joined the W.A.A.F., but now I have left the old luxurious habits behind me for ever. I shall sew and dust and cook – I had a year's domestic training in Switzerland, you know, darling, so I *can* cook.'

Adrian smiled at her and buried his face for a moment against the soft hollow of her throat.

'I think we will be able to afford a maid or

something,' he said presently. 'I've a certain amount of private income you know.'

'Would we be able to afford a baby?'

'Sweetheart, you can have anything you want,' Adrian said, and meant it. 'But let's not have a kid too soon.'

'No!' she agreed. 'We'll get to know each other first.'

'I shall love you too much, I think,' Adrian said with a little sigh.

'Too much?'

'Yes! I shall be like a cave man. Suddenly in the middle of the day I shall want to make love to you. Then I'll leave my work or whatever I'm doing and carry you upstairs to the divan!'

'Adrian! Which end shall we sleep?' Jonquil asked with a breathless little laugh.

'The top end!' Adrian said airily.

'But I shall want to be the other end,' Jonquil said. 'You'll have to give in to me.'

'I will not! I shall tie you down with dressing-gown cords and tickle you until you cry for mercy.'

'Then what?'

'Then this!' Adrian said and bit at the top of her ear before he turned her face up to his and kissed her lips.

This time it was Jonquil who drew away.

'No, no more!' she said, putting her hands against his chest to prevent him drawing her back into his arms.

'Scenic railways?' Adrian asked huskily.

Jonquil smiled and nodded her head.

For some minutes they lay side by side in silence. Jonquil traced the lines of his face, her fingers running across his eyebrows and down the bridge of his nose.

'When shall I see you again, darling?'

'As soon as I can get some more leave,' Jonquil said. 'I should get a forty-eight in about six weeks' time, too.'

'A month and two weeks!' Adrian sighed. 'That's a horribly long while.'

'I'll write every day,' Jonquil promised. 'And as soon as you are allowed up, we can telephone.'

'Perhaps there is another room with a telephone installed in it,' Adrian suggested. 'I will have to ask Matron.'

Jonquil looked at her watch and gave a little cry.

'It's a quarter to three!' she said. 'I'll have to go in a minute.'

She buried her face in his shoulder and he rubbed his chin against the top of her head.

'Darling, I shall miss you dreadfully,' he whispered against her hair. 'I shall be lying here all day thinking about you and imagining things we will do together when I am well again.'

'I'm glad I know where you are,' Jonquil said. 'I shall be able to picture you here. Oh, Adrian! I don't want to go.'

'Your country needs you!' Adrian said with a humorous twist to his mouth, and added softly, 'but not half as much as I do!'

'Oh, I'm tired of being a Waaf!' Jonquil said childishly. 'I want to be silly and wear feminine clothes again, and not have to carry all my parcels in the left hand so that I'm ready to salute with the right! And I'm tired of doing everything by the clock and rushing my meals and night watches...'

'Heh! What is this?' Adrian asked laughing. 'Revolution?'

'Oh, I don't mean it really. At least, I *am* tired of all those things but I realise they are a necessary part of my service life. At least I don't have to scrub floors any more! No, what I really meant was that I didn't want to have to go back to camp – to leave you.'

'You know, Jonquil, darling, that I'm awfully proud of you? You will be a squadron officer next and then where will I be... No more orders, not to Squadron Officer Mathews!'

'Heaven forbid!' Jonquil said with a smile.

'Might as well make hay while the sun shines,' Adrian said. 'Flight Officer Mathews, I hereby detail you to give Wing Commander Hepworth one kiss, large, his, for use of, as they would say in equipment!'

'That would be a pleasure, sir!' Jonquil said, and planted a light kiss on the top of his nose. But he pulled her closer to him and held her tightly against his heart.

'There will never be anything worse for me in this life than having to be parted from you,' he said huskily.

'I shan't really go, my dearest,' Jonquil whispered. 'Only my person will be gone, but my heart and mind and soul, and all my thoughts will always be with you.'

'Don't say "goodbye"!' Adrian said suddenly. 'Just so "so long" or "au revoir" or something like that. But never "goodbye".'

'All right, darling. I won't.'

'Promise?'

'I promise! Adrian, I shall have to go…'

'No, not for a minute!'

'One minute more then. Oh, my dearest, don't make it more difficult for me. It's hard enough…'

Adrian released her and she slipped off the bed and he lay watching her as she put on her shoes and tunic and powdered her nose. As she ran a comb through her short, fair hair, he said:

'I shall comb it for you when we're married. You have lovely hair. In fact you're altogether beautiful.'

She turned her head and smiled at him over her shoulder. When she was ready to go, she went back to him and their lips clung in a last, long kiss. Then she drew back and smiled a little crookedly as she said:

'So long, darling!'

'Au revoir!' he answered, and followed her with his eyes as she opened the door and closed it gently behind her.

For a little while he lay quite still, reliving in his mind all the beautiful moments of this last week with Jonquil. He could see her as she moved across the room to open the window for him, as she sat in the chair by his bedside, talking and smiling down at him. He could see her rearranging the roses in their glass vases, and remembered that she had pricked her finger on a thorn and sucked it for a few minutes like a small child. He could see her as she tempted him with some delicacy, or removed the pips from the grapes with long slender fingers.

'You spoil me!' he had said, and she had answered him:

'Nothing could spoil you, Adrian!'

'Oh, Jonquil! Jonquil!'

He buried his face against the pillow where the perfume of her hair still lingered barely perceptibly, and within a few minutes he was fast asleep.

Em could hardly contain her excitement when she learned from Jonquil of her engagement to Adrian.

'He has loved you so long!' she said. 'And I had almost despaired of you ever coming to your senses. He *is* going to be all right, Jonnie?'

'Oh, yes! The second operation was a great success and now it is only a question of time. We are planning to be married in the autumn.'

Em clasped her friend round the waist and they laughed together and danced round the room before subsiding breathlessly on to Em's bed.

'Oh, I meant to tell you, Marion is coming over after tea. With Hurry of course!' Em said. 'She told me she has some wonderful news for us. Wonder if she has been promoted. Surely not so soon?'

But Marion's news was not of promotion.

'It's far more exciting than that,' she said, when their preliminary greetings were over and Hurry had calmed down a bit and lay panting at their feet.

'Do tell us quickly, Marion!' Em and Jonquil cried laughing.

'I'm going to be married!' Marion answered with sudden shyness. 'Oh, Jonnie, Em, I never thought any man would – could love me with a face like this … but John does. And I love him. I'm so happy, I'd like to die right now so that it can never be spoiled.'

'Marion, how wonderful!' her two friends cried in unison.

'Who is this, John?' Em asked, and Jonquil added:

'Are you sure he's good enough for you, Marion?'

'Good enough? Why, he's far, far too nice for me,' the girl cried eagerly. 'He's – he was a night fighter pilot. He crashed and his face was terribly burned. I met him at the clinic where they make new faces for people like him.'

'But what were *you* doing there?' Em asked gently.

'I went with some books and magazines,' Marion admitted. 'You know there has always been a special bond between people like us...' she pointed unselfconsciously to her face. 'But while I was in Matron's room, a specialist came in and caught sight of me. Within a few minutes he had told me he could give me a new face if I wanted one. *If I wanted one!* I think I told you Mummy took me to some doctors when I was quite small, but they couldn't do anything and I never thought of going again. Of course, the whole profession has progressed unbelievably since then and what wasn't possible then can be done now.'

'Marion, that's the best news of the lot!' Em cried happily. 'When is the transformation going to take place?'

'He said I could have it done any time I could be spared from the W.A.A.F. for a few months. He said he would squeeze me in somewhere among the boys as it was more important for a girl to have a pretty face. But I talked it over with John and decided to wait until the war is over.'

'But why? Why?' Jonquil asked, not understanding.

'Oh, well! I don't suppose they'll much like my leaving the W.A.A.F. for all that time just when I've got my commission. And – well, the boys come first really. They're not used to their disfigurements, and I am to mine. Besides theirs are so much worse...'

The three girls were silent for a minute, Em and Jonquil too full of admiration for Marion to find words to express it.

'I was telling you about John,' Marion said breaking the silence. 'This specialist I met in Matron's room offered to take me round the wards. We had just arrived at John's bed when he was called away and we were left to make our own acquaintance. In those first five minutes I knew I loved him just from the little he had told me of himself. His eyes were covered in bandages, you know, and he couldn't see me. So I told him about myself and what a sight I looked! But he said, "It doesn't matter what your face is like. It's you. You sound nice. Half a year with no eyes has developed my other senses and they're all telling me you're the sort of girl I always wanted to meet..."'

'Marion, how romantic!' Jonquil cried. 'Do please go on.'

'I didn't really expect to see him again. I suppose, to be honest, I both hoped and prayed I would. But he didn't write and the weeks went by. Then the other day he just turned up. His eyes were all right and his face ... well, I didn't know what it was like before, but it was delightful now. "Let's have a look at you," he said. I wanted to bury my head under ten feet of earth and then suddenly I thought, if he can't love me with this face, he won't love me at all. So I looked at him, fair and square and then ... oh, Jonnie, Em, he laughed a great noisy laugh and put his arms round me and kissed me and said, "Proud little devil, aren't you?" And then I think I cried a bit and he lent me his handkerchief and asked me if I loved him enough to marry him. It was only the second time we'd met, but I was sure, sure, terribly sure...'

'It's just like a story!' Em said with a sigh. 'I suppose now you'll get married and live happily ever after?'

'We hadn't really decided,' Marion said. 'I wanted to wait until I had my new face, but John says I mightn't be so nice then and I'd better marry him quick while he still loved me. But there isn't really any hurry. He's off ops for good, of course, and won't leave this country. What of your husband, Em?'

'Oh, he's fine,' Em said, her eyes glowing. 'He doesn't seem to think he'll be going overseas yet.'

'And that nice friend of his – Adrian

someone-or-other?'

Em and Jonquil laughed, and Jonquil's cheeks were a rosy pink when she said:

'I'm engaged to him and getting married next autumn!'

'Jonnie! You're not joking?'

'Better tell her the whole story,' Em suggested.

'We'd never have imagined all this possible if someone had foretold it the day we met,' Marion said when Jonquil had finished her account of the last few months.

'No, we certainly wouldn't!' Em agreed. 'Our Jonnie a Flight Officer and about to marry Wing Commander Hepworth. Marion an A.S.O. and also about to be married to a fighter pilot. And me an old married woman and hoping to produce something in miniature before the year is out!'

'Curious how Fate works,' Marion said thoughtfully. 'If I hadn't joined, I don't suppose I'd ever have met John.'

'Nor I Charles!' Em said.

And I, Jonquil thought, would never have met Bill and Brian and would therefore never have become the me whom Adrian loves. And I should never have understood or appreciated him. Oh, Adrian, my darling. Are you thinking of me now, I wonder?

Far away in Exmouth, Adrian was struggling with his first love letter. Writing from the position he was in, lying on his back,

required considerable effort, but he kept
determinedly at it.

My dearest (he wrote),
'I love you. I love you. I love you. I am
thinking of you every hour of every day and
wonder if you have a moment sometimes to
think of me.
   When shall I see you? The days go so
slowly now you are not here to share them.
   I am getting better as quickly as I can.
Matron says I am doing remarkably well. It
is all for you – and for me – so that I can
soon get up and come and see you.
   Writing is still a little difficult, but it is a
link with you. When I seal the envelope I
shall wait, counting every second until your
evening 'phone call comes through. I cannot
wait to hear your voice.
   Darling – I love you!
   Yours always,
   ADRIAN.

He put the letter in an envelope and gave it
to one of the V.A.D.s to post when she went
off duty. Then he settled down to wait with
impatience for Jonquil's telephone call.
   He loved her very much.

Chapter 20

'I, Adrian Allan Hepworth, take thee, Jonquil Susan Mathews, to have and to hold from this day forward, for better for worse, for richer for poorer, in sickness and in health, to love and to cherish, till death us do part, according to God's holy ordinance; and thereto I plight thee my troth.'

'I, Jonquil Susan Mathews, take thee, Adrian Allan Hepworth, to be my wedded husband, to have and to hold from this day forward, for better for worse, for richer for poorer, in sickness and in health, to love, cherish, and to obey, till death us do part, according to God's holy ordinance; and thereto I give thee my troth.'

Adrian placed the thin, gold band on the third finger of Jonquil's left hand, saying as he did so:

'With this ring I thee wed, with my body I thee worship, and with all my worldly goods I thee endow; in the name of the Father, and the Son, and of the Holy Ghost. Amen.'

Then they knelt and the priest said some prayer that Jonquil could not afterwards remember. But she recalled his last words as they struck suddenly on her ears...

304

'...I pronounce that they be Man and Wife together.'

Man and wife. Adrian's wife!...

Then the organ was playing 'The King Of Love My Shepherd Is', and she was walking down the aisle with her arm tightly clasped in Adrian's, and they were out in the blazing hot August sunshine. After the dim half-light of the church, they were blinded a little at the sudden glare and stood blinking and rubbing their eyes.

The clicking of cameras and excited chattering of the photographers as they pushed and pulled the wedding groups into their positions seemed to come from a long way off. For Adrian and Jonquil there was consciousness only of themselves. Adrian held her hand more tightly in this own and her fingers gave him the reassurance of their answering pressure.

I will always remember this moment, Jonquil thought. The little grey-stoned village church with red roses clustering over the portal. The Reverend Miles, so fat and dumpy and benign in his snowy-white cassock. Daddy in his pin-striped trousers, waistcoat and tails (which are much too big for him now!) and the white carnation in his buttonhole. And Mummy, looking dignified and smart in her pale-blue 'Digby' costume and straw hat. (Two years ago she'd have worn a long, flowery, flowing gown of mauve chiffon!)

And Em, her matron of honour, looking charming and still extraordinarily slender in spite of the coming baby, in a long corded silk picture frock which she would later be able to use as a dinner dress. And there was Charles, not far off, looking pale, but cheerful and elegant in his uniform. And Adrian...

Her eyes came to rest on this man who was now her husband, and it seemed to her that she could never again be as happy as she was at this moment. He looked fit, sunburnt from his long convalescent leave, amazingly attractive in his uniform, loving and beloved.

This is the greatest, happiest moment of my life, she thought.

Adrian, too, was lost in his own thoughts, unaware of the people talking to him, pushing him here and there, shaking his hand and congratulating him. He was re-membering an evening in the Manor House, in the days when he had first known Jonquil. Charles had been playing 'I'll Follow My Secret Heart' and he had thought of those words, 'White, white for a bride,' and longed without any real hope, that one day Jonquil would be *his* bride. Now that dream had come true. She stood beside him, unbeliev-ably lovely in a pure-white gown and veil, with the traditional wreath of orange blossom crowning her short, curly fair hair. There seemed to him to be a halo of purity round her that made him want to fall at her feet and worship her. He did not feel worthy of her and found it hard to believe she really did belong to him. 'To love and to cherish,' he had promised. Always, always would he do so.

Charles was escorting them down the flagged path to the waiting cars. The crowds cheered and Mrs Mathews surreptitiously wiped her eyes as the doors closed and one of the cars drove away with the bride and bridegroom.

'Adrian!'

'Jonquil!'

His arms were about her and his lips met hers in a long, passionate kiss.

'Let's not go to the reception,' Adrian whispered against her hair.

'But, Adrian...'

'Let's elope, Mrs Hepworth.'

'Say it again!'

'Mrs Hepworth! My wife! Oh, Jonquil, I love you so.'

'And I love you.'

They kissed again, but the journey from the little church to the Manor House was a short one, and soon the car drew up outside Jonquil's home.

'Never mind, dearest,' Adrian whispered as he helped her out of the car. 'We'll be alone together soon.'

In a kind of daze, Jonquil took up her stand beside Adrian in the large flower-filled drawing-room, and shook hands with her guests, answering their congratulations with suitable conventional remarks and thanks.

Mr Mathews had unearthed some now priceless bottle of champagne which he had buried at the first hint of invasion, saying:

'Rather the worms have them than the Boche!'

Now they had come in useful.

Toasts were drunk, speeches made. Jonquil, with Adrian's hand guiding hers, cut the three-tiered wedding cake. Impressions came and went. Mrs Mathews, saying:

'You ought to go and change in a minute, darling.'

Adrian's C.O. drawing her aside, saying:

'You've shot down our best pilot. Takes a clever woman to do it! Hope you'll always be happy, Mrs Hepworth!'

Mrs Hepworth! Adrian's wife. Mrs Adrian Hepworth. She would have to get used to the name. Jonquil Hepworth.

'Darling, oughtn't you to change?'

'Yes, Daddy, I'm going now.'

I'm going now, I'm going now, I'm going away now.

'Careful, dear, don't tear the veil.'

'You forgot to throw your bouquet to the bridesmaid, Miss Jonquil.'

'Oh, Helen, how could I? Mrs Lewis was my matron-of-honour. You only throw your bouquet to bridesmaids, then the one to catch it will be the first to get married.'

'What will you do with it then, Miss Jonquil?'

'She is Mrs Hepworth now, Helen.'

'Would *you* like it, Helen?'

'Oh, Miss Jonquil – Mrs Hepworth, I mean. Could I reely?'

'Catch!'

'Darling, do hurry. Your train goes in under an hour.'

'Mummy, where are my stockings? My best, thinnest, only pair of silk stockings…'

'We laid them out on your bed this morning, darling. They must be there somewhere.'

'Mummy, where *are* they?'

'Now, darling, don't panic…'

'Remember you are British!'

'Here they are, Miss Jonquil.'

'Oh, Helen, thank you.'

'Darling, you look lovely!'

'Do I? Well, so do you!… Mummy, you're crying … on my wedding day.'

'No, I'm not! It – it's hay fever. Jonquil, don't hug me like that. I've no breath left.'

'Mumsie, I wish you and Daddy were coming, too.'

'Now, darling, don't be silly. Fancy what Adrian would think, having his in-laws on his honeymoon!'

'You'll write?'

'Of course! Every day!'

'Mummy, I'm scared!'

'Darling, there's nothing to be frightened of. I told you last night...'

'No, no. Not about that side of it! I'm just frightened that this can't last.'

'Of course it will last if you make it. Now run along down like a good girl.'

'I love you, Mummy.'

'Be happy, darling.'

'Goodbye, Helen!'

'Goodbye, Miss Jonquil!'

'Darling, you look lovely!'

'Adrian, do I? It's all for you.'

'Kiss me!'

'Oh, I can't – not here!'

'Rubbish! You're my wife.'

'Adrian!...'

'Well, well, well – the newlyweds!'

'Charles, you old scoundrel! Can't I kiss my wife?'

'Certainly! Can I?'

'Well, only a peck! A nice, brotherly one on the cheek!'

'Selfish old dog, you!'

'Where's Em? *I* shall kiss *her.*'

'Goodbye, Em, darling. Take care of yourself.'

'I will, Jonnie. Best of luck!'

'Daddy, you've been marvellous. It's all

marvellous! Thank you, so much.'

'Happy, Poppet?'

'Gloriously!'

'So am I! And I have a sneaking suspicion it's the champagne!'

'Daddy!'

'Where's your mother?'

'She'll be down in a minute. Mummy? Mum–mee! We're just going.'

'Coming, darling!'

'Charles says the C.O. himself tied the old boot on to your car.'

'Em, he didn't! I hope there isn't a kipper, too.'

'No, but there's a nice "Just Married!"'

'Come on, darling. Let's go!'

'Goodbye. Good luck.'

Goodbye! Goodbye!'

'For they are jolly good fellows ... and so say all of us...'

'Alone at last!'

'Darling?'

'Yes, darling?'

'Only darling, darling.'

'I love you, Jonquil.'

'I love you, Adrian.'

They went to London for the first night of their honeymoon and travelled down to Mullion in Cornwall the following day. The train journey was long and tiring but Jonquil was able to sleep against Adrian's shoulder part of the way and he was happy to have her there.

At times she just drowsed – her mind chasing back over these last few months, reliving the precious moments of her leaves when she had hurried down to the hospital to find Adrian so much better. And later, when he had moved to a convalescent hospital near Wodecot in Kent, and she had been able to visit him from home. And the very last week or two before their marriage – a wonderful week which she had spent in London with Adrian, buying her trousseau. The family had been marvellously generous about coupons and of course Adrian gave her nearly all his, and somehow or other they had been carefully panned out to buy a complete new outfit of civilian clothes for her.

She had also a good many of her pre-war dresses renovated and remodelled, and now her wardrobe was smart enough to satisfy any bride.

'Isn't it a bit of a waste, dear, when you spend so much time in your uniform?' Mrs Mathews had asked. But her husband broke in with a twinkle in his eye.

'Got to be prepared for the future – and future generation,' he had said mysteriously. 'I've always wanted to be a grandfather.'

Jonquil had blushed and denied that this had been at the back of her mind. But secretly, ever since she had heard Em was going to have her baby, she had thought about her own and Adrian's child and known how much she wanted one herself.

'It would be such fun, Em,' she told her friend in confidence. 'Our children would be the same age and could have marvellous times together.'

'They might even get married!' Em had said, laughing.

'Let's not have a baby too soon,' Adrian had said that day in hospital just after they had become engaged. But last night, holding her in his arms, he had whispered huskily:

'I'd love our children so much, dearest, since they would be part of you. I want a little girl who looks just like you in miniature.'

'Adrian, if I did have a child, I would be out of the W.A.A.F. and we need never be parted again.'

'Jonquil, I love you so much that it hurts!'

'I love you more than my life! Adrian, I know now what it means to reach the stars.'

'What were you thinking of?' Adrian had asked. 'Our R.A.F. motto? But those sort of stars are different, Jonquil. Through hardships to the stars – that means something greater and bigger than self. It means ... oh, I can't explain. One day, my darling, you'll understand.'

'Explain to me, Adrian. I want to know.'

'I can't, darling. You have to feel it for yourself.'

313

'I can't feel anything but you!'

'Darling!'

And they had forgotten everything in the wild ensuing tide of passion which had enwrapped them both, body and soul.

Jonquil stirred against Adrian's shoulder and her fingers sought and found his hand. They were quite alone in the first-class carriage.

'Tired?' Adrian asked tenderly, settling her more comfortably against his shoulder.

She smiled and nodded, and in a minute was fast asleep.

Throughout their ten days' leave, the weather was at its best. Adrian and Jonquil spent nearly every day lying on the sands, tanning a golden brown, climbing over the rocks and exploring caves. Once or twice they took the proprietor's two small boys for a picnic on the cliff-tops. In the evening, they went for long walks or sat in the lounge listening to the wireless recording some symphony or concerto that they were particularly fond of.

'This is my idea of real life!' Adrian said. 'We must definitely come here for our summer holidays in peace time. You'd like that, wouldn't you, darling?'

'Yes!' said Jonquil absently. 'Adrian, when do you go back on ops.?'

'When I'm fit, I suppose.'

'When will that be?'

'Well, I'm fit now. I'll have a board when I get back and all being well... Jonquil, you wouldn't want me grounded, would you?'

'No, no, of course not,' Jonquil answered quickly. 'I know how much flying means to you.'

'You must try and be a fatalist, my darling,' Adrian told her. 'That's the way I look on things, and it's the only way to avoid worry. I say "If it's written in the stars, then nothing I can do will alter it!"'

'Your C.O. was very nice to me on our wedding day,' Jonquil said, bravely changing the subject so that he should not see how worried she was to learn he might soon be back on operational flying.

'I'm glad!' Adrian said. 'He doesn't really approve of our getting married ... thinks it's bound to affect our flying.'

'But Adrian, why on earth...'

'A woman's influence is softening!' Adrian quoted with a smile, and added more seriously: 'A man won't take the same risks, when he has a wife he wants to get home to. It's subconscious, really. When he's free and unattached, then he will play up the devil for a bit of fun!'

Jonquil rolled over in the sand and propped herself up on one elbow so that she was looking down at Adrian's face.

'I never want to be a handicap to you, darling,' she said. 'When you fly you must forget all about me. No, not that. You must remember that I am fighting with you so that you can take twice as many risks, have twice as much courage.'

'Jonquil, do you really mean that? Suppose – suppose anything should happen to me, you wouldn't blame yourself for saying such a thing?'

'No!' Jonquil said with a smile. 'I shall shrug my shoulders and tell myself "it is written in the stars!"'

'You're teasing! Darling?'

'Yes, darling?'

'Nothing, darling. Only that I love, admire, respect, adore, cherish and worship you, and I'm going to kiss you.'

He drew her into his arms and as she closed her eyes and surrendered her lips to his in a long kiss, every fibre of her body, every beat of her heart, cried out silently:

'Oh, take care, my love. Promise me you will take care for I cannot live without you.'

And she pressed closer to him, winding her arms about him as if to protect him from some unknown danger of which she was only instinctively aware.

This fear is one of the things I cannot share with him, she thought. For as long as the war lasts, I must bear this alone and never let him know how afraid I am – how horribly, dreadfully afraid. Em, now I understand what you have been suffering all these months with Charles in the air...

'Jonquil, you're miles away! You didn't hear what I said to you just then, now did you?'

'No, darling! I'm sorry! What was it?'

'I said I love you.'

'Adrian, you didn't. I know I'd have heard that!'

'All right, I admit I didn't! I asked you if you'd mind very much leaving here a day earlier than we had arranged. I would rather like to spend one day in Cambridge.'

'No, of course not, if you want to go, Adrian,' Jonquil said, rather puzzled by his motive.

'I'd like to go and say goodbye to Uncle Eric...'

'Goodbye?' Jonquil broke in quickly. 'Adrian, what do you mean?'

Adrian turned away and said with forced casualness:

'Oh, he's getting old, you know, and just in case I should be posted off to some remote part of the country at a moment's notice...' his voice trailed away unconvincingly.

'Don't lie to me,' Jonquil said, clenching her hands against her sides. 'It isn't fair of you, Adrian. If you – if you think you might be going ... overseas or something ... tell me now. I'd far rather know.'

Adrian turned and studied the back of her head with eyes that were compassionate even while they were adoring.

'I don't know anything definite,' he said quietly, and she heard the truth in his voice.

'What do you suspect, then?' she asked, still not looking at him.

'I had a letter from Charles asking me if I thought I'd pass an overseas medical ... he said he went for his yesterday. I surmised from that that the squadron might be making a move. Of course, it may mean nothing at all.'

'Adrian, do you think you would pass your medical?'

'I don't know, darling. Probably. My injuries were severe, but only in much the same way as an appendicitis. Once the operation was over, so was the danger and everything else. I wasn't going to mention it, but I suppose my mind was on it and it slipped out. Jonquil, look at me.'

He turned her round to face him and her eyes were full of tears. She flung her arms round his neck and hid her face against his chest.

'I'm not crying,' she said, sniffing audibly. 'Anyway, there's nothing to cry about – yet. I don't suppose you'll go for months and months ... and the war will be over soon ... oh, Adrian...'

He let her cry for a minute or two, then he produced a large handkerchief and pushed it into her hand.

'It's full of sand,' Jonquil said, blowing into it. 'Adrian, I'm so very sorry. I thought I'd stopped being hysterical and emotional.'

'It's just reaction,' Adrian said understandingly. 'You've been pretty pent up for months about the forthcoming wedding, and working very hard as well. No one expects you to be made of steel. It's the last thing I should want.'

She smiled up at him and suggested a quick swim before supper. She laughed a good deal and teased Adrian unmercifully, splashing him with water and diving out of his reach. As they rubbed themselves down with rough towels, she noticed the look of relief in his eyes. He was happy now that she no longer fretted.

But underneath the gay exterior her heart was full of foreboding – and the fear of being parted from Adrian for the duration far exceeded the unhappiness she felt when she thought that this wonderful fortnight's honeymoon was fast approaching its end.

That night, held tightly in Adrian's arms with his kisses still warm and sweet on her lips, she told herself that now – *now* was the only time that mattered. The past was forgotten and the future she refused to anticipate.

'Jonquil!' Adrian was whispering softly. 'Love me! Love me!'

And her mind ceased to be a single unit

but became one with Adrian's, obeying his will, and her whole being answered with equalled passion the intensity of his desire.

Chapter 21

The months flew by, winter following autumn with startling rapidity. The wind blew icy gales round the camp and the roads became squelching rivers of slimy mud.

Jonquil envied Em who now had a tiny furnished flat within a few miles of where Charles was stationed, and was awaiting the arrival of her baby with a happy calm and longing. Jonquil had had but one week's leave since her honeymoon and although it had been a deliriously happy one and free from worry of Adrian's posting overseas – this scare having died down completely – she felt now she was back at work almost as if she had never been away.

Being married, she reflected, had not made any great difference in her life. She saw so little of her husband and it was only when she glanced at the wedding ring on her finger, or saw an envelope addressed to herself as Mrs Hepworth, that she realised she really was Adrian's wife. She took a childish pleasure in talking of 'my husband' whenever there was an opportunity, but somehow Adrian did not seem to her to be her husband – only her lover. To Jonquil, having a husband meant seeing his toothbrush lying alongside yours on the bathroom shelf; waiting for him to come home from work in the evenings; someone with whom you went over the household accounts and discussed alterations to the house.

At times she felt very bitter towards the fates for robbing her of those months of Adrian's company and home life. Then she would remind herself that she was only twenty-two and that although the years of her youth were passing (and horribly quickly at that!) there would be many more years after the war.

'I'm lucky to have Adrian in this country,' she told herself, thinking of some of her W.A.A.F. friends who had been parted from their husbands since the outbreak of war. Adrian was within 'phoning distance, easily callable in an emergency...

She wasn't quite sure what she meant by 'an emergency', but in the back of her mind she was certain there would come a day when she would need him.

Always a person of tremendous vitality and glowing health, she was upset to find herself feeling tired and irritable and generally run down. In defiance, she worked twice as hard, blaming the cold weather and the mild attack of 'flu to which she had succumbed some weeks earlier for her listlessness. When she most felt like curling up in bed with a hot-water bottle and a book, she forced herself to accompany the administrative officer on her inspection of the hostels where the girls were billeted, making sure they were warm and comfortable. She had not forgotten the conditions under which she and Em had lived that first winter at 'The Yews'. But they were vastly improved now and Jonquil found the airwomen without any worse complaint than that they could not have their own sweet coupons.

'We get the same old thing, week after week, from the N.A.A.F.I., M'am,' they said. 'And the shops are full of marvellous looking toffees and boiled sweets. Can't anything be done about it?'

Jonquil promised to make inquiries, but there wasn't very much she could do, since it was a matter for Air Ministry. But she did visit the head of the N.A.A.F.I. and asked him if he would try and produce more of a variety. That was one of the reasons Flight Officer Hepworth was so popular – she never left anything undone.

It was following an inspection of the chocolate and sweets stocks, that Jonquil had her first attack of sickness. She had also had a queer feeling of faintness, and decided to see the M.O. at sick parade the following morning.

The doctor gave her a thorough examination, and after a few questions, informed Jonquil that she was going to have a baby, and that she had better put in for her discharge right away.

'In the meantime,' he said, 'take things gently, Mrs Hepworth. There's no need to treat yourself as an invalid, but don't go overtaxing your strength.'

'When – when do you think it will be born?' Jonquil asked, trying to conceal her immense excitement.

'May, June next year,' the M.O. said cheerfully. 'You seem very pleased, anyway.'

'Oh, I am, I am!' Jonquil told him with a smile.

Her first impulse was to telephone the news to Adrian, but she changed her mind and resolved to write. After three attempts, she gave it up, deciding to wait and tell him when she saw him on her next forty-eight.

But she wrote to Em, a happy, excited letter, cautioning her not to tell Charles in case he should break the news to Adrian. 'I want to do that in person,' she wrote.

The following day, she filled in the forms for her discharge. The Senior Waaf officer congratulated her on the news, but frankly admitted how sorry she was to lose her.

'You have always been one of our most conscientious and reliable officers, Hepworth,' she said kindly. 'We shall all miss you. In case you should feel like joining up again, I shall recommend you highly for enrolment.'

'Thank you, M'am! It's very good of you, but I don't think I shall ever leave my husband and child. I think it is very courageous to leave one's children to their grandparents and do a war job, but personally I feel one's first duties and responsibilities are to those children. No one can replace a mother, and one can always replace a Waaf officer!'

'We shall find it exceedingly hard to replace as efficient a one as yourself,' the C.O. said with a smile. Then she dropped into a less formal tone and, taking Jonquil's hand, wished her the best of luck and every happiness.

When Jonquil left the room, she felt a lump in her throat which she would never have believed possible. Leaving the W.A.A.F. was going to be like leaving school. One grumbled and complained all the time and it wasn't until the moment came to say goodbye that one realised how attached to everything one had become.

Several weeks later, when her discharge had come through and all her *adieux* made, Jonquil talked it over with Em.

'To think how we used to say to one another, "Oh, to be a civilian again! Oh, to be out of the W.A.A.F.!" Why, I feel as if I have left part of me behind!'

'I understand,' Em said. 'I felt just the

same, Jonnie. We had some grand times and I made some wonderful friends. I wouldn't have any of it different if I had to go through it again – not even those two weeks at the depôt.'

'I still *feel* a Waaf,' Jonquil said. 'When I see an airwoman coming down the street, I invariably shift all my parcels over to the left arm, so that I can take the salute, and remember in the nick of time that I'm no longer in uniform.'

'I used to wake up in the middle of the night with that dreadful feeling we used to get, "Lord! I should have been on night-watch and I've overslept." Do you remember, Jonnie?'

Jonquil nodded her head.

'I still have a personal pride in the R.A.F.,' she said thoughtfully. 'As if I still belong. I suppose once a Waaf always a Waaf – like the Girl Guides!'

'Well, I think it's a good thing,' Em remarked. 'It gives one standards of courage and loyalty and all that sort of thing. Does that sound silly?'

Jonquil shook her head, laughing.

'It sounds silly!' she said. 'But that's just how I feel, too.'

It was early December, and Em and Jonquil now shared Em's tiny flat. It wasn't very often that Charles and Adrian came on leave together, and, though small, the flat could hold three comfortably. There was a double room and a single room upstairs and a large sitting-room and minute kitchenette downstairs.

Em's baby was expected in February, and Jonquil had arranged to go to her own home when she came back from the nursing home so as to leave more room for Em and Charles and their offspring. But, until then, Em wanted Jonquil's company and Jonquil was only too ready to go.

But a week before Christmas, their plans were suddenly and abruptly changed. Adrian and Charles unexpectedly arrived home together one evening and announced that they had fourteen days' embarkation leave. The squadron was going overseas.

The four of them discussed their future with a lack of emotion they certainly did not feel.

'If you'd care to, Jonnie,' Charles said. 'I suggest you and Em stay here together. You'll be company for each other and can fight over the babies' bottles and things...'

'What about it, darling?' Adrian asked gently.

'If you'd rather go home, Jonnie, I can always do the same,' Em said. 'Mother is pretty busy, but I don't know she'd have me.'

'I'd like to be here!' Jonquil said slowly. And added to herself, 'Here, where I have so many memories of Adrian to keep him with

me; here, where Em and I can talk about
them both to our heart's content; where we
can let down our back hair and cry every
time we feel like it!'

'Yes, here!' she said firmly.

Em went over to her and put her arms
round her friend's shoulders.

'I'm so glad, Jonnie,' she said. 'That's how
I want it, too.'

'I thought I'd take Jonquil down to Mullion tomorrow,' Adrian said. 'I know it's
December and that Mullion is a summer
resort, but ... well, what about it, darling?'

'I'd love it!' Jonquil cried eagerly. That
would mean they would spend their last
days alone, quite alone. Mullion would be
very bleak and cold at this time of the year,
but with Adrian...

'If I have to go before the kid is born,'
Charles was saying, 'You'll look after Em for
me, Jonnie?'

'Of course, Charles,' she said simply, and
seeing the tears in Em's eyes, she added
hastily: 'Let's all go out to dinner somewhere and be gay. You feel well enough,
don't you, Em?'

Em nodded gratefully. She felt very near to
tears, and she didn't want Charles to know.

Charles went out to get a paper so that they
could see what was on at the local cinema,
and Em went upstairs to change her frock.
Jonquil was left alone in the sitting-room

with Adrian.

'We'll spend a day in town, won't we, darling?' Jonquil asked, with forced cheerfulness.

'Yes, I'll have to get my tropical kit,' Adrian answered automatically.

'That will be fun,' Jonquil went on, determined not to give way. 'We'll do a show and...'

She saw the sudden droop of his head and hurried to him, words of comfort tumbling over one another in their hurry to reach him.

'It won't be for long!' she said, drawing him into her arms. 'Think of the fun you'll have, too! Masses of action which you've always craved for. And they say the mails are wonderfully quick, now...'

Now it has happened, I am the stronger of the two; she was thinking with surprise even while she was talking to him. Perhaps it was the child that made the difference. It was that which was worrying him – leaving her in this state. She would have to be brave for all three of them now.

'There is no need to worry about me – and the baby, Adrian,' she said carefully. 'I'm as strong as a horse, and Em and Mummy will both be looking after me. Now you won't worry, darling, will you?'

He shook his head, still not trusting his voice.

'Daddy wrote and said he thought the war would be over by '43,' Jonquil went on. 'So you'll be home for the Christmas after next.'

'I'm going to miss you so!'

The words went straight to her heart, piercing through the armour she had been building round it. But still she would not give in.

'I'll send you lots of photographs of myself and the baby when he's born!' she went on bravely. 'I'll write every day, darling, so that we won't lose touch with one another. Not that we ever could, really, but letters will help.'

She went into the little kitchenette and came out with a bottle of whisky and a siphon of soda, and poured him out a drink. He took it in one gulp, then lit a cigarette and inhaled deeply.

'Nobody ever had such a wonderful wife!' he said presently. 'You're so strong and brave...'

'No, no, I'm not!' Jonquil cried. 'I'm an awful coward inside. You mustn't think I don't mind so much because – well, because I appear indifferent. Inside I feel just as you do...'

'I know!' Adrian said. 'That's why you are so brave. You're much stronger than I am.'

'No, I'm not, Adrian!' she protested. She wanted him to have confidence in himself, to show a touch of the old daring. He mustn't be weakened because of her.

'Adrian!' she cried eagerly. 'You do want to go, don't you?'

He hesitated for a moment, then he said with his half-smile:

'No! Now I have you, I don't want anything else but to be with you always. There isn't much point being falsely heroic. Oh, I want a crack at the Hun all right, and by God, if I get near one, I've got a few debts to repay. I'll fight all right ... but I don't want to go. I'm not afraid to die, but I don't *want* to die, Jonquil, not now that I have you, and the child is coming... We've had such a short time together and I want to go on living with you and for you... I want to see our baby born safely; to have our own house and garden; somewhere we can call home, our home. Oh, God, I want to live!'

Jonquil was staring at him, her eyes wide with surprise, question, fear.

'You'll come back to all that, Adrian. We're both young and at the most the war won't go on for more than two or three years. You speak as if you won't be coming back.'

'If – if I shouldn't,' Adrian said, speaking slowly and with difficulty. 'No, don't interrupt me, darling. I must say it ... if I shouldn't get back, you mustn't be unhappy. I shall be with you always, wherever you go, whatever you do, for as long as you want me. You will have to live for both of us. If you

331

want to marry again, I shall understand. I shall expect and want it. Financially you will be fairly well-off. I'm leaving everything to you, of course, and that amounts to about eight hundred a year, and with my life insurance, you won't be too badly off. If our child is a boy, I'd like him to go to Winchester, where I was. If it's a girl – well, if she grows up like you, she'll be all right with me … Jonquil, my darling! You're not crying? Why, sweetheart, this may never happen. I didn't mean to frighten you…'

'You – you sounded so – so certain you … you…' She couldn't bring the words out. 'I w-was q-quite all r-right until you st-started talking like th-that,' she added reproachfully.

'I'll never do it again,' Adrian said, his arms tightly round her and his cheek against hers. 'I promise!'

And he kept his promise faithfully during the following two weeks of his embarkation leave. They were not perfectly happy weeks. How could they be with the threat of his departure so close to their hearts? But neither allowed the other to know how much they dreaded the impending parting, and the days passed in quick succession, each filled with some specially precious moment that they could treasure in their minds when they were no longer together.

Mullion was, as they had expected, quite

deserted, and their Christmas was quiet and uneventful. But they were content in each other's company and would not have had a moment of any of the days otherwise. They travelled back the last day of their leave and spent the night at Em's flat. Em was white and her eyes were strained, and Charles looked worried and pleased to see Jonquil.

'She refused to see the doctor while I was home,' he told her anxiously. 'She admits she hasn't been feeling too well, but won't waste a moment of our time together. Will you make her see him tomorrow after we've gone? I'll phone during the evening if I can and ask you how she is.'

'Of course I will,' Jonquil reassured him. 'Don't you worry, Charles. She'll be all right.'

For Jonquil, that last night with Adrian was one of both agony and perfection. They had never seemed so close, so near and dear to one another before, but through the long hours of the approaching dawn she lay wide-eyed and wakeful, unable to shake off the nightmarish feeling that this was the last time she would be in Adrian's arms. He was sleeping fitfully, and awoke an hour or so before it was time to rise, and clung to Jonquil like a small boy who doesn't want to go back to school.

'Promise me you'll never forget me,' he kept saying. And although she was frightened by his words, she answered calmly:

'Never for as long as I live.'

'Whatever happens?'

'Whatever happens!'

'Oh, I love you so much, my darling. So very much.'

'I love you, too.'

'I'm glad about the child,' Adrian said.

'I shall have part of Adrian whatever happens,' Jonquil thought, and, beside her, Adrian said to himself:

'Part of me will live on. My life will not have been in vain now that I have shared in the creation of another being.'

And the fear of death was overcome by the joy of the new life to come.

Em and Charles and Jonquil and Adrian had breakfast together in the little sitting-room. Charles and Adrian tried manfully to keep the atmosphere gay and humorous. But Em was silent and tearful and would not eat anything. Jonquil did her best to cheer her up, but Em seemed to have collapsed completely, and for Charles's sake, Jonquil took her upstairs and put her back to bed.

'Try and be brave, Em darling,' she whispered before she went downstairs. 'Send him off with a smile.'

Charles went up to say goodbye and Jonquil returned to the sitting-room where Adrian was stacking the breakfast things on to a tray.

'It's all right, darling. Mrs Alsop will do them when she comes in,' Jonquil said.

'I don't mind doing it,' Adrian said obstinately, and she realised that he was glad to have something to occupy his mind.

She stood in silence, watching him as he carried the tray through to the kitchenette. Then she helped him fold the tablecloth and push the table back against the wall. Now there was nothing more to be done.

For a moment, they stood facing each other in silent misery, and then she was in his arms and the tears she had so bravely withheld forced their way out of her eyes. Neither of them spoke. There was no comfort for them in words. Adrian kissed her forehead, her eyes, her ears, her cheeks, her lips. Upstairs a door closed and Charles came slowly downstairs.

'Coming, old chap?' he said, and with a smile at Jonquil, he opened the front door and went out.

'I must go,' Adrian said huskily, and drawing her into his arms, he kissed her with a rough hard passion that bruised her lips. Then he put her gently from him.

'Take care of yourself, my darling!'

'Adrian...'

She reached out her arms as if to hold him back, but he was already at the door, his hat a little to one side of his head, his respirator slung over one shoulder.

'Goodbye, my dearest love,' he said, and closed the door softly between them.

'No, no, not goodbye!' Jonquil whispered. 'Adrian, not goodbye. I mustn't let him go with those words.'

She hurried towards the door, but before she could open it a voice from upstairs, from Em, called her name:

'Jonnie, Jonnie, come quickly. Oh, for God's sake, do come here...'

She turned up the stairs and hurried into Em's bedroom.

'The doctor!' Em gasped, the sweat pouring from her face. 'Oh, God, the pain...'

'But Em, the baby shouldn't be here for another two months. The doctor said...'

Em was past hearing. She seemed to have sunk into a little world of her own, a world of biting, searing pain. With a last worried look at the figure writhing on the bed, Jonquil turned and went downstairs to do her bidding.

At seven o'clock that evening a little girl was born to Em. And although it was only a seven-months child, it was the most beautiful baby Jonquil had ever seen.

But no word came from Charles, and although she telephoned the camp again, always she received the same answer.

'I'm afraid neither Wing Commander Hepworth nor Squadron Leader Lewis are available.'

And she realised with a sinking heart that Charles and Adrian had really gone.

'For how long?' she asked herself as she climbed exhausted into bed. 'Oh, Adrian, for how long? For how long?'

Chapter 22

December moved into January and with the third week of the new year came news from Adrian and Charles. They cabled once announcing their safe arrival, and Jonquil had one glowing account from Adrian of their journey out.

There was a short gap of a week before they heard again, and from then onwards mail came in fairly regularly. Jonquil and Em always read the 'newsy' bits aloud, and it was Em's idea that they should compile a kind of diary from the interesting part of the letters, so that they would have a record to show their children – and grandchildren!

On cold evenings, they would sit around the fire in Em's little bedroom and scribble new entries into their book. They did not try to make a story of it, nor follow any particular dates. This was impossible, anyway, because sometimes a letter would arrive back-dated several weeks, and long after the arrival of more recent air-mail cards or airgraphs.

The diary read like this:

DIARY – 1943

…We are in the middle of the rainy season and suddenly violent storms appear from all directions and are as quickly gone. They leave the place in an awful mess – a glutinous yellow morass in which we go slipping about; the planes sink and have to be dug out, and life is made generally damp and unpleasant. Still, I suppose we shall be complaining about the heat soon. The weather has driven a lot of the local birds to seek sanctuary in the camp, and after every storm I have the pleasure of the company of four jolly little crested larks who sit on the guy rope of my tent to dry themselves off. They are so hungry they will almost feed out of my hand, but not quite; they are just too shy. We also have herds of starlings and sparrows about the place, and, of course, the vultures out on their scavenger duties…

…I have got a new toy – a Jeep! I am absolutely thrilled with it and it steers almost as well as the old Morris! But not quite!…

…We came through Baghdad, but have left there now and are out under canvas again. It is the same wild, barren country, which I find rather exciting and stimulating, although most of the boys seem to loathe it. I climbed to the top of the hills behind the camp at sunset yesterday, and it was like standing on top of the world. The vast, desolate plain behind me and in front range after range of red granite hills rising up to the snow-capped peaks, all rosy in the after-glow of the sun. There was a small, cold, keen breeze, clear and exhilarating as iced champagne, which came creeping down on me from the North. I love it...

...The weather is warmer. The boys all went off to the showers this afternoon – a great event these weekly washes. I took my Jeep and whistled off down to a wide bay I know of, took off all my clothes, and wallowed in the marvellously warm blue sea. Then I lay and sunbathed and swam again. It was lovely, all alone in the deep wide bay with a ragged fringe of palm trees round the edge. How I wished you were here with me...

...About seven it begins to get dark, and it is in this period between tea and seven that I do most of my letter-writing. As the sun goes down you see some marvellous colour effects. The desert cools off quickly and a little breeze comes in off the sea, and every-thing is very quiet. It is like that now, and I am sitting at the door of my tent, the flies having packed in for the day, and the mosquitoes not yet being on parade! You will understand that I cannot tell you about our work – only these 'days off'. I expect you hear all the 'War' side of it that you supposed to know from the B.B.C. But we *are* working...

...I had a few days off and was lucky enough to get back to Cairo. While there, I spent a morning around and in the Great Pyramid. I think it is just about the most imagination-stirring thing I have ever seen. I shall never forget it. I hope to be able to send you some snaps soon...

...Monty came and talked to us yesterday evening – a remarkable man, with a magnetic personality. As he left the men swarmed round him shouting and cheering, determined to show him that they thought he was a jolly good fellow. He chatted and laughed and told us a bit about the Eighth Army, then drove off, amid thunderous cheers. An inspiring man...

...I have just been on forty-eight hours leave – the first since I came here, although Adrian wrangled a few days some weeks ago, as you probably know. What a joy to get away from all things Air Force and be free again! The first thing I did on arrival in Alexandria, where I was staying, was to have an enormous bath, a real wallow, and my first in weeks! It was heaven to eat off china and drink from glasses – and we had a nice French (sort of!) cook. After the almost invariable bully beef and stewed tea off chipped enamel utensils, you can imagine how lovely it was. But in a way I'm glad to be back with the squadron, and there were some letters waiting for me from you, which would make anything worthwhile... It was gloriously hot, and the Mediterranean was as blue as you see it on picture postcards at home. We had dinner at the Officers' Club on Sunday night, and a very excellent one it was, too. The whole place was staffed by Italian prisoners who perform just as well as their brethren in London's best hotels! They are quite happy to have something to do, and only too pleased to be safely out of the war... On the way down, I stopped at an old monastery kept by Franciscan monks. There is always one of the Brotherhood watching and praying in the chapel, day and night, and the one who showed me round asked if I would like to say a prayer for the safety of my loved ones at home. I did. I was not a little moved by his kindness and supreme faith. He was very dignified and radiated charm like an aura, and I was glad I had taken time to stop there...

...Don't worry if letters stop coming through for a while. No news is always good news, and I think you will find this is so...

Here Jonquil and Em had ceased writing, hoping that the next letters would bring them tidings that they could add beneath the last paragraph.

'No news is good news,' Jonquil repeated over and over again.

But she could not cease to worry.

February brought with it cold winds and rain and white, hard frosts.

Em's baby was six weeks old and had been christened Joanna Mary Lewis – Jo after Em's eldest brother who had been killed over a year ago now.

Jonquil felt dull and listless and roused herself from this apathy only when she had news of Adrian. In the ensuing weeks, she listened with unfailing regularity to the news bulletins, following every details of the North African campaign, and even going so far as to purchase a map of the area and moving the flags when Allied victories or losses were reported.

'I'm living it with Adrian,' she told Em. 'Then I shall understand his letters better, and when he comes back I shall be able to share this part of his life with him, too.'

Em was content just to lie and watch the baby. She was still weak herself, although the baby was healthy enough, and the nurse would not allow her to get up. Em did not mind, since it afforded her every opportunity to play with and look at her child. Joanna was certainly enchanting, always laughing, always hungry, always willing to be picked up and cuddled. She was ridiculously like Charles, and Jonquil found herself wishing that her own baby, when it was born, should be as like Adrian as Jo resembled her father.

For the first two or three weeks after Jo's birth, the nurse had slept in the little room next to Em's, and Jonquil had slept on the divan in the sitting-room. But now Em was so much better, the nurse came only in the day-time, and Jonquil went back to the little room upstairs. She spent long hours with Em, sitting and sewing baby clothes, writing up their 'diary', and talking about Adrian and Charles and the wonderful days they had all spent together.

Em's mother was a constant visitor, and Mrs Mathews came every Sunday, which was the only day she could spare from her committees and institutes and evacuees. She always arrived with large stacks of fresh fruit and vegetables from the Manor House garden and hot-houses, and some gift of chocolates or a cheque from Robert Mathews. Both parents tried hard to persuade their daughter to come home, but Em and Jonquil refused to give up the little flat and could not be persuaded to leave. The place had so many memories for them both, and no amount of persuasion was of any avail.

As the weeks went by, Jonquil found herself growing more restive, more nervy every day. Em's nurse cautioned her severely, saying:

'You must try and take things more calmly, Mrs Hepworth, or it will affect the health of the baby.'

Jonquil made an effort, but still she would wake in the night, sweating and crying out after some nightmare which she could not remember, knowing only that it had to do with Adrian. And during the day, she would stop suddenly and listen, although Em could hear no sound in the room.

'I thought I heard someone call me,' she would say apologetically.

Em was worried and spoke to the nurse about it. But the nurse was reassuring.

'Expectant mothers do all sorts of queer things,' she said cheerfully. 'She will be all right again as soon as the child is born.'

'Well, it gives me the jitters!' Em said. 'I'm beginning to have premonitions of dreadful things to come myself!'

'Perhaps if you had a talk with her?' the nurse suggested. 'If she's worrying, it may help her.'

But their talk was not enlightening.

'I don't know what it is, Em,' Jonquil said. 'It's just a constant dread of something awful happening, and I don't know *what*. I dream about it, and can't remember the dream. If only Adrian hadn't said good-bye...'

'But I don't understand,' Em protested. 'He couldn't go without...'

'No, it's just a superstition he had about the word itself,' Jonquil interrupted. 'He never used it – until the morning he left... Oh, I'm silly to worry, Em. I know it! But I just can't help myself.'

'Jonnie, dear, look at it this way. You had a letter yesterday not two weeks old. He must be all right. Besides, you know Charles promised to wire me if anything should happen.'

'Yes, Em, I know!' Jonquil said. 'But whatever it is hasn't happened yet. I shall know when it does.'

'Jonnie, be reasonable! You can't go on like this. You'll make yourself ill.'

Jonquil shrugged her shoulders and smiled with tired eyes.

'I wish I *could* stop worrying,' she said.

The news that evening was excitingly optimistic. Montgomery was advancing, Rommel retreating on all fronts. The Allies were reported to be in complete mastery of the air. For a few days, Jonquil seemed more cheerful. She had another letter from Adrian, saying he was safe and well, and although he was still missing her, he was having a fine time. 'Don't worry if the mail doesn't come through regularly,' he repeated. 'We're so busy out here I don't always get time to write. But I'm thinking of you constantly, my darling, and of our child. Remember that I love you now and always.'

Jonquil took the letter to her room and fell asleep with it clutched tightly in her hand, like a child with some favourite toy. Em was up and about, now, and seeing Jonquil lying so contentedly asleep, she closed the door gently and took Jo out in the pram.

'Jonnie's going to be all right!' she told herself happily, and turned her attention to the child.

In the little flat the telephone was ringing sharply and insistently. But Jonquil slept on exhausted. She did not even wake when the doorbell rang and the telegraph boy pushed an orange envelope through the letterbox and rode away on his bike, whistling cheerfully. Em had been out over an hour before she stirred and woke suddenly as if someone had called her name. She sat up in bed, rubbing her eyes, wondering what it was that had woken her. There wasn't a sound in the house, and with a little feeling of panic growing inside her, she slipped on a warm coat and skirt, and went down to the sitting-room.

'Em, are you there?' she called.

There was no answer. She went into the hall and noticed that the pram had gone. So Em was out. She turned back towards the sitting-room, and, as she did so, her eye was caught by the bright orange envelope lying on the coconut matting. She stared at it for a moment, feeling her heart beating wildly against her ribs.

'This is what I've been waiting for,' she thought without emotion. 'All these days of worrying have been working up for this moment.'

She could not take her eyes off the envelope. It lay upside down and a sudden overwhelming curiosity swept through her to know who the telegram was for.

'It might be from Mummy to say she can't come on Sunday,' she said aloud. 'She said she would wire if she couldn't make it. Or it might be from Marion ... she said she'd wire if she managed to get her forty-eight. Or it might be from Adrian...'

But she didn't really believe these suppositions, and she bent down with difficulty because of the child within her, and picked up the envelope with hands that trembled a little as she did so.

It was not for her. It was addressed to Em.

She walked into the sitting-room and put the telegram down on the table. Then she sat down heavily in one of the chairs and studied it.

'You know Charles promised to wire me if anything happened,' Em had said. The words came back and repeated themselves over and over again in her overwrought brain, until they seemed to be coming from the room itself.

'I've got to know,' Jonquil whispered, her

hands reaching out for the envelope. 'I've got to know...'

She tore the flap and pulled out the slip of white paper inside, and with an effort forced herself to read the printed words.

'Darling prepare bad news. Adrian killed on twentieth in heroic flight. Deepest sympathy Jonnie. My love you and Jo. Charles.'

'No!' she whispered. 'It isn't true. It isn't true. Em? Em, where are you?'

Every other emotion faded into this one great desire to find Em. She must find her and ask her if it could be true. Em would known. Em would tell her it was all a joke.

'Em! Em!' she cried, her voice rising as her panic took possession of her. 'Em, Em, *Em?*'

She ran out into the hall and opened the front door. Outside, the air was sharp with frost, and the pavements were shining with patches where the puddles of last night's rain had frozen hard into little pools of ice.

'Em, Em, Em!' she called, running down the steps and heedless of the people in the street who turned to stare at her. The child was heavy, and her breath came in little short gasps. The road was slippery and she put her hand out to steady herself, but there was nothing to hold on to, and with a little lurch forward, she slipped on the icy surface and fell with a sickening crash, striking her head against the pavement. Em, returning with a smiling, rosy-cheeked Jo, turned the corner into the street just in time to see her fall.

It was two days before Jonquil recovered full consciousness. Her head ached and she felt weak and sick. She remembered her fall and her first thought was of the child. Underneath the bedclothes, her hands moved down and, unbelievingly, felt the slim loose lines of her body.

'The baby...'

The nurse at her bedside turned quickly and laid a restraining hand on Jonquil's arm.

'You're going to be all right, dear,' she said soothingly.

'But the baby...' Jonquil cried, still not understanding the lines of her body.

'I'm afraid ... there won't be a baby now, dear,' the nurse said kindly. 'But you're going to be all right.'

She saw the expression in Jonquil's wide, staring eyes, and in her anxiety to relieve her suffering, she blundered horribly.

'Never mind, dear,' she said. 'You'll be able to have other babies...'

Jonquil turned her head and the tears forced their way weakly down her cheeks. She was unconscious of them.

'There won't ever be any other babies,' she said pitifully. 'My husband ... Adrian ... was killed on the twentieth in heroic flight. Deepest sympathy Jonnie. My love to you and Jo. Charles.'

Her voice trailed away and her eyes closed. She seemed to have lost consciousness. As the nurse went out to find the Sister, her own eyes were filled with tears. She was herself married to a man in the Air Force, and she could imagine what it would mean to lose him. And to lose one's child as well...

Jonquil had a severe hæmorrhage, and for a week her life was in danger. Em was frantic with worry and came every day to the hospital for news.

'If only she had some incentive to live,' the doctor said.

'I don't see that she can possibly wish to go on living,' Em said bitterly. 'I shouldn't!'

'Perhaps if you would talk to her,' the doctor said. 'Take your child, perhaps. Let her think you need her help.'

'I'll do my best,' Em promised.

She went along to the private ward where Jonquil lay, and sat down by the bedside, taking one of the limp hands in hers. She saw, with a deep ache in her heart, that Jonquil's fingers were so thin she had difficulty in keeping her wedding-ring from slipping off.

'Have your parents been to see you?' she asked.

Jonquil nodded her head.

'They're terribly worried about you,' Em

said gently.

Jonquil did not answer.

'For Adrian's sake,' Em went on in her quiet, forceful voice, 'please make an effort, Jonnie, darling.'

'I don't want to live without him.'

'I know, I know!' Em cried. 'I should feel just the same if anything happened to Charles...'

'No, you wouldn't!' Jonquil interrupted quickly. 'You have Jo to live for.'

Em was silent. She didn't know what more she could say.

'May I bring Jo to see you?' she asked presently.

'If you like!'

'I would love to,' Em said. 'She has grown so, you won't recognise her, Jonnie. When I gave her her bath last night ... why, Jonnie...'

She broke off, seeing the tears which had sprung into her friend's large, shadowed eyes. Her first impulse was to throw her arms round Jonquil's shoulders and hold her to her, comfort her and sympathise. But some instinct deep within her, forbade her to do so.

'Have courage, Jonnie!' she said quietly. 'You know I had a letter from Charles today. He says Adrian is being recommended for the V.C. – the highest honour there is. Apparently their squadron of fighter-bombers was sent out to a very special target which they were told to bomb at any cost. It wasn't by any means undefended, and, long before they got there, they were met by a formation of enemy fighters. Nearly all our boys were shot down. Adrian's 'plane was hit in one of the petrol tanks. He knew that if he turned back, he could reach base; that if he went on, he could reach the target, but not home. He told the other chap to bale out, and he went on alone, and bombed the target, flying so low that he couldn't miss. You see, he had nothing more to lose, knowing he couldn't get back, so he made sure of his target... Oh, Jonnie, aren't you proud of him? Such courage, such disregard for his own safety! Be worthy of him, my dear. Don't let him down.'

Jonquil was crying quietly, and, unable to bear it any longer, Em left the room, closing the door gently behind her.

'I can do no more,' she said to herself, as she made her way home. 'Jonnie must do the rest for herself.'

In the hospital, Jonquil lay, exhausted by her own tears. She could cry no more.

'I want to die!' she told herself. 'Why can't I die? Oh, Adrian, Adrian...'

She closed her eyes and tried hard to conjure up his voice, his image, but only his words came back to her:

'If I shouldn't come back, you mustn't be

unhappy. I shall be with you always, wherever you are, whatever you do, for as long as
you want me. You will live for both of us...'

No! No! I don't want to live!

'You're so strong and brave, Jonquil...'

Not any more, she thought bitterly.

'You must try and be a fatalist, my darling.
It's the only way to avoid worry. Say, "if it's
written in the stars, there's nothing I can do
will alter it".'

How true! What could she have done to
make things different?

'Don't say "goodbye". Just, "so long", or
"au revoir", but never "goodbye".'

Oh, Adrian, it was you, *you* who said goodbye.

'Pearls mean tears!'

'Pearls for our engagement and autumn
for our wedding. Can we overcome all this
superstition, darling?'

Oh, it isn't fair; it isn't fair! she cried,
brokenly. Then hearing the words, she
thought suddenly, I've said that before!
When was it? The day after Simon was killed
... Adrian came to talk to me. She could
remember easily now.

'Don't fight me. Fight the people responsible,' he had said.

A sudden, burning wave of hate swept
through her, hate for every German, every
Italian, every man and woman responsible
for the war, for Adrian's death, for the death

354

of her child. As suddenly, she wanted to be well and strong, to be fit enough to fight back, to fight again...

'I want to live!' she cried aloud, to the empty room. 'I will! I'll make munitions, scrub floors. I'll do anything. I'll...'

'If ever you should feel like joining again, I shall recommend you highly...'

That was what the Waaf C.O. had said.

'I'll rejoin the W.A.A.F.,' Jonquil thought. 'That will need courage. I'll show Em I'm worthy of Adrian. Oh, yes, yes, yes! I'll rejoin the W.A.A.F.'

She wanted very much to tell Em of her decision and rang for the nurse, and asked her to telephone Em and tell her to come round first thing in the morning.

Em came early, bringing the now three-months-old Jo with her. She found Jonquil with flushed cheeks and a feverish, excited light in her eyes.

'Em, I'm joining up again,' she said. 'As soon as I'm fit enough, I'm going straight to Victory House...'

'Jonnie, darling! Do you really mean it?'

'Yes, I'm deadly serious, Em,' Jonquil said. 'I have some debts to repay, and what you said yesterday made me remember them. Oh, Em, Adrian shall be proud of me! As proud as I am of him.'

Em held Jo tightly to her, and her eyes were suspiciously bright.

'We'll go round together,' she said. 'Oh, Jonnie, your cheeks are almost as rosy as Jo's. Now you really are going to get well.'

'Yes,' Jonquil said quietly. 'As quickly as I can!'

Ten weeks later, with the prospect of an Allied invasion in the near future almost a certainty, and with the victory of the desert army as a torch of encouragement, Jonquil and Em made their way towards Victory House, and Jonquil offered her services to the Women's Auxiliary Air Force for the second time. Em's eyes were soft and misty with memories.

'If it weren't for this…' she said, giving her daughter a little hug. 'I'd come with you.'

But Jonquil knew she would come through the months ahead of her without Em's company, much as she would have liked it. Adrian walked with her, was with her always so it seemed to her, and now she never really felt alone. Looking into the future, she saw only the work she was going to do, her reward being the victorious conclusion of the war. She refused to think further than that.

But Em saw beyond Armistice Day. Jonquil was only twenty-three, and although the hardships she had been through made her seem older than her years, she was still young, and more beautiful than she had ever been. Her eyes held a wistful, haunting loveliness that few men would be able to resist.

'Some man will fall in love with her and Jonnie ... well, she would never love anyone as she loved Adrian, but...'

Em's eyes were full of hope as she and Jonquil walked out of Victory House and made their way home to tea.

Chapter 23

The invasion had started. Already Lampedusa, Pantellaria and Sicily were in Allied hands, and a small part of Italy as well. The crowds that stood outside Buckingham Palace were cheerful, excited and optimistic about the war in general. At last we really did seem to be getting somewhere.

The sun was hot and bright and only the faintest of breezes stirred the flag above the Palace. It was at top mast. The King was in residence, and the crowds outside were waiting for a glimpse of the heroes who were receiving their medals somewhere inside the royal home. There were always crowds when an investiture was taking place, and one is apt to wonder whether it is curiosity or patriotism or a little of both that never fails to bring the people surging round the gates.

They were a little restless. It was some time now since the cars drove in with their uniformed passengers, and the few visitors who were allowed in with them.

'Wouldn't say "no" to a nice cup o' tea,' said one of England's cockneys.

'Awh! They won't be long naow,' said her husband, shifting his weight on to the other foot. ''Ere, lean on me.'

'Say, d'yer think we'll see George?' an American officer asked his neighbour.

'If you mean the King, the answer is probably "yes",' said the Englishman with dignity. But his superior attitude was forgotten as he turned excitedly to the girl on his other side.

'Look!' he said. 'They're coming out!'

The American forgot his annoyance and lifted the small boy in front of him on to his shoulder so that he could better see what was happening in the large courtyard.

'Well, kid,' he said cheerfully. 'What's to do?'

'I can't see!' the child squealed. Then he gave a little bounce of excitement. 'It's the King – *and* the Queen,' he shouted.

The crowds burst into a loud cheer and the American put the child down and reached for his camera.

'Gee, this is swell!' he said. 'Won't the folks be pleased if I can get a picture.'

The Englishman who had been on his dignity tapped the American on the shoulders, and said half apologetically:

'Take my place. You'll get a better shot!'

'Gee! Thanks!'

The gates swung open and the cars moved slowly out. The King and Queen went back into the Palace and, after a little while, the crowds dispersed. The American, pleased with his camera shots, wandered into the park. His quick eye noticed a girl in W.A.A.F. uniform sitting alone on one of the park benches. She had a small box in her hand, and she was looking at it as if it were very precious. He thought he recognised her face, and then as quickly remembered that he had seen her go by in one of the cars. She must have been at the Palace.

'Pardon me!' he said, going up to her without the slightest trace of shyness. 'Would you mind if I took your photograph?'

She looked up quickly and he was surprised to see her eyes were full of tears. But she smiled at him and said gently:

'Why do you want it?'

'Well, I guess you've got a medal there, huh?' he asked, sitting down beside her.

She nodded her head.

'I kinda thought it would give the folks at home a thrill,' he said. 'Would you mind?'

'I'm afraid I didn't win it!' the girl said. 'It's my husband's.'

'Oh, I'm sorry!'

He was quick to realise his mistake. He'd read about posthumous awards. He wondered whether he ought to get up and leave her, but something prompted him to stay.

'Would "the folks at home" be interested in the story?' she asked, a little smile playing at the corner of her lips.

'Say, you're making fun of me now!' he

said, but laughing at himself.

'I'm sorry! But I meant it, if you want to know.'

'Sure,' he said quickly. 'Sure, I want to know.'

So she told him about Adrian and how he had won his V.C. She found herself telling him, too, about the baby. He was easy to talk to, and she wanted to be sure she *could* talk about it without breaking down.

'What made you join the W.A.A.F. again?' he asked when she had finished her story.

She shrugged her shoulders.

'I should have been called up anyway,' she said.

He looked at her and his eyes smiled.

'No, that wasn't the reason,' he said with his quick intuition. 'My! I'm mighty proud to have met you!'

She looked at him curiously.

'Proud to have met *me?*' she asked.

'Yes! I know courage when I see it!' he said simply. 'Could I take the picture now?'

'For the "folks at home"?' she asked, smiling.

But he wasn't laughing when he answered: 'No, for myself!'

He took the picture and snapped the camera back into its case.

'Would you think it impertinent of me if I asked you to come and have a cup of tea with me?' he asked.

Jonquil looked up at him, and again her eyes smiled.

'No!' she said. 'But I'm afraid I can't have the cup of tea. I've got to catch the four-thirty from Paddington. I'm on duty tonight!'

His face fell, but he was still unbeaten.

'Then can I take you to the station?' he asked.

She looked at him again, judging him, and liked his honesty.

'That would be very kind of you.'

In the taxi, he turned to her eagerly.

'Gee!' he said. 'Your husband must've been a swell fellow.'

She liked him for that.

'For more reasons than one,' he said. 'He must've been swell for a girl like you to care so much for him. When I'm flying my little old kite around I shall think of this afternoon and feel all good inside!'

'You fly?' she asked.

He pointed to the wings on his army tunic.

'Fortresses,' he said proudly. 'Say, would you like to come over some time to our 'drome? I'd love to show you my kite. Maybe we could fix a trip?'

'Oh, I'd love to,' Jonquil said. 'But we aren't allowed to fly without permission.'

'We'll get permission,' the American said easily. 'Is that a date?'

Jonquil hesitated.

The American pulled out a card from his

wallet and scribbled his address on the back.

'Think about it!' he said. 'You can always let me know.'

Paddington Station was crowded. Jonquil was glad she had told her mother and father not to come with her.

'I'd like a few minutes in the Park by myself,' she had said. 'You go on home.'

They hadn't wanted to go, but she had been glad of the chance to be alone, to remember the words of praise the King had spoken for Adrian. He had even bothered to ask her how long she had been in the W.A.A.F., and finding she had joined again, he had said:

'With men like your husband and women like yourself to fight for England, we shall surely win.'

Then – *then* had she known and understood what Adrian had meant when he had said, 'Through hardship to the stars – that means something greater and bigger than self.' It did! For Adrian, it meant the supreme sacrifice, and for her – the praise from her King.

'I'll try and find you a seat,' the American was saying. 'You wait here.'

She watched his tall, broad back disappearing into the crowded carriage. Presently he returned, his face flushed with triumph.

'I made it!' he said. 'With a struggle!'

He shepherded her into the carriage, then went round to the window.

'You know, you never told me your name,' he said.

'Jonquil – Jonquil Hepworth!' she told him.

The train started to move, and she held out her hand.

'I'm awfully pleased to have met you, Jonquil,' the American said. 'Perhaps we'll meet again?'

'Perhaps!'

He was walking along beside the train.

'Well,' he said, and his face crinkled into a smile. 'So long!'

'Goodbye!' she said, drawing back from the window. Then she leant out again swiftly, and called to his receding figure:

'No, no, I didn't mean that. Not "goodbye"… So long.'

He knew that he would see her again.

This Large Print Book, for people
who cannot read normal print,
is published under the auspices of

THE ULVERSCROFT FOUNDATION